THE RUSSIAN

Русский язык

Thomas J. Nichols

The Russian

ISBN-13: 978-1-955937-09-2 (*Paperback*)

ISBN-13: 978-1-955937-13-9 (*eBook*)

Published by Defiance Press and Publishing, LLC

Bulk orders of this book may be obtained by contacting Defiance Press and Publishing, LLC.

www.defiancepress.com

Defiance Press & Publishing, LLC

281-581-9300

info@defiancepress.com

CONTENTS

ABOUT THE BOOK

The Russian continues Thomas Nichols' fact-based novels of the border wars along the southern boundary of the United States. Beginning with *Color of the Prism,* continuing with *We Were Young Once* . . . and concluding with the third of these spellbinding stories, Nichols's readers experience an insider's view of cartel-controlled human and drug trafficking.

In *The Russian,* New Mexico State Trooper Enrique (Ricky) Basurto joins other local, state, and federal agents in the Multi-Agency Human and Controlled Substance Interdiction Task Force. Focused along the desolate NM Hwy. 9 (New Mexico State Road 9) from Columbus to Animas, Ricky and his colleagues face the dangers of the powerful cartels, their heavily armed militias, and the innocent men, women, and children who are their victims.

The near ghost town of Hachita, New Mexico, is the bull's eye in the war. It is here in the remote Chihuahua Desert where life and death intersect, bringing unexpected challenges to Ricky and his colleagues' professionalism, ethics, and personal goals and fears.

THE DESERT

The Chihuahua Desert was, and in many ways remains, one of the richest and most beautiful desert landscapes in the world. Bounded by the Sierra Madre Occidental mountain range to the west and the Sierra Madre Oriental range to the east, this unique bionetwork has existed for over 9,000 years as a desert ecosystem. It is a land in which the beautiful darkness of the night sky is diluted by the array of stars and planets—Aquarius and Capricorn, Ursa Major and Orion, Mars and Jupiter, and the endless scope of planets and constellations.

The ravages of nature and human development have not been kind to this strong yet delicate ecoregion. Water usage, agriculture, urban growth, and mining have taken their toll. Nevertheless, a more sinister and unnatural series of events have taken a devastating levy on the men, women, and children who live in this inimitable desert.

Whether *cartel*, *mafia*, or any other designation, this nearly 680,000 square miles of Mother Earth has become the handmaiden to the most power-hungry and violent people on earth—the cartels.

The desert and its people are ours to save or to destroy.

CHAPTER ONE

Oleg Krutoy was as ordinary and non-descript as a man could be. His neighbors thought him to be in his late 60s or early 70s. A bit on the portly side, the broken blood vessels on his nose and cheeks gave him the appearance of too many vodkas over the years. Nowadays, no one ever saw him the slightest bit tipsy. He had lived in the neighborhood for more than ten years, just off Broadway and Swan Road in Tucson, Arizona. Everyone thought he was a widower, or maybe a bachelor, from Brighton Beach in New York City where he ran a shoe store. He talked about the old days back there when he could go to the Russian Orthodox Cathedral of the Transfiguration, though that was a different time, back in '07. Tucson was a lot different. They didn't have a *Russian* Orthodox Church. The Holy Resurrection Orthodox was close by, but it wasn't Russian—just a generic substitute.

Nobody knew him well, but they were in total agreement on one point: There wasn't a better neighbor than Oleg. They found him to be a kind and gentle soul. He'd pick up your mail and newspaper if you were gone a few days, make sure the flowerpots were watered, or maybe have a key and walk through the house to be sure there wasn't a water leak or some other calamity.

*

It was a Thursday morning, like any other Thursday. Everyone needed a routine, and Oleg had his. Every Thursday was just like it was last week and would be next week. There's nothing wrong with good habits. That's how life was supposed to be lived.

Barefoot but wearing his boxer shorts and undershirt, the old man rubbed the small of his back and looked at the clock on the oven. Seven o'clock. It was time to put *Собака*, the dusty gray and black miniature Schnauzer, in the back yard to do his duty. Of course, the neighbor kids couldn't say his Russian name, but they weren't far off: *Sobaka* is what they called him, and they were pretty close to right.

Today was going to be another hot day, "104," they say. "It's going to be hot, but it's a dry heat so it isn't too oppressive." That's what those weather people always said. He chuckled to himself. "Anyhow, I'll stay inside and watch the U.S. Open up north in Wisconsin. I like that Koepka kid."

He unplugged his old percolator coffee pot, dumped the grounds in the trash, then rinsed and dried his cup and put it in the drain rack next to the sink. Shuffling to his bedroom, he donned his favorite cotton sports shirt, a pair of freshly pressed khaki trousers, calf-high silk socks, and his dark brown Mephisto Oxford shoes. Pausing, he took in his reflection in the mirror, brushed aside an errant hair from over his ear, tucked his wallet and handkerchief into his pockets, and snatched his keys from the dresser top. He exited the carport door, taking time to lock it behind him before unlocking his car. Glancing at his watch, he smiled. Seven-twenty. Right on time.

That was important to him. Everyone should lead an orderly life. He backed his 2016 Volvo out of the carport, negotiated the curves and roundabouts in the neighborhood, and blended into eastbound Broadway lanes toward the rising sun. Traffic was light this time of day, but bumper to bumper westbound toward the city.

Oleg hung his ADA permit on the rearview mirror, slipped into a handicap parking spot at NYC Bagels, and found an empty table with a copy of *USA Today* left behind by a previous customer. He smiled. It was a good day. He enjoyed a cup of espresso along with a hot buttered garlic bagel. They were delicious.

*

Saguaro National Park was a beautiful, relaxing drive out the Spanish Trail east of the sprawling suburbs and strip shopping malls of the city. It was a world within itself, home to thousands of towering saguaro cacti, deer, javelina, birds, coyotes, and the occasional mountain lion. It also was a Mecca for bicyclists with its twisting ups, downs, and arounds for a nine-mile circular tour of the park.

Oleg turned cautiously into the park drive, watching for cyclists or long-distance runners absorbed in their own world, oblivious to traffic. With his "America the Beautiful Pass" adhered to his windshield, he slowed and was waved through by the Park Ranger. They acknowledged each other as they did every Thursday with a soft salute from the Ranger to which Oleg responded with a tip of his chin, a smile, and a wave.

Then it was on to the narrow, paved route—slow and relaxed, ever watchful for the covey of quail scurrying across the road, or the beep-beep of a roadrunner dashing after whatever roadrunners dash after. Midway through the route and on the long incline on the easternmost boundary of the trip was a turnout. It served as an interlude for tourists to stop and absorb the beauty of the Sonoran Desert, or for the cyclist and runners to stop and catch their breath for the long, final push to the top.

As was his habit, Oleg paused at this peaceful vista to inhale the silence and smells of the rugged desert foothills. More than once he was rewarded with a glimpse of a javelina or coyote at the bottom of the canyon. Down there, a hundred yards or more, and safely away from the gawkers on the road, the wildlife could quench their thirst from a trickle of water ebbing down the rocky canyon bottom.

Today was like any other bright, wonderful Thursday. He nosed his Volvo into a parking slot facing the retaining wall overlooking the canyon below. With a little grunt and groan, he eased his tired body out of the car and took the half-dozen steps to the wall. As he always did, he sat down and swung his feet over the edge, taking a deep breath to enjoy the freshness of the desert. All was quiet and peaceful with the world. A little movement near the bottom caught his eye. He smiled. Mother Nature would reward him today with a quick peek of wildlife scurrying along the canyon bottom.

He held his breath in anticipation. He was right. From beneath a mesquite tree and some wild grasses, a covey of blue quail dashed to the water's edge. Oleg smiled inwardly. How fast they could run—dash, splash, and they were gone. It was over in a few seconds.

4

A couple of cyclists, a man and a woman, were nearing his position, huffing and puffing and ready for a well-deserved respite before they completed the second half of their ride.

He gave them a quick glance, then turned his attention back to the canyon below. The quail covey was gone, but there might be others. Maybe even a coyote or fox. Oleg glanced as the couple propped their bikes against the retaining wall and retrieved their water bottles from the bike frames. The old man turned his attention back down the canyon, casually aware of the woman walking behind him doing stretching exercises while the man sat on the retaining wall looking toward the bottom.

Oleg never heard the gunshot. He pitched forward with his weight catapulting him down and almost completely hidden beneath a patch of prickly pear and jumping cholla cactus.

He was dead. His debt was paid.

*

Everyone was surprised Thursday evening when the police came around asking questions and going through his home. "Dead?" they asked. "How? Where? When?"

"Shot?" they exclaimed. "Oleg? That can't be. Everybody loved Oleg. He wouldn't hurt a flea."

But it was true. *Someone* didn't like him.

Vengeance is a hunter.

CHAPTER TWO

Wearing his Stetson hat, crisp white western shirt and Levi's, Ricky Basurto was enjoying a cup of coffee with his mother, Sophie, at her home near Hachita, New Mexico. His two-year-old daughter, Guadalupe, was oblivious to the world, lying on her pallet on the floor and playing with her Lilly doll. The house was quiet but for their soft conversation, one of many they had over the years since Lupe, as they called her, had joined the family. "Tell me about Muncie's new job," Sophie said while she poured a fresh cup of her favorite Piñón Coffee.

Looking over the rim of his steaming cup, Ricky paused to savor the smooth, nutty flavor. He leaned back in his chair and slipped his hat to the back of his head. "She worked her tail off having the baby and studying for her Ph.D. at the same time, but it worked out. She's in seventh heaven, and we're both happy the way it turned out. She's teaching upper-division Anthropology Linguistics this semester." He paused with a soft chuckle. "I know *she* knows what it means, but I think I'll stay with English and Spanish."

Glancing down at Lupe who was beginning to grumble, he continued with a shake of his head. "The only thing that bothers us is leaving her every day. But," he said when he looked into his mother's eyes, "it's a blessing we have *you*."

Sophie placed her cup on the saucer and spoke as only a grandmother can. "She's my daily blessing, *Hijo*. I wouldn't have it any other way."

Ricky lifted his cup and just as quickly put it down when his cell phone buzzed a message. Pulling it from his hip pocket and giving it a cursory glance, he shoved it back in his Levi's. "Gotta go, Mamma. They've got something for me near Antelope Wells." He scooted down on the floor, nuzzled little Lupe, then hopped up.

Sophie followed him to the door while Lupe scurried along on her hands and knees. "How much longer are you going to stay on this Task Force? I don't like it. It's too dangerous."

He turned to hug his mother, then using both hands, he carefully aligned his Stetson on his head and straightened his belt buckle on his trousers. Stepping outside, he spoke over his shoulder as he reached for the door of his pickup truck. "Mamma, it's a long-range project that could go on forever. We'll be in business as long as the cartels and the *coyote*s keep pushing narcotics and little girls into hell on Earth." He shook his head as he climbed into his truck. "It's a war that'll never end."

Still wearing her nightgown, robe, and slippers, Sophie stood in the doorway and waved forlornly when her son eased his truck down the dirt road that led away from her little refuge and across the lonesome desert to NM Hwy. 9. She leaned down to pick up Lupe. Holding her to her breast, she whispered a prayer for Ricky and the people he encountered. The world was an ungodly place.

7

Ricky hit the *Return* button of his cell phone to reach his supervisor, Border Patrol Supervisory Agent Miguel O'Rourke. "What do you have for me, boss?"

"*Buenos Dias*," O'Rourke replied. "Border Patrol has a dead body with suspicious circumstances. Check your odometer. They're 7.4 miles south of Highway 9 on Highway 81 going toward Antelope Wells. You'll have to leave your truck on the road and hoof it in for about two-thirds of a mile. Be sure to put on your snake chaps and gaiters."

"Sounds interesting," Ricky replied.

"Yeah, it is. They're in a place called *Cañón de la Muerte* and the name is meaningful. The friggin' place is infested with rattlers, so be careful."

Twenty minutes and 7.4 miles later, Ricky eased his trusty F-150 pickup onto the shoulder of the road, a stretch of blacktop visited by few others than the occasional Customs or Border Patrol Agents.

Carefully going through the assortment of equipment he carried on the rear seat and floor, he found his thigh-high snake pants and Velcro snap-on shin guards. After adjusting them for a tight but comfortable fit, he rummaged around in the truck bed and found exactly what he needed: an eight-foot length of garden hose, an ideal weapon for killing snakes. Finally, with his Stetson fitted perfectly on his head, a 2-liter Camel Water Pack on his back, a .40 caliber Glock and portable radio on his belt, the hose in his left hand, and a trekking stick in his right, he set off—up the rocky, cactus-strewn incline to the east toward the canyon.

Cresting the hill, he spotted two Border Patrol Agents about 400 yards southeast of his position in the sandy wash at the bottom of the ravine. Each of them sat astride a 4-wheel ATV several feet away from what looked like a clump of rags propped up against the side of the wash.

Seconds later, one of the agents looked in his direction, gave a wave of his hand, and started up the hill to give him a ride. Simultaneously, Ricky's heart ran cold when he heard the distinct buzz of a rattlesnake. He froze, then lowered his eyes to the scrub brush directly in front of him. There, coiled with its head lifted and tongue darting was a Mohave Rattlesnake, one of the most toxic and aggressive members of the rattlesnake family.

The ATV rider apparently was cognizant of the situation, slowed, and made a circular maneuver placing him several yards behind Ricky. "Stay steady, my friend," he said.

With his eyes glued on the snake and his lips dry, Ricky gave a soft, "Yeah." Concurrent to the explosion of the agent's .40 caliber H & K handgun, the rattlesnake's head disappeared in a vapor.

Ricky remained frozen. Even the blast of the gunshot and the impact of the bullet passing within two feet of him did not break his concentration. Seconds that seemed to last forever ticked away in his brain. Finally, he took a deep breath and stepped back toward the ATV. He steadied himself on the driver's shoulder and cracked a sick smile. "I gotta pee," he uttered, turning around and relieving himself on a flat rock. Afterward, he took a deep breath, held it, then slowly exhaled: He was alive and well.

Following a circuitous route along the rocky slope and sitting astride the back of the ATV, Ricky and his newfound friend, Armando Ochoa, rolled to a stop in the wash. Armando introduced him to his co-worker, Axel Wolff, a German Mexican American. Sliding off the 4-wheeler, Ricky stepped toward what he previously thought was a pile of rags. It wasn't. It was the animal-ravaged, decomposed body of a human being. "Son of a bitch," he murmured. "It's been here a while." Looking at the two agents, he asked, "Any idea how long?"

Axel shook his head. "It's hard to say. We almost never come this way. The *coyotes* know it's a snake din, so they stay out of it." He took a deep breath and spit into the sand. "We can't tell if it's male or female, but there's a handgun partially under the right side of its head. That's why we called for y'all. Usually, when we find bodies out here, they either died from the heat or fell off a cliff." He paused, twisted his lips, and continued. "When we saw the gun, it changed things for us, but we're not sure how—murder or suicide, could be either."

"Give me your guess," Ricky replied.

Armando nodded. "Suicide. Maybe lost. Maybe snake bit. Maybe just decided nothing was worth it. The ground temperature out here hits about 120 degrees." Pointing to two canteens and a water bottle next to the body, he continued, "The bottle is empty, but we haven't touched the canteens or anything else—just waiting for you in case it's a murder."

"One thing, though," Axel said, "makes me lean toward suicide. From the size of the person, I'm guessing it's a female and we didn't find any other footprints in the wash besides what we think are hers.

Maybe, just maybe, she got snake bit. There're dozens of them within fifty feet of us right now." Nodding his head, he continued. "Maybe she was in a hell of a lot of pain and knew she was a goner. So, she took a quick way out and ate her gun."

Scanning the ground with a quick search for snakes, Ricky dropped his water camel and took his iPhone from his pocket. Flicking on his camera app, he moved in a clockwise pattern about ten feet from the body taking pictures, then repeated the action from about fifteen feet.

Looking at the two BP agents, he asked, "Is it safe to scrounge around the body, or might there be snakes under it?"

Axel gave a strong belly laugh. "We didn't touch that maggot-eaten thing, so you look around to your heart's content. I 'spect you'll let us know if you find a snake or two under it."

Ricky gave a disgusted little guffaw, extended his trekking stick, and slipped it under the body, holding his breath because of the thick odor that rose from the decayed mass.

Death is a hunter.

CHAPTER THREE

Ricky covered his mouth and nose with a handkerchief and stepped back. Taking a moment to gather himself, he glanced at the Border Patrol Officers and gave a muffled, "At least there weren't any more snakes."

Without warning, Axel lurched forward and nearly fell off his ATV as he spewed vomit down the front of his shirt and onto the sandy wash. Armando started to laugh, then caught himself, took a deep swallow, then backed up a dozen feet to find a breath of fresh air. "Lord, have mercy. That's awful," he bellowed.

With his face still covered by his handkerchief, Ricky enjoyed a private laugh at his newly found friends. Even in the face of whatever wickedness they discovered, they could still laugh at themselves. Each of them took a few moments to refocus on the task at hand and to allow Axel time to clean off his uniform shirt.

Stepping further back, Ricky spoke. "Did you put in a call to the Medical Examiner?"

"Yeah," Armando answered. "Did it when we called you. They're sending a Deputy Medical Examiner." Nodding his head, he continued. "I know him—Danny Trejo. He's a sharp young medical student working part-time for the M.E. He's out of the Hidalgo

County Office in Lordsburg." Looking at his watch and shaking his head in exasperation, he commented, "Should be getting here pretty soon. He'll take the body and whatever else we find once we move the carcass. They will be responsible for transporting it to the lab in Albuquerque. From then on, it's up to you and him to figure out who and what we've got here."

The three federal agents moved down the gulch away from the odorous human remains and sat in the shade of a mesquite tree. They sipped their water, munched on power bars supplied from Axel's pack, and kept a close watch on the time. The day was warming, and the body would only become riper in the heat. Patience was not one of their virtues. They wanted it over, the sooner the better. An hour later and drenched in sweat, they heard music to their ears: the grumbling sound of an ATV. The cavalry arrived in the form of Danny Trejo and a colleague riding in their Yamaha four-wheel-drive ATV.

Moments later, they bounced off the hillside and into the wash. Climbing off, Danny shouted a greeting to the BP officers who were coming back up the wash to what they now called a crime scene. "*Was geht?*" he shouted in bastardized German.

Axel shook his head. "And the dumb fuck is going to be a doctor?" He shouted back, "Why don't you kiss my ass, *der Doktor?*"

After a good laugh, Axel introduced Ricky to Danny, and his assistant, Deidre Cruz. She was a new medical student and part-time M.E. staffer in her mid-twenties, tall and slender, eager to join an investigation from the original crime scene to the lab.

13

After reviewing the agents' notes, the two medical professionals retrieved a body bag and their personal apparel from the rear seat of the ATV. It took a few minutes in the now-sweltering heat to don their blue, plastic hooded, one-piece suit, booties, gloves, goggles, and facemask.

Circling the body much as Ricky had done, Deidre began taking close-up and distant photographs of the body and surrounding area. Stepping back with Danny looking over her shoulder, they reviewed her work. Satisfied, Danny directed her to stow the camera while he laid out the OSHA-approved, liquid-proof body bag next to the body. Sweat dripped from around their headgear when they unzipped the bag directly alongside the body. Looking over his shoulder at Ricky, Danny spoke. "Do you want the gun now?"

"*Seguro.*"

Danny lifted the head a few inches while Deidre used a sterilized set of forceps to grip the trigger guard and lift the gun, in the process dragging coagulated blood onto the sandy soil. She gripped it firmly while Danny opened an evidence bag and held it out to her.

"Remember, it's loaded," she commanded when she eased it into the bag.

Ricky took it from Danny, sealed it, and initialed it across the seal. He gave a condescending smirk, shaking his head and speaking as much to himself as to his colleagues, "I'm no firearms expert, but this is the damnedest looking gun I ever saw. It's nothing like what we studied or fired for familiarization."

He and the others stepped back while the M.E. personnel lifted the body onto the bag. Unfortunately, the body shredded as they

14

lifted it, so it became a piecemeal effort of body parts, a baseball cap, clothing and boots, a backpack, a water bottle, and one water camel.

Ricky and the BP agents moved farther back as the odor wafted with the gentle breeze that came down the gulch. With the body sealed in the bag, Danny and Deidre each pulled a rake and hoe from the cargo bed of the Yamaha and began sifting through the sand where the body had lain. For the others, the smell became more putrid with each stroke of the digging tools, so they moved safely upwind. There was no value in getting sick again.

After twenty minutes, Danny shouted, "Got something."

Ricky and the BP agents returned, finding Danny and Deidre leaning against their ATV. Danny held out his open, gloved palm showing them a brass cartridge. "It was directly beneath her shoulder. It should be the expended brass from her gunshot."

Ricky approached them, visually examined it, and directed them to bag it and he would take it as evidence. His voice was nearly inaudible as he shook his head. "That's a weird-looking cartridge. I never saw anything like it. An expended brass should have an open end, but this one is clamped shut as if the ejector did it."

*

The deceased was loaded into the cargo bed and was unceremoniously hauled on the back of the ATV over the rocks and cactus to the waiting truck on the highway. Following an invitation, Ricky crawled onto Axel's ATV and went up the trail behind the guest of honor who was yet to be identified.

Standing alongside their vehicles while they stripped off their work clothes, Danny provided a quick overview. "Just from a cursory look, I'd say you have a female, very fit even before whatever it was happened to her, and with the placement of the gun under the head, it's likely a self-inflicted wound." Throwing his gear in the back of the truck, he continued. "We'll get to the morgue in Albuquerque today. With any luck, the preliminary autopsy will be done this evening, but it'll be a couple more days before toxicology is complete." He looked at Ricky. "Do you want to come up, or just do this on email, or phone?"

Ricky looked at his watch. "By the time you get to Albuquerque, today will be about shot. This is Monday. What about if I come up there Wednesday mid-morning?"

Nodding and extending his hand, Danny replied. "That should be perfect. We can go over whatever we know about her, go through her clothing and pack, and see where that takes us."

"You're on," Ricky said.

Inquisitiveness is a hunter.

CHAPTER FOUR

It was five o'clock Wednesday morning when Ricky backed out of his driveway. A faint glimmer of sunlight poked the summit of New Mexico's Florida Mountains, a prelude to the unrelenting heat that would bathe the Chihuahua Desert. It would be a long drive up Hwy.11 to I-25, and then follow the Rio Grande for 225 miles to Albuquerque and the Medical Examiner's office. There wasn't a shortcut. Five hours later, he found a parking spot at the Medical Examiner's building, a modern multi-story facility holding some of the most delicate and private secrets of a person's life—the cause and manner of their death.

He met Danny in a second-story conference room, a standard government-neutered meeting room with a six-foot conference table, eight straight back chairs, a framed picture of the Governor in one corner and the President in the opposing corner. Ricky took it in with a quick glance. *Appropriate,* he thought. *A liberal in one corner and a conservative in the other.* He smirked. *It was fitting.*

"Okay," Danny said when he passed a facemask to Ricky and donned one himself. "Let's get started." He ripped the tape off a cardboard box and carefully laid out the dead person's backpack, cell phone, water camel, and water bottles. Pointing to the second of his two sealed boxes, he said, "We removed her clothing before we could do the autopsy, so we went through her pockets. There wasn't anything in them except some money—three ten-dollar bills, one twenty, and five one-hundred Peso notes. All total, it equals about sixty-five dollars. No wallet or purse—*nada*. Anyhow, it's all in that box with her clothes," he said as he nodded toward the second box. "If you want to open it later and sort through it, you can, but not now. The stench will be stronger than what is on these things here. It'll drive us out if we don't wear extra breathing gear."

Scooting his chair around to the open box, he spoke. "She— yes, it was a woman—was between 25-35 years old. Her estimated height and weight were 5' 4", 125-135 pounds, with no identifiable marks, scars, or tattoos. The M.E. places her death approximately ten days before being found, so that puts it on or about June 15th or 16th. The cause of death was a gunshot wound inside her mouth exiting out the top left of her skull.

"Something very unique was that we couldn't find traces of GSR, that's gunshot residue, on either wrist. Most of her hands were missing from decomposition and scavengers. The point is, though, if she shot herself, we should have found *some* GSR on her wrist." Nodding his head, he continued. "But she either ate her gun, or it was fed to her. There were significant amounts of GSR in her mouth. Assuming she was right-handed, that's ninety percent of the population, she held the gun in her right hand, put the muzzle in her mouth, and fired. That would make it a suicide, plain and simple. However, what we found is confusing. Could somebody have shot her?" Bewildered by their findings, he shrugged. "Anyhow, you know what I know, so tell me about the gun and the cartridge we found with the body."

Ricky pulled his cell phone from his pocket, commenting softly. "Something is really screwy about this. It's all new to me." Giving a little shrug as he scrolled down his notes, he said, "I think we're on to something out of the ordinary for *coyotes* or illegal immigrants, or even a drug deal gone bad. This investigation is going to be an outlier." He leaned back and took a deep breath as he shook his head. "I'm saying this, but I hardly believe it myself. Yesterday an agent from Alcohol, Tobacco and Firearms looked at the gun." Reading from his notes in a monotone voice, he continued, "The gun is a Russian-made 7.62 semi-automatic especially designed for KGB assassination teams. It's known as a PSS, or what is commonly called a *silent pistol*. That's why you didn't find GSR on her hands or wrist." He shook his head. "The gun's design blocks it from emitting GSR with the intent to protect the assassin from being linked to the weapon. But, of course, fired at close range there would be GSR on the victim."

Taking another deep breath, he continued, "That's what explains the unusual spent brass you found under the body. It trapped all the GSR that otherwise would have been expelled with the ejected brass." He gave a little smirk and went on, "The Russians were ingenious in the design and manufacture of this gun and bullet, but that gives us a tangled web to work on. What did this woman have to do with the Russians?"

Flicking the cell phone off, he continued, "In all likelihood, she committed suicide. Unfortunately, we'll never know for sure since the spent bullet wasn't recovered because it passed through her skull and into never-never land."

Danny interjected, "Good point. You have a lot of work ahead of you. For our part, it'll take a few days for toxicology, but the pathologist found multiple snakebite wounds on her legs, arms, and hands. The doctor's educated guess is the victim was bitten one or more times, went down, and was bitten again, then put herself out of her misery, which would have been horrible from the snakebites. The doctor was at a loss about the lack of GSR anywhere except in her mouth, but your explanation will go a long way in explaining it.

"Now, let me add a couple more things to your problems. We found the cell phone in her pack, so our IT personnel worked on it. The phone number is in the 4-3-2 area code, so that puts it in or around Marfa, Texas. The name associated with it is Maria Espinoza."

Danny sat back in his chair, took a deep breath, and continued. "We generally don't investigate names, so that's going to be another starting point for you. However, IT found two numbers: one in her contacts and the other in her notes. For whatever it's worth, the contact number had been called on the 14th at 8:20 p.m. It went to the 4-3-2 area code to a cell phone in Boquillas del Carmen, a very small berg on the tip-end of the Big Bend across the Rio Grande. Technically, the number is in south Texas, but in reality, it's on the other side of the river. The name associated with it is Pablo Gonzales." He smirked and gave a wise-guy chuckle. "That's about like Joe Smith, so I doubt there's much to chase down on Mr. Smith.

"But" a smile crept across his face. "The other number is in the 5-2-0 area code. That's Tucson, Arizona. It was listed to a man named

Oleg Krutoy. It had an address of 4822 Calle Julio." Danny leaned back in his chair to enjoy his moment. "Guess what?" He didn't wait for a response. "I ran a record check on that name and scored big-time. It came up on the computer that he was a murder victim. It happened on June 15th, but that's all I got. I figured I needed to bow out because I was getting in over my head." He paused to wet his lips, then continued, "That puts it about two weeks before your people found Jane Doe in the desert, roughly 400 miles east of where Mr. Krutoy bought the farm.

"Nevertheless," he continued, "we collected blood samples from her body and clothing. I've got them in our evidence locker, so you can take them with you." He shrugged and offered a consoling smile. "But you've got to take it to the crime lab in Santa Fe. Your lab in Las Cruces doesn't do DNA, and we can't do it for you."

Ricky nodded. "There's just one more thing to do before I head home." He looked at Danny as they rose from their chairs. Looking at the clock, he continued, "I'm not going to make it home until late tonight. Sixty miles north to Santa Fe, an hour at the lab, then about six or seven hours to get home; maybe more if I stop to eat." He gave a half-hearted frown as they left the office. "There's something not right about this case. Too many twists and turns. It's like writing a straight line with crooked letters."

*

It was four o'clock before Ricky guided his pickup truck onto I-25, southbound from Santa Fe toward Albuquerque and on to the long stretch home. The time-consuming, tedious trip gave him time to consider his dilemma. The Jane Doe case had been elevated from one of a found body in the desert to a death brought on by snakebites that led to a possible suicide but was catapulted into a now mysterious death with international espionage implications. What would a Russian agent be doing in the desolate Chihuahua Desert, and what was her connection to a murder in Tucson?

Ricky shook his head and muttered his thoughts aloud, "A Russian assassin's gun; a dead woman alone in the desert; a dead man in Tucson with a Russian name; and a cell phone with the names Krutoy and Gonzales in it." He chuckled and nodded approval of where his investigative mind was going. *Are Jane Doe and Maria Espinoza one and the same? Why was she here?*

*

The Task Force's desert headquarters on New Mexico Highway 9 was bathed in the glare of a dozen overhead lights creating a never-ending daylight over their compound. The nation's first line of defense along the New Mexico border was once the headquarters of *El Rancho Agua Dulce*. Now, though, this lonesome sentinel was the heart and soul of the border wars. *Agua Dulce* had fallen victim to the war: the wrath of the cartel, the hazards of the influx of immigrants, and the loss of peace of mind—they had all taken their toll.

He tapped his code into the keypad, then sat silently in his truck while the gates slid open, welcoming him into the Task Force's inner sanctum. Other than a scattering of Customs and Border Patrol Agents stretched over the countryside, the facility would be staffed by a handful of support personnel monitoring the surveillance cameras and motion detectors spread over the desert. Parking near the door, Ricky slipped out of the front seat and pulled the two evidence boxes from the rear set. Setting them aside, he tapped his code in the keypad, hoisted the boxes, and carried them down the dimly lit hall to his workstation. Always cognizant of his manners, he continued into the far wing of the building housing the communications staff, offered them his greetings, then returned to his work bay.

An hour later with his property documented and placed in the evidence locker, he retraced his steps bidding a 'goodnight' to the communications officers, made his way back to his pickup and started for home. It was midnight, a nineteen-hour workday behind him. His wife and daughter would be asleep when he got home—just another day in the life of a Task Force Agent.

Tomorrow promised to be a challenging day—tomorrow and many tomorrows to come.

Anticipation is a hunter.

CHAPTER FIVE

The alarm clock buzzed at 6:00. It didn't care if Ricky had only five hours of sleep. He rolled over to find Muncie already up. Then it hit him: the smell of bacon. Grabbing his robe from the bathroom door, he padded down the cold vinyl hallway to the kitchen in his bare feet.

Muncie looked over her shoulder as he slipped up behind her and wrapped his arms around her waist. "What do you want, lover boy?" she asked.

He chuckled. "How about an appetizer?"

"Not today," she whispered in her sexiest come-on tone. "It's a workday. You've got to get Lupe to your mom's before eight o'clock or you'll be late for work."

"Seguro," he commented as he poured his coffee and took a seat at the table. "But why do you always have to be right?"

Muncie tossed a sidelong glance at him. "Because guys think about sex like it's the only thing in the world."

"Isn't it?" he cracked.

Placing a plate of fried eggs, bacon, and toast in front of him, she asked, "Now what's more important?"

Leaning over his plate, he looked up into her eyes. "I love it when you talk dirty while you're fixing my breakfast."

*

Almost on time, Ricky wheeled into the parking lot at the Task Force compound, entered through the back door, and went directly to the break room. After filling a Styrofoam cup with what passed for coffee, he strolled casually down the hall greeting his colleagues, then tapped on the doorframe to the office of his supervisor, Agent Miguel O'Rourke.

Miguel looked up from his computer screen. "*Pasa, mi amigo.* Take a seat and fill me in on your trip to the M.E."

Ricky pulled up a chair, sitting opposite O'Rourke. Tilting his head and smiling, he spoke. "Well, it was a hell of a long day, but we got some good work done. I picked up Jane Doe's personal items which didn't amount to much. She had some pesos and U.S. currency totaling about sixty-five dollars. I also picked up her blood samples and personal items from the Medical Examiner and took them to the crime lab in Santa Fe." Leaning forward with his elbows on his knees, he continued. "I still had the gun and magazine in my custody. It's a unique weapon: Russian-made. ATF inspected it before I went up to Albuquerque. It's known as a PSS: a silent 7.62 killing machine. It has a six-round capacity, but only had four rounds in the magazine—but let me go back and correct myself. It's not actually a magazine. The Russians catalog it as a detachable box, but we call it a *magazine*. Its serial number is a simple four-digit figure, 1574. If nothing else, that indicates this is an early model, probably put into use around 1983 or

25

1984. We didn't strip it down, but the lab will. If it's a complete factory package, each part should have the same number on it."

Each man drank another cup of coffee while Ricky described the unusual aspects of the investigation—the strange connection between Jane Doe, the gun, and the Tucson murder case.

Miguel leaned back in his chair and folded his arms across his chest. Looking up at the ceiling he spoke to himself as much as to Ricky. "Okay, we make a connection with the Tucson cops, enter a cartridge and a fired bullet into the National Integrated Ballistic Information System (NIBIS), and submit Jane Doe's DNA to the Missing Person File of the Combined DNA Index System. From NIBIS and CODIS, we should get a boost forward, and with you teaming up with Tucson, this case should be . . ." He paused. "I don't have the slightest idea where this is going to take you, but it sounds like you're in for a wild ride."

*

Following a quick succession of phone calls, Ricky spoke to Lt. Sandra Igo, Commander of the Violent Crimes Section at the Pima County Sheriff Department. "Yes," she said. "I'm familiar with the Krutoy case. I'll let you talk with Deputy Anaya as soon as he gets back. He's working on Krutoy along with the FBI since the crime occurred in Saguaro National Park. Larry Summers is their agent assigned to it. Both of them are out of the office at the moment, but they should be back within the hour." She paused for a moment, then continued. "Agent Basurto, I just received a message from your Santa Fe lab. They said they submitted a cartridge and slug from a 7.62

pistol yesterday and it's a match with the bullet our lab submitted on Krutoy's case."

"I'll be damned," Ricky said. "That's fast."

"Indeed, it is. What about this?" Igo said. "I'll set up a meeting here at our office tomorrow. Can you drive over here this evening? I'll get you a motel room. We can put our heads together, see what we know, and make an outline of where we go from there. Will that work for you?"

"Perfect," he said. "It's about a five-hour drive, so I'll be there and have my material ready to discuss."

"Great. I'll book a room for you and get back to you."

"No, that's not necessary. I've got a great-aunt there. I'll give her a call and spend the night at her place."

"Say," Igo uttered. "Are you the same Basurto who is related to a Tucson narc who was murdered several years ago?"

Ricky's voice suddenly became somber. "Yes, ma'am. He was my grand-uncle, Antonio Castaneda." He paused, then spoke softly, "I'll see you in the morning."

*

The sun had set by the time Ricky arrived at his great-aunt's home on Tucson's east side. *Tia* Elizabeth, as he referred to her, opened the door when he was parking his pickup at the curb. "Welcome, Ricky," she called out. "Bring your suitcase. I've got your bedroom ready."

After a hug and kiss on his cheek, she led him down the hall to a bedroom opposite hers. She gestured to his room. "A real B&B. It comes with a Mexican dinner and drinks, plus a first-class breakfast."

He laughed. "Can't beat that," he said, dumping his suitcase on the bed.

"C'mon, margaritas on the patio while we watch the moonrise," she said when she turned back toward the family room and the windows overlooking the patio. "Dinner is in the oven. We should be able to catch up on everything by the time it's done."

*

After two margaritas and a *chili relleno* each, they were up to date on her sons Matthew and Mark and their families, Ricky's family, plus a quick sketch of the Krutoy case that brought him to Tucson—a murder only a ten-minute drive east of where they sat in this peaceful ambiance.

When the conversation dwindled, they turned their attention to cleaning up the kitchen before calling it a day. Deep in his heart, Ricky knew tomorrow would open a new chapter in his life as well as for Jane Doe and Oleg Krutoy.

*

Sitting around the conference table were Lt. Sandra Igo, a trim, thirty-something, wearing a navy skirt and white blouse with a silver and turquoise necklace; Deputy Pepe Anaya, a stout forty-year-old with well-groomed dark hair and wearing a light blue guayabera shirt and tan khakis; and Special Agent Larry Summers who wore typical FBI attire, a starched white shirt with a blue and red striped tie, navy blue trousers, and tan Cole Haan loafers with a tassel. Ricky wore his standard uniform, a white cowboy shirt with pearl buttons, Levi's,

28

well-worn classic black and brown cowboy boots, and a handgun affixed to his belt.

He was impressed with the setting where they found themselves. It wasn't the standard government-neutered meeting room. Rather, it was an elegant, wood-paneled room with Arizona and American flags alongside each other, and photographs of the governor and the sheriff at opposite ends of the room.

Igo called the meeting to order in a professional yet polite manner. "Gentlemen," she said, "with the bits and pieces of scattered information we possess, it appears we face a murder case that goes beyond our normal run-of-the-mill killing." Shaking her head, she continued, "I don't see this as a family feud or an unhappy neighbor, and it's not likely to be a jilted lover's triangle or a drug deal gone bad. This was a targeted assassination."

Pursing her lips, she laid out the bare details of the known facts. "We have an elderly Anglo man, possibly of Russian descent, killed in a national park with a single gunshot to the back of the head. To be precise, the entry wound was pointed slightly upward at the point of the brain stem. Clearly, a well-intended shot. Four hundred miles to the east, we have an approximate thirty-year-old Hispanic female found dead and decomposed in the desert. Maybe suicide and maybe not. However, we have a match on the murder weapon used to kill Mr. Krutoy and the gun found with Jane Doe."

Igo tossed a sidelong glance to Deputy Anaya, "And we have a strange little Russian handgun manufactured especially for the KGB and their dirty work." She smiled. "Pepe, we've worked a lot of cases over the years, but nothing quite like this. Do you have a starting point for us?"

Nodding his head and laying his arms on the table, Anaya spoke with command and self-assurance, "Yes, ma'am. With three of us, we can stay coordinated and move this case along—ideally to a good conclusion, or at least take it to a dead end where we have exhausted all normal investigatory protocols. Then, when all else fails, we move outside the box into unknown waters." Nodding again, he continued, "Only then will we see how deep it really is."

Igo shivered and gave them a half-hearted smile. "I hate to think of what that might be. But, if you're correct, the waters will be very deep."

Skepticism is a hunter.

Chapter Six

Summers handed out copies of the search warrant he had obtained from the U.S. Magistrate authorizing a search of the house, outbuildings, and curtilage of the Krutoy property on Calle Julio. "I've got the key," he said. "One of our agents, along with a couple of deputies, made a cursory search the day Krutoy's body was found. They were looking for any other victims or obvious evidence, but it took only about twenty minutes." Making eye contact with Pepe and Ricky, he continued. "We can do a thorough search looking for letters, cell phones, computers, or something that might give us a nudge in the right direction. I suggest we go right now."

"I agree," Ricky said. "The longer we wait, the colder the trail gets." Scooting his chair back, he continued, "Somebody wanted him dead. We don't know who or *if* it was our Jane Doe who pulled the trigger, but somebody or some group wanted him out of the way."

Pepe joined in, "But an old man like that? He shouldn't be much of a threat to anybody."

Standing up and adjusting the knot on his tie, Summers commented, "Yeah, but being an old codger doesn't exclude the possibility that someone from a long time ago just found him." He gave a wry chuckle, "Maybe this was an overdue debt."

*

Following a quick lunch at the Lucky Wishbone, the three officers arrived at Krutoy's home. Parking at the curb, Summers nodded a polite, "Hello" to the old man across the street who was sweeping his sidewalk. "Give it five minutes," he mumbled, "and the whole neighborhood will know we're here."

"Make it two," Ricky said as he watched an elderly lady two doors down approach her car parked at the curb. She started acting busy and dusting the taillights as she watched the three of them walk up to Krutoy's front door.

Stepping inside, Summers closed the door behind them. Ricky followed, then did a quick visual and mental inventory. The houses in the neighborhood were of similar layout and about forty years old. While clean and neat, the house bore no evidence of the feminine touch—no floral arrangements or family pictures, no knick-knacks, no evidence of a family unit or workplace associates. It was an old bachelor's house, tidy and comfortable, but suited to his basic needs.

Summers pulled a notepad from his pocket and began with a general division of labor. "Anaya, why don't you take the living and family room? Take your time. Go through the credenza drawers, look under every piece of furniture, inspect the bottom side of the drawers, cushions, everything. Do you have your camera?"

Anaya gave a Cheshire cat grin as he produced his Sony camera from his pocket. "A good Boy Scout is always prepared."

Great," Summers replied. "Go through the house and document the rooms as they are before we touch anything."

32

Deputy Pepe Anaya proved his skills as a Crime Scene Investigator, meticulously going room to room, shooting from different angles, and making a permanent record of the layout of the victim's residence, including the coffee mug on the drain rack alongside the sink.

Twenty minutes later, he went to the front porch where Summers and Basurto sat on Krutoy's Adirondack teakwood chairs. "Done deal," he said. "I'm ready if you are. Let's take a look at what secrets our old fellow may have stashed away." He lingered a moment, then turned back to the living room and paused as though in deep thought.

He chewed his lip and took a deep breath, absorbing every aspect of the room—the globe ceiling light, the light switches and plugs, a coffee table and the area rug it rested on, and a stack of travelogue magazines on the coffee table. He exhaled with a hardy blow and commented with a joking, "I think we're going to be here a while."

"Okay," Summers continued, "there are two bedrooms, but one has been turned into an office of sorts. Ricky, why don't you take it?"

"*Seguro*, I'll take it apart and then put it back together."

Summers chuckled, "*Porque, no.*" He gave a polite smirk, "My mom was born in Mexico City, so I grew up speaking Spanish."

"Got me," Ricky cracked.

"Okay, and I'll start in his bedroom. When we find something of interest, give a call so we can photograph it before we handle it."

The buzz of the doorbell caught them off guard. Summers turned on his heel with the others following behind. When he opened the door, he was greeted by the old man from across the street. "Hi, sir," the old fellow said. "I'm Tommy Gerard and I live right across the street. I assumed you people were the police and wanted you to know something."

"Yes, what is it?" Summers replied while showing his identification to the man. "I'm Special Agent Summers with the FBI." Looking quickly over his shoulder at his colleagues, he continued. "These gentlemen are also law enforcement officers. Can we help you?"

The old man gave a nervous little chuckle. "Yes, sir. You sure can." Pointing to his house, he spoke confidently. "You see, I have Oleg's dog. I don't know the damned thing's name. It was some funny sounding Russian word, so I just call him Shitter, 'cause that's all he does. Shits all over the yard. What am I supposed to do with him?"

Deputy Anaya stepped around Summers and introduced himself to the neighbor. "I'll have Animal Control come out in the morning and pick up the little shitter for you. Will that be okay?"

Holding his side in laughter, the elderly gentleman blurted out his thanks, then turned to go home.

*

Ricky went to the hallway off the living room, turned to his right, and found the home office much as he expected—an inexpensive, oak, two-drawer desk, a folding chair, and a pair of two-drawer file cabinets side by side to the right of the desk. A floor lamp stood next to the desk and, like in the living room, a globe light hung from the ceiling. A small window looked out over the back yard which was a sickly presentation of splotchy Bermuda grass and a China Berry tree. A four-foot-high block patio wall surrounded the yard with a wooden gate providing access to the alley.

Like the living area, in the office, there were no pictures or mementos to be seen. He judged it simply as utilitarian. No frills.

Taking a pair of latex gloves from his hip pocket, he sat at the desk to peruse a small scattering of papers and sticky notes and sensed that all but one were of no apparent use. They were odds and ends: a reminder to get the dog shots and license renewed, a grocery order of normal food items, several crossword puzzles apparently cut out of the paper, and a note to get the car lubed. However, one page was different. It was a list of what he guessed were names, but they were written in a foreign language. *Russian Cyrillic? Might make sense,* he thought while inspecting them without a clue as to what language it was. The words were written on a sheet of notebook paper, one beneath the other in handwriting that differed from the handwriting on the other papers.

Канзас-Сити

Жители Нового Орлеана

Майами

Империал Бич

"In here," Ricky shouted, then stood aside when Summers and Anaya came in.

"What's up?" Summers asked.

"Beats me. This piece of paper was front and center on his desk. Russian, I assume. We'll have to get somebody to translate it for us."

Nodding approval as he looked at the list, Pepe took his camera from his pocket. "I got a couple of overall shots of the room, but I'll take a close-up shot of the desk and the papers."

"Good," Summers said. "I'll get an evidence box out of my car, and we can start cataloging things and boxing them."

*

After the picture taking, Ricky logged the paper and sealed it in an evidence envelope. Continuing the slow, meticulous search of the desk drawers, he realized Oleg was a pack rat, but a neat one—everything orderly and in its place. The drawer was only partially filled with individual manila folders: property tax forms for the last several years, car title and insurance; separate files for water, telephone, and electricity; receipts for every little thing he purchased in recent years—clothes, shoes, car repairs and tires, a new roof, house repairs, yard and garden supplies, and telephone bills.

Taking a short break, Ricky pushed back in his chair and did a quick inventory of what he did not see—a computer or evidence of a cell phone; nor were there records of Oleg ever having them.

He was a well-organized man, but no cell phone or PC. He shrugged and let out a deep breath. *Too old to care? Too old to get into the clusterfuck of the computer world? Ricky's* mind raced. *Or too careful to leave electronic footprints?*

He turned to the two file cabinets. Getting down on his knees and opening the first one, he found both drawers empty. To be sure he hadn't missed anything, he removed the drawers and examined them top to bottom, and front to back. Nothing.

Scooting over to the other cabinet and opening the top drawer, he found it to be a pile of old travel receipts dating back five years— hotels and motels, airlines, bars and restaurants, car rentals, and two hotel room fobs, one for the Charm Inn in Imperial Beach, California, and the other for the Laredo River Inn in Laredo, Texas. One point struck him—they were border towns. *Tucson's not exactly a border town, but close to it.*

Sorting the receipts on the floor didn't reveal a particular system to Oleg's travels. He would leave that for the Crime Analysis (CA) Unit to find any common denominators.

The fobs, he thought, *most likely something any of us can do at any time. Just forget to turn them in when we check out.* Nevertheless, it was something else for the CA unit to work on. He bundled them up in another evidence envelope and sealed it with his initials, then turned to the lower drawer.

Like the first one, it was a disheveled assembly of travel receipts, but these were from six to seven years ago. *Hmm,* he thought, *at least he was organized enough to lump them by the year. Seven years on the road. What was the old shoe salesman up to?*

Stuffing them into an evidence envelope and sealing it, he tossed them aside. Now was the time to go deep. He spent the next hour taking the plugs and outlets off, searching the underside and backs of the drawers, taking the ceiling light apart and looking beneath the electrical outlet there. Nothing of value. Just Tucson dust bunnies.

Anaya and Summers had the same results—nothing of evidentiary value. Oleg Krutoy kept a neat house. If there were any leads into his murder, it would come from his travel history.

"What about his car? Ricky asked.

"We have it at the Department of Public Safety lab," Summers replied. "They'll go through it with a fine-tooth comb and let us know what they find." He looked at his watch. "Nearly five o'clock. What about we knock off to get something to eat and come back here around 6:30? Most of the neighbors should be home and finished with their dinner. We can see what they know."

"Fernando's Hideaway," Pepe blurted. "Good Mexican food and prices."

*

After a leisurely dinner, they returned to the victim's house. "I'll take the houses on this side of the street," Summers directed. "Pepe, take the houses across the street." He glanced at Ricky, "Take the block across the alley on Calle Luna. We'll meet back here later and see where we go from there."

Pulling his pickup around the corner, Ricky draped a lanyard with his badge around his neck. He took a quick count—only five houses on the block, one directly behind Krutoy's home. With notebook in hand, he began the door-to-door interviews, working the block from the west end toward the east. The first house was dark. No one answered the doorbell. "Off to a bad start," he mumbled under his breath. The second house was no more promising. The occupants were an elderly couple, Henry and Mildred Martin. The interview was over almost before it started. Mildred was bedridden. Henry didn't know anyone on the other block and didn't care to. "No," he snapped. "I don't know that fellow. Now, if you will excuse me, I've got to clean up the kitchen." With that, he stepped back and slammed the door.

It'll have to get better 'cause I've struck out so far, Ricky thought as he approached the third house, the one directly behind Oleg's.

A spry little old lady answered the door almost immediately. Her hair was white as snow, cheeks alive with color, and attired as if she were a living promotion for a catalog. "Good evening, young man. Can I help you?"

Presenting his badge, Ricky introduced himself. "If you would have a minute, I'd like to ask you some questions about an incident involving your neighbor, Mr. Krutoy."

Stepping back and gesturing him inside, she spoke melodically, "Please come in and sit down. I heard about poor Mr. Krutoy. Isn't that a shame?" She didn't wait for a response before she continued. "Make yourself comfortable. Can I get you something to drink?"

"No, thank you," he replied. Sitting on the edge of an occasional chair with notepad in hand, he asked, "Did you know Mr. Krutoy?"

"Oh, indeed I did. My name is Mrs. Phillips, Margaret Phillips. I've lived here almost forty years and have known Oleg ever since he moved into our little neighborhood. I was married at the time, but my Seth passed away twenty years ago." Shaking her head, she continued. "Isn't it terrible what happened to Mr. Krutoy? Why, I just cannot imagine anyone wanting to hurt the dear, sweet man."

"Yes, ma'am. Anything you can tell me might help us solve this case and bring peace of mind for everyone who knew him."

Sitting forward on the couch, Margaret's lips quivered as she held back her tears. She dabbed her eyes with a tissue, then spoke

39

softly. "He was a wonderful man. We were friends, Oleg and me." She caught herself, gave a twinkle of a smile, and continued. "Oh, no. nothing like that. We were just friends. Old folks that no one much cared about, but we liked each other." She paused, reminiscing, while Ricky sat unobtrusively, waiting.

Nodding her head, she continued. "He was a good man. Not that he'd ever go to church with me. I'm a Methodist, you know. He was Orthodox, so he didn't bother about going to church. Not even on Christmas or Easter. He'd stay home, but he wasn't a bad man. He liked to cook, and sometimes on special days he'd invite me over for dinner." Once again, she gave a little embarrassed giggle and continued. "Our alley gates sit opposite each other, so we could go to one another's house without neighbors sticking their noses into our business."

Sensing this could be a long story, Ricky sat back in the chair with a smile creasing his lips. She looked like a sweet little lady. *But time will tell,* he thought.

"Anyway, Officer Basurto, I liked Oleg. It tears my heart out to hear somebody would kill him. He's the only person in this whole city who would take time to be nice to me."

"Did he ever talk to you about his business or where he lived before he moved to Tucson?"

"Oh, yes indeed. He was a lovely man. He owned a shoe store in Brooklyn but retired and came to the desert—like so many older people. Get away from the crowds and the snow, you know." She smiled. "That was one thing about Oleg. He always wore good clothes, and *especially* shoes." She nodded approval of her own statement. "Really nice, expensive shoes."

"Can you tell me anything about his family or his business associates?"

Margaret shook her head. "He didn't have family here. If I understood it, and we didn't talk about it much, he had family in the old country. But we really didn't go into that sort of thing. It made him fidgety, so I just left it alone."

"What about his shoe business?" Ricky asked.

She smiled and looked down. "Now, Oleg did keep his toe in the business. That's how he said it. Sometimes he'd take a trip—always business, he said. Be gone for one or two days, then home." She looked into Ricky's eyes. "He always seemed happy when he got home. He'd fix me a Russian dinner sometimes. We'd eat, and I learned to drink vodka—just sip it, of course." She gave another embarrassed chuckle and continued.

Ricky sensed she was enjoying herself, so he allowed her to talk. Realistically, it was in these types of conversations that true colors were often revealed. While she was so 'into it,' he slipped his hand in his pocket and texted a message to Larry that he was making headway and would see them later.

"Please sir, understand, we were the best of friends but nothing beyond that."

Ricky responded with a nod and smile, "Certainly, I understand. Everyone needs a friend."

"He was so kind. Sometimes he'd call me, and I would go over there and the two of us would have dinner." Smiling and gazing toward the ceiling as though she could picture it this very moment, she continued. "Quite a cook, he was. I could never pronounce those hard Russian words, but he'd tell me what was in it and how to prepare it—it was so wonderful."

Instantly sitting upright and bright as a child on Christmas morning, she continued. "I must tell you this. It shows what a kind gentleman he was. Why, do you know he was even teaching me to write those awful Cyrillic letters?" Giving a humble little chirp, she went on. "Cities. That's what he was teaching me to write. The names of cities here in America, but he had me use the letters of his native tongue."

"Any cities in particular?"

"Oh, yes. He'd always teach me the word; then he'd use it in a sentence." She chuckled again before she returned to her monologue. "They were cities where he traveled for his business. I remember them well 'cause it was so darn hard to learn them—Miami, New Orleans, Imperial Beach, and Kansas City. Those were the places he went to check on his shoe business."

"Recently?" Ricky asked.

"Oh, yes. Every three or four weeks he'd have to go. He must have been very successful with all the nice clothes he wore and that spotless car he drove." Nodding in self-approval, she smiled and sat back. "I'll miss Oleg. He was so nice to me."

"Did he ever talk to you about his trips?"

"Oh, sometimes he would be a bit exasperated about the way people, I guess his employees, were doing things. But, overall, he was a happy person."

"What caused his exasperation?"

"Oh, my goodness," she replied. "I don't want to say unkind things about him. He was so nice, but sometimes he would get upset and drink that terrible vodka—he really liked it. It was just a week ago that he got home from Kansas City. We had already planned on dinner before he left, so of course, I was right on time. I went through the alley gate right up to his back door. He was standing in the kitchen on the telephone and was really upset with whomever he was talking to. Of course, I didn't want to overhear his conversation, so I stepped back a bit but I could still hear him."

She shook her head, wetting her lips and continued, "My goodness, he was upset. I never heard my Seth use that type of language, but I couldn't help but hear he was barking so loud." Mrs. Phillips paused, looked down at her feet and composed herself before continuing,

"Sir, he used the "B" word when he was talking about a woman, but I don't have any idea who it was."

"What else did he say," Ricky asked.

"I can tell you exactly what I heard. He said, 'You've got to move them across the border. I don't give a—then he used an *F* word. 'I don't give a *f* but I pay you to do a job, so do it.'"

At that point, Mrs. Phillips sat back. Tears dripped slowly down her cheeks.

"Can I get you a drink of water?" Ricky asked.

She half laughed and half cried, pointing to a credenza across the room. "No, but I'll take a shot of Scotch."

He poured one for each of them, sat alongside her, tipped their shot glasses together, and gave a toast. "To Mr. Krutoy."

"To Mr. Krutoy," she responded. "I loved him so much."

Remembrance is a hunter.

CHAPTER SEVEN

The three officers met for breakfast at the *Perezosa Café,* only a block away from the sheriff's office. Between sips of coffee and bites of his *huevos* and *tamales,* Ricky sorted through the drawn-out evening with Mrs. Phillips. Shaking his head, he mumbled more to himself than to the others, "I thought she'd never quit talking, but I didn't want to shut her up. Every once in a while, she would toss me a bone to keep my interest, then get back to what it's like to be an old widow." He gave a half-hearted laugh and continued, "It took nearly two hours and three shots of Scotch, but by damn she knew Oleg pretty well. Those cities she wrote down—those are the places where he invited her to go with him."

"Did she actually see him conducting any business?" Pepe asked.

Ricky shook his head. "Nope. He'd have a nice hotel for them but left her there when he went about his business."

"New Orleans, Kansas City, Miami, and Imperial Beach," Summers mumbled. "How long would they be gone?"

"Usually just overnight. They stayed in New Orleans a couple nights on her only trip there, but he took her sightseeing the second day."

"So, she just hung around and he went about whatever business he supposedly had?" Anaya asked.

"*Exactamente*. He never talked to her about what he was doing—just going to meetings. Then they'd have dinner and come home the next day."

"Did she ever see him use a credit card?" Summers asked.

Ricky finished his coffee, set the cup down, and leaned back in the booth, relaxed. "She said she never saw a man with so much cash, and that's how he paid for everything. Cash on the barrelhead—that's her exact wording."

Summers leaned his elbows on the table. "Wasn't she suspicious?"

"Very," Ricky said.

Summers glanced at his watch, then spoke very purposely in a quiet, business-like tone. "Gentlemen, I am the bearer of bad news today." He took a deep breath and exhaled slowly. "They pulled me off the case. I'm not even supposed to be here. They think I'm on my way to Phoenix to assist in a case they're working and are short-handed. My supervisor said you two had this well in hand and the Bureau could better use me elsewhere." He chewed his lip and shook his head. "I hate to sound paranoid, but there's more to this than meets the eye. It gets more complex every day."

"What happened?" Ricky asked.

Summers shook his head, bewildered. "He didn't say, and I didn't ask. It's clear to me that I—or *we* got too close to something. Special Agent Thompson, my immediate supervisor, called me in first thing this morning. He was straight and to the point, 'We've got better things for you to do than be on this Krutoy case.'"

With that, Summers reached into his shirt pocket, retrieved the door key to Oleg's house, and slid it across the table to Anaya. He gave a half-hearted chuckle, "The keys to the kingdom." He leaned back with his hands folded behind his head. His eyes bounced back and forth from Pepe and then to Ricky. "You're too close to something, but I don't know what that something is."

Summers leaned in across the table and continued, his voice little more than a whisper. "When we finished in the neighborhood last night, I went to the office to do some background on our deceased, Mr. Krutoy. I hit something that somebody doesn't want us to know about." He grimaced as he continued. "You don't know where you got this, but your man Oleg Krutoy had been in Witness Protection. About ten years ago, he told the U.S. Marshall who was supervising him to go screw himself. No explanation, he just packed up and left town for parts unknown. That is, unknown until now."

"That's it?" Pepe fired back.

"Yep," Summers replied. "He'd been in the Russian Mafia working along the Atlantic seaboard from South Carolina to Massachusetts. His cover there was a Tommy Tucker Shoe Outlet he owned. It was a multistate/federal task force that built the case against him. They finally arrested him in Boston where he was involved in human and drug trafficking. They had him cold and he was facing years in the joint. Being a smart guy, he accepted the deal they offered and testified as a prosecution witness. That's when he went into Witness Protection. They moved him to Miami and set him up

47

managing the shoe department in one of those big box stores. Here's where it gets a little complicated. Apparently, he was recognized by somebody in Miami, so he was moved to New York but remained under the protection program. He lasted almost five years there; then he told the U.S. Marshall assigned to him to *fuck off* and disappeared."

"They didn't track him?" Ricky asked.

"Nope. It's a fact of life. Snitches come and go. He went, and that was the end of the story." A hint of a smile creased Summers' lips. "Actually, I think the guys in New York were glad to see it when he bought the farm. That's a good incentive for the next guy they're trying to twist. Stay with us and we'll protect you; get out and it's only a matter of time before somebody finds you and settles the debt."

After shaking hands, the trio separated and each got into their own vehicle. Ricky watched in silence as Summers backed out of the parking lot and turned north on the Interstate toward Phoenix.

*

Meeting in the conference room with Lt. Igo and Pepe, they brought her up to speed, tiptoeing around the Summers situation, only revealing that he was needed in a case of higher priority and would not be available on the matter of Mr. Krutoy.

Lt. Igo cocked her head and gave a Cheshire cat grin to her deputy. "I didn't fall off the hay wagon this morning, but I know what you mean. You got too deep into something the Bureau would rather forget."

Pepe nodded in agreement. "*Seguro que sí.*"

"Then let's get to work," she intoned.

48

She looked at Ricky. "Does your sweet little old lady recall the names of the places where she and Krutoy shacked up?"

He nodded. "In Miami, KC, and New Orleans, they stayed in a Royal Viking hotel. She went with him to those three places, but never to Imperial Beach. She was scheduled to go with him but got sick and missed the trip."

Igo sat back in her chair with her hands folded on her lap. Looking inquisitively, she asked, "Do you think she's being open and truthful with you, or would a female deputy put her more at ease?"

Ricky shook his head. "No. No female investigator. Let me handle her. I'll get everything out of her but I will have to take it at a pace she's comfortable with."

Igo looked at Pepe. "The Charm Inn. It sounds like a lovely place with an ocean view." She frowned and shook her head. "But not in Imperial Beach. It's not very high on anyone's vacation agenda." She paused and looked at her fingernails as if in deep thought, then turned her attention back to Pepe. "You don't need me to tell you what has to be done. Actually, we might be better off without the FBI on this. They can have the worst bureaucracy in the world. They can be great on one hand, but a millstone around the neck on the other."

She scooted her chair back, rose, and eyed Deputy Anaya. Standing six feet tall, she exuded command presence with her dark hair pulled into a ponytail secured with a turquoise and silver grommet, and her badge pinned to her starched, white shirt,. Her voice was sharp and to the point. "Keep me posted."

Authority is a hunter.

49

CHAPTER EIGHT

"I've got an idea," Ricky said as he and Pepe walked into the sheriff's parking lot. "I thought about it last night but couldn't get it out of my head. Now, though, hearing about Oleg's history, I know it in my bones. We missed something." Shaking his head as they went to their respective vehicles, he commented, "We looked at the obvious, but we need to think like Krutoy. He survived all these years by being smart, but we can't let him outsmart us. We missed something, but what?"

Twenty minutes later, they pulled to the curb on Calle Julio and started up the walkway to the front door.

"Hey, fellas," a voice called from behind them.

Spinning around, Ricky saw old Mr. Gerard quick-stepping across the street. "Don't you boys ever sleep?" he asked when he approached them.

Anaya responded. "Good morning, sir. How are you today?"

Gerard chuckled. "A man my age is doing great if he's vertical, but what about you fellows? Don't you ever sleep?" He continued before they could respond. "Wasn't that you boys here at two o'clock this morning? I was up taking a pee and looked out the window," he said when he turned and pointed back toward his house. "Said to myself, why those boys are working too hard."

Ricky interjected before Mr. Gerard could continue. "No sir. That wasn't us. Could you tell us exactly what you saw?"

The old man shuffled his feet and adjusted the belt beneath his well-fed stomach. "Officers, I think there's more to this than what I imagined." He paused, then spoke hesitantly. "When I first heard that something happened to Oleg, I just hoped against hope that maybe some dope fiend tried to rob him and killed him. That was wishful thinking, but I knew better. Now seeing you here and what happened last night," he paused again, looking down at his feet before looking directly into Ricky's eyes. "I know this is a lot more than some dope fiend trying to rob an old man." He paused again and looked back toward his house. Like Oleg's, it was a well-kept, flat-roofed tract house with a well-trimmed Bermuda lawn. Clay flowerpots and a veritable kaleidoscope of Wandering Jews, Marigolds, and Poppies sprouted color along the front porch.

"Let me pour a cup of coffee for you—fresh right before you drove up." He turned toward his house as he spoke over his shoulder. "There're some things you might need to know. Maybe Oleg wasn't such a great fellow after all."

*

Entering the kitchen, Ricky recognized the effect of the 'woman's touch,' much unlike Oleg's tidy but tired old house. Gerard introduced his wife when she entered the kitchen from the laundry room. Dressed in a bright yellow housedress, but prim and proper with a little white apron draped around her waist and her silver/gray hair tied into a bun, the spritely octogenarian's smile lit up her face. "My better half," Gerard said, "Mollie, these fine gentlemen are police officers. After what I saw last night, I think we might ought to tell 'em what we've seen over there."

Nodding in agreement while she took three mugs from the cabinet, she gestured to the circular oak table and chairs. "Sit yourselves down and I'll pour some coffee for you." Glancing first at Pepe, then to Ricky, she spoke with a soft, melodious voice. "Straight up, or with milk and sugar?"

"Straight up," Pepe replied.

"Make it two," Ricky added.

She poured for the men, then took a small china cup for herself, and the four of them sat around the table. Ricky sipped his coffee, then spoke. "Last night. Tell us about it."

"As I said," Gerard replied. "Old guys have to get up in the night and last night was no different. By chance, I looked at my clock on the nightstand and it was two o'clock on the nose. I was going into the bathroom when I noticed car lights coming down the street." Nodding approval of his own statement and scratching his unshaven chin, he continued. "This is a quiet neighborhood. There aren't many young families around anymore. Just us old folks, and we aren't running around in the middle of the night. So, I went to the living room window where I had a clear view, and the car pulled up and parked right where you fellows are parked.

"Unusual," I said to myself. "Those cops sure must have something going." So, I sat on the edge of my chair and watched. I

52

saw one person, a man stockier than either of you, get out. I don't know if there was anyone else in the car, but the one gentleman went to the front door. He had a little flashlight and he turned it on so he could get his key into the lock. I watched him go in and I could tell he was moving around the house because he turned the lights on when he went from room to room. Of course, I couldn't see exactly what he was doing because the drapes were pulled, but he was in there a good ten minutes—maybe even fifteen.

"Now, I needed to take a pee, but came right back here and nothing had changed. He went to all the rooms I could see; then he turned off the lights and went to his car and left. He didn't look like he was in a hurry. He just went about his business and skedaddled."

"Was he carrying anything when he left?" Pepe asked.

Gerard shook his head. "Not that I could tell."

Ricky sipped Mollie's steaming hot coffee, then rested the mug on the paper coaster she placed in front of each of them. Glancing first to Mollie, then to Tommy, he asked, "But there's something else. What was it that aroused your curiosity?"

The elderly couple exchanged glances, then Mollie answered. "Forgive me, Lord, if I say something wrong about Mr. Krutoy, but," she said when she looked directly into Ricky's eyes, "there was something evil about that man. I felt his spirit, and it wasn't anything like he pretended to be. It was an evil spirit—dark and mean. That's what I felt, but whenever he spoke or just said hello, he was as nice as an angel. But inside, I knew different."

"What was it?" Pepe asked, "that gave you that feeling?"

Mollie's smile disappeared. "It was seven years ago," she remarked. "I don't like a sneak, and he was one." She grimaced as if it hurt her to talk. She sipped her coffee, put the cup down, and looked directly at Pepe.

"My sister, bless her soul, she's gone now. We celebrated her birthday. Just us girls. We went to the Tiki Club to have a nice quiet dinner together and have one of their wonderful desserts." She paused and looked around as if to be sure no one else could hear her comments. "Well, we were at a corner table beneath some palm fronds. It was a little dark where we sat, so probably Oleg and his two friends didn't see us when they came in. The maître d' seated them at a table across from us. We couldn't hear a word they said, but *oh*," she emphasized, "they looked really nasty. Mean men, that's what they were."

Ricky shook his head. "I don't understand, Mrs. Gerard. What are you implying? Can you explain it a little more for us?"

Mollie sipped her coffee, then took a deep breath and exhaled. "Oleg's back was to us, but I could see the expression on the other two men's faces and they looked very stern. The waiter took their order and brought their drinks; then all three of them hunched forward and were really jabbering. Of course, I didn't hear a word they said, but those were some mean-looking and very angry men." She sat back and gave a sick little chortle. "They certainly weren't celebrating anybody's birthday."

"Can you tell us about the two men? Their age or anything?" Anaya asked.

Mollie sipped her coffee and very carefully put it down on her coaster. "Indeed, I can," she spouted. "They were a lot younger than Oleg, but they both were as big as a barn—big, husky fellows. The way they were dressed looked like they came out of a Humphrey Bogart gangster movie—silk shirts, they both had gold chains around their neck, and greasy black hair combed back." She chuckled. "Maybe I'm aging myself, so let's say they were gangsters in the Soprano TV show."

The three men chuckled in unison. She had described them accurately.

She continued, "They talked a long time. They were yapping so long and hard that they even let their meal get cold. But, anyway, we finished our meal—we shared a chocolate and strawberry dessert—and paid our bill and left."

"Have you seen those men again?" Ricky asked.

She gave him a quick smile and nodded her head. "Oh yes. I ran into them one day at the grocery store about two years ago. It was just one of those fellows and Oleg. They didn't see me, but they were sitting at a table in the coffee shop. It looked like Oleg was making some notes on a napkin, but I didn't stay around. I just got my things and came home. But there was one more time about a year ago. I couldn't sleep and had gotten myself a cup of warm milk and was sitting on the chaise lounge on the front porch. It was the middle of the night and it was beautiful. A full moon night." She sat back in her chair, adjusted her apron, and sipped her coffee.

Ricky watched her carefully as she appeared to be steeling herself for what she was about to say.

She paused for a long moment, then spoke so softly they almost couldn't hear her. "A car pulled up at the curb right in front of Oleg's place. Indeed, two men got out and went to the door. Now, Oleg's house was dark but no sooner did those men reach his porch than the door opened. I could hear Oleg's voice. He was saying something, but I'm not certain what he said. It sounded like he wasn't speaking English. Anyway, those men went in and the living room lights came on.

"By this time, I was curious, so I stayed put on my lounge and waited. Of course, I wasn't wearing a watch, but it was about ten minutes later when those men came out and left." Shaking her head, she looked down at her now empty cup. "Those were evil people. I never saw them again and am glad of it.

"But, in fairness," she said, "every once in a while, I might be out taking a walk when Mr. Krutoy would be in his yard, which he really didn't keep up very well, but he'd smile and say a nice little greeting. So, he wasn't all bad, but I don't think I'd trust him too far."

"Well, look there," Tommy interjected as he pointed his short, stubby finger toward the front window. "It's those Animal Control people. I reckon they're here to get Shitter."

*

Fifteen minutes and minus one little Shitter, Ricky and Pepe returned to Oleg's front porch. Opening the door, Ricky commented as he shook his head, "Something's here, but what the hell is it and where would he have hidden it?"

"In plain view," Anaya replied. "With eyes wide shut and it's so obvious we're walking right past it. *If*," he emphasized, "that other *hombre* didn't beat us to it."

The two investigators spent the next two hours with their latex-gloved hands feeling every cushion seam; the upper and lower wall edgings of each room; removed the covers on the oven and microwave; removed everything from the kitchen counters to search for hidden compartments; examined each canned and bottled food and drink container looking for contraband holding devices, and finally searched Shitter's dog house in the back yard for anything of evidentiary value. In the end, there was nothing.

Hot and tired, they sat in the living room, Pepe on the couch and Ricky in a lounge chair.

"Something's screwy," Pepe commented softly. "If we don't find anything here, I'll have the crime lab take his car apart." He gave a strong exhale, "Something's somewhere."

Ricky nodded. "*Seguro que sí.*" Then, as if hit by a bolt of lightning, he lurched forward, staring at the fireplace. "It's a friggin' gas fireplace."

"Too hot for that now," Anaya replied.

Ricky jumped to his feet, reached out and lifted aside the heavy bronze-colored fireplace screen. "Inside, Pepe. It's going to be in here."

Pepe leaned forward, staring into the fireplace. "Son of a bitch. I think you're on to something."

Crossing his legs, Ricky sat in front of the fireplace and removed the six artificial ceramic logs from the top of the grate and handed them to Pepe.

"Look at them," Ricky uttered. "They're like new. Never been used."

Together, the two men slowly examined each log but found nothing. They appeared to be standard ceramic logs, albeit unused.

"Give me a hand," Pepe said as he grasped the end of the heavy metal grate that held the logs. They pulled it free from the fireplace and sat it on end on the floor where they could examine it thoroughly. "Nothing," Pepe blurted as they finally laid it flat on the floor. "Fucker's solid steel."

"I need a flashlight," Ricky said when he hopped up and went to the kitchen. "There's one beneath the sink." He chuckled. "I know, 'cause I already checked it out."

He returned moments later, sat cross-legged on the floor, and flicked the light on. The beam of the three-cell flashlight pierced the darkness on the fireplace as he leaned in with his upper body. The light shown across the clean, gray, clay fireplace bricks—one side to the other, top to bottom. Shaking his head, his voice was little more than a whisper. "*Nada*. Clean as a whistle and never been used."

"*Abajo*," Pepe said. "*Por la chiminea.*"

Ricky rolled over on his back and scooted into the fireplace with his light shining up to the damper and chimney. His comment was instantaneous. "Home run," he barked. Reaching up with his empty hand, he pulled down a bundle of string-wrapped butcher paper the size of a football, and a smaller one similarly packaged.

Passing them to Anaya, he slid out and sat on the floor as Anaya gingerly placed the packets on the floor between them. Laughing, he joked, "Are we making any bets on what's in them?"

"The real Oleg, or whatever his name is," Ricky said as he began to untie the larger bundle. It was simply tied with a bowknot holding it together. With a minimum of melodrama, they eased the butcher paper free and spread the contents on the floor . . . money, and more money, and passports—five of them.

Anaya stood over the treasure and began taking photographs of their newly found evidence of the life of Oleg Krutoy. When he finished, they scooped everything up and took it to the kitchen table along with the smaller packet. Anaya stacked the money, then separated the denominations into stacks of 20s, 50s, and 100s. He paused to take another picture, then they counted it out—$21,650.00.

"Not bad for a little pocket money," Ricky joked. Scooting the money aside, he pulled the passports from the table's edge to lie directly in front of him and spread them out, face up.

Again, Anaya stood over them and took a photograph.

"Here we go," Ricky commented when he picked up the first one. "Romanian," he whispered when he opened it and found it bore the photograph of the man they knew as Oleg Krutoy. The name on it was Andrei Popescu. "Interesting," he said tossing it aside and picking up the next one: Russian in the name of Dusa Bobrov. He gave another half-hearted chuckle and picked up the third passport, this one from Azerbaijan. It bore the name of Raul Mammadova. The fourth one was a Turkmenistan passport under the name of Eziz

Petelol, and like the others, it had a photograph of the man they knew as Oleg Krutoy.

"Who is this son of a bitch?" Pepe asked.

Grabbing the last passport from the table, this one from the United States, Ricky flicked it open, then gave Pepe a sidelong look. "Oleg Krutoy."

Pepe tilted his chair back on its rear legs with his hands over his head, stretched and yawned. "Damned if I know," he said. "I'll tell you what I *do* know . . . old man Krutoy was an enigma. He was whatever he had to be with whomever he was with, but however he covered his tracks, somebody from his past caught up with him: a very professional hit."

Stacking them in his hand like a deck of cards, Ricky scrutinized the passports one at a time, starting with the U.S. passport. It was issued in 2010 and showed multiple travel dates to Venezuela, Azerbaijan, Germany, Russia, and Italy, with the most recent trip nine months earlier to Grozny, Chechnya.

The expired Turkmenistan passport was issued in 2002 and listed only two round trips, both in 2004: one to Madrid and the other to Berlin. Both started and ended in the capital city of Ashgabat.

The Romanian passport was issued in 2013. The last documented trip on it was in 2015, a one-way to London, England.

Reaching for the next passport, Ricky smirked and held it to his forehead ala Johnny Carson, "Azerbaijan, where oh where did Oleg go?" He placed it flat on the table, and with a melodramatic flip, opened it. Glancing at it, then to his colleague, he gave an angry little remark. "The bastard used it once in 2018 on a one-way trip to Frankfurt. *Entonces, nada.*"

Ricky gave a disgusting blow of his breath and picked up the Russian passport. He carefully opened it, paused, and gave a Cheshire cat grin. "What did we expect?" he asked while glancing at Pepe. "Dusa Bobrov." Thumbing through the pages, he read off the ports of entry: Frankfurt, Paris, Chicago, Dallas, Kiev, and Grozny. "He was in Grozny on January 17th of this year, and in Dallas on the 20th." He smirked again. "He was a busy old fart."

Pepe nodded. "Sure, but where does it take us?"

"To packet number two," Ricky replied as he untied the string on the second bundle.

Spreading the contents onto the tabletop, Anaya cracked a satisfying grin. "Gotcha, you old coot." He glanced at Ricky. "His bank statements." The two men methodically began to separate the stack of papers into two piles: one for each of the bank records—Rincon National Bank, and another for Ridgeline National Bank.

"I know both of those places," Anaya interjected. "Rincon is down here on the corner of Broadway and Swan, but the Ridgeline National Building is downtown on Stone Avenue."

Still sorting the records, Ricky found a business card. Lifting it up, he read it aloud. "Leonard Lazzarato, Attorney at Law."

Pepe snatched the card from Ricky's hand. "Look at that address: 604 Ridgeline National Building." They eyed each other and gave satisfying little smirks. "We're closing in," Pepe said as they continued sorting the documents. Moments later, they sat back as a victorious air swept over them.

As he organized the balance sheets on the table, Ricky said: "$2,268.45 at Rincon."

Anaya laughed at him, "Too bad we're not playing cards, 'cause I beat the crap out of you. A total of $403,965 at Ridgeline." He paused momentarily, then commented. "Not bad for a retired shoe salesman."

An hour later, they had photographed their findings, locked up the house, and marked and secured Oleg's money and documents into the Evidence Division at the Pima County Sherriff's Department.

"*¿Ahora que?*" Pepe asked.

Sitting at Deputy Anaya's cubicle, they called the office of Leonard Lazzarato, Attorney at Law. In what amounted to a somewhat humorous five-minute back-and-forth with his secretary, Anaya finally settled with a meeting the next morning at 10 a.m.

Joy is a hunter.

CHAPTER NINE

After hearing about Lazzarato's reputation from his great-aunt, Muncie, and even more from his *compadre*, Deputy Pepe Anaya, Ricky was not surprised by Leonard's office suite. It was his private little kingdom with oiled mahogany walls, autographed photographs of famous Arizonans, politicians, car dealers, movie stars, professional athletes, All-American athletes from the university, and a personally autographed picture of the President of the United States.

One thought was clear to Ricky—Leonard was not a man to be taken lightly. Following a greeting between Pepe and Monica Rosas, the lawyer's striking secretary, they were shown into the inner sanctum. She closed the door behind her when she left.

Their introductions were brief and to the point. With a minimum of fanfare, the tycoon invited them to join him for coffee at a circular conference table which was adjacent to the windows and overlooked downtown and the mountains to the west. The two officers took their seats while their host poured coffee from a sterling silver pot into monogrammed cups bearing a swirled "L."

Ricky smiled inwardly. *Lazzarato enjoys flexing his ego.*

A silver serving tray in the center of the table held a creamer and sugar bowl. Lazzarato heaped two spoons of sugar into his cup. Glancing at his guests, he offered the condiments to them. Each of them declined, then sipped their steaming, hot beverage.

"Perfect," Anaya said when he slowly placed his cup on the paper coaster.

Leonard cupped the hot mug in front of him, glanced casually at the two men, then spoke in a measured tone to Anaya. "My secretary informed me you wanted to discuss a Mr. Oleg Krutoy, but I do not know the gentleman. Might he be known by something else?"

Anaya sipped from his cup again, carefully preparing an appropriate response. "Krutoy. That's how we know him, but since he is deceased, we were under the belief that you might offer some insight about this man we know only as Oleg Krutoy."

The lawyer and the officers were aware they were playing a cat-and-mouse game: Who would blink first?

"Krutoy, you say? I don't know anyone by that name."

"Your business card was found in his effects."

"Many people have my card. That's how I earn a living."

"This man was murdered."

"Are you implying anything about me?"

"He's dead. He lived an underworld life. He had your card, a significant amount of money, and a variety of passports. He was Russian. I meant that as a question."

"I have clients all around the world."

"Dead ones in Tucson?"

Leonard shook his head and leaned forward with his elbows on the table, smirking. "Gentlemen, let's come to the point. Are you here concerning the murder I read about in the paper? The man at Saguaro National Park?"

Ricky nodded approval. "Known to us as Oleg Krutoy, but likely has a variety of names. We have no idea who he really is or why someone would want him dead. That's why we're here. We believe he was your client." Ricky caught himself and quickly gave the attorney an easy out. "Of course, you may never have known him as Krutoy, but if you can put us on the right track, we could possibly make some progress on his murder."

Lazzarato sat back and folded his arms over his chest. He dipped his chin to Ricky. "Indeed, I never heard the name by which you identified him, but yes," he smiled and nodded, "I probably know your Mr. Krutoy." He smiled again. "But, not by Krutoy." He paused for effect, then continued. "*Obasi Kaupin*. Not far removed from Oleg Krutoy, but I'm sure they are one and the same. It clearly was an alias, but that's how he chose to be known."

"Do you have a next of kin for him?" Anaya asked.

The lawyer turned in his chair and reached for the intercom on the credenza behind him. "Monica," he barked. "Bring me the Kaupin file."

Moments later, Monica came in carrying two large manila folders.

Leonard scooted his chair back and stood as he motioned for her to put them on his desk. "Shall we, gentlemen?" he inquired as he gestured for them to be seated in the dark leather armchairs in front of his desk.

Pulling up his matching, high-back executive chair, he placed the folders directly in front of him, examined the notations on each of them, pushed one aside, and opened the other. Holding the dozen or so papers like it was his poker hand, he examined them one at a time.

Ricky was aware of him absent-mindedly nodding as he perused the papers. The moments crawled while he scanned them, backtracked, scanned again, and finally slipped the lot of them back into the folder. Nodding approval of himself, he leaned back looking over the rim of his spectacles at the officers. "What is it specifically you want to know about my client?"

Ricky responded quickly. "Any names besides Krutoy and Kaupin?" Without allowing Lazzarato to respond, Ricky shot another question to him. "Who is his next of kin?"

"Let's be certain we are speaking of one and the same person," he replied as he slipped his hand into the folder. Pulling out a single sheet, he placed it face up on the desk. It was a black and white copy of a New York driver's license. Both officers nodded, glanced at each other, then back to Lazzarato.

"It's got the name of *Fadric Kaslov*," Anaya said. "But that's our man."

"Very talented fellow," Lazzarato replied. "He could have been a millionaire if he used his talents within the law, but he was impatient, very impatient."

"So, who was he?"

Leonard chuckled. "I can't say for sure, but I believe it to be *Makar Popov.*" Clearing his throat, he continued. "Since my client is deceased, I have no obligation to protect his and my otherwise confidential information, so I will tell you what I know and what I think."

He tapped a button on the side of his desk. Moments later, Monica returned. "Yes sir?"

Lazzarato pointed to the coffee. "Our coffee."

Without uttering a word, Monica promptly but professionally removed the cups, coasters, and the coffee set from the table and placed them near the edge of her boss's desk.

Raising his hand, he ordered. "Pour."

She dutifully carried out her task before Leonard gestured for her to leave. Sipping his coffee, he turned his back to them and looked at the distant mountains. His voice was solemn. "He was a bastard but knew how to make money. I'm sure of that." Turning to face them, he continued. "He made enemies. Plenty of them, and in his business that can have long-term negative consequences. "

Pepe quickly interjected, "What business was he in?"

Lazzarato broke out with a long, deep laugh. "I'll be damned if I know. We met when he was in Witness Protection. He had been a mid-level Russian Mafia gangster. He hailed from Moscow but was working along the Atlantic seaboard. White slavery, they called it. To make a long story short, he was apprehended on a federal charge. As I said, he was an impatient man, and that type doesn't do well in prison, and he was looking at twenty years. So, he did what people do in that position. He twisted—turned state's evidence against some high-ups, did everything the feds wanted him to do, and ended up in protection."

"Where did all this happen?" Ricky asked.

"Boston about fifteen years ago. He did a good job for the feds and they treated him quite fairly. They set him up in the shoe business in Florida, then a few years later in upstate New York. He was happy for a while. Like I said, he was impatient and decided to leave the program. I had handled some organized crime cases in the Northeast. He knew my name; got in touch; I guided him through the process; and, about a year later he was out and on his own. I don't know for a fact, but assumed he bounced around setting up some of his old type of business, then settled here in Tucson."

Leonard chewed his lip before continuing. "He contacted me eight years ago. We never discussed his business, but he came in once or twice a year. Over time, he became a changed man. He thought about his future—the afterlife. He knew deep inside they would never forget him, nor would they ever forgive him. His time was coming. He knew it. It was simply a matter of how soon."

"Any associates or family?" Ricky asked.

He gave a nearly imperceptible shake of his head. "I have no doubt your victim was a violent man, at least in his younger years. Reading between the lines of the few conversations we had over the years, I deduced that when he spoke of buying and importing shoes, he actually was referring to human beings, specifically women. Nevertheless, from his very guarded comments, I concluded some of his unnamed associates informed him that someone or some organization was looking for him." The attorney paused, turned again

68

to look at the distant mountains, and finally spoke with his back to his guests. "He would go out of town periodically, but I didn't want to know where he went or who he was contacting. Also, there were times when his associates would come to Tucson." Leonard paused at length, then continued, still looking into the distance. "The last time my client came in was six months ago. He was calm on the outside but undoubtedly suffered inner turmoil. We discussed his finances and how I should handle it when he died." He chuckled and turned around facing the officers. "*Voilà*, here you are."

"Any hints of who was looking for him?" Ricky asked.

"Yes. You beat me to the punch. Assuming it was female sex slaves he was importing into the United States, it would be fitting if the assassin was a female. An Eastern European. We never discussed specifics, but his roots are from that region and he let slip just one time that his *shoe* factory was in Chechnya." Smiling and leaning forward on his desk, he continued, "So, let's put the parts of the puzzle together and see what we have: He is Russian and tied into the mafia; his *shoe* business is in that part of the world; and his specialty is the importation of women.

"Gentlemen, I have no doubt that in the sordid world of white slavery, they—whoever they are—thought it would be sweet justice for a woman to put a bullet into his head."

Anaya gestured toward the second folder. "And that?"

"His financial records, and likely significantly more than what you found in his home." Letting out a deep breath, the tycoon continued. "Of course, I will take my fee, but most of his money will be distributed as he requested. Having no next of kin, it is to be donated to several charitable causes—legitimate ones here in the United States." Nodding again, he spoke with a tone of finality. "He was an evil man but he saw the light and tried to do the right thing. I will sort out his Will and file it in Probate Court in the next few weeks.

"In the meantime," he said as he rose and gestured toward the door, *"Удачи."* He chuckled softly. "It's Russian for 'wow.' Your Mr. Krutoy taught that to me. Nevertheless, I wish you good luck with your investigation."

Evil is a hunter.

CHAPTER TEN

From the attorney's office downtown, the officers began the long drive through the city en route to Saguaro National Park. With Pepe at the wheel of his unmarked sedan, Ricky called the park office. After a brief interchange of bureaucratic transfers from one desk to another, he finally spoke to Randy Peoples, the Supervisory Ranger at the park. Ricky explained the purpose of the call was to allow Peoples reasonable time to prepare to meet with the two officers.

After a quick drive-through lunch at Lucky Wishbone, they arrived at the park at one o'clock. Peoples, dressed smartly in his park ranger uniform complete with the Smokey Bear cap, greeted them at the Visitor Center. Following brief introductions, he led them to a small but professional conference room overlooking the vista of mammoth saguaro cacti.

Looking at Ricky, he spoke. "Thanks for the heads-up on your visit. I've been expecting somebody—a Fed or one of you guys—to come out for a follow-up on our murder." He sat back and exhaled. "It's not unusual for us to deal with a death. We might get four or five a year—a senior citizen keels over with a heart attack, or a hiker takes a giant step off a trail and goes end-over-end off a cliff, but this is our first murder."

Pepe nodded. "Yep, our Search and Rescue group is familiar with this place, but they're glad to be of service when needed. I understand they even assisted in removing Krutoy's body from down the hillside where he fell."

"We couldn't have done without them, but now let me see if I can help with your investigation. We routinely have a twenty-four-hour video camera recording of all entries and departures at the security booth. The camera is affixed to a utility pole just east of the booth. It's motion activated, so it gets reams of data, most of which are the after-hours visitors—deer, coyotes, and javelina that prowl around at night. Our IT staff maintains the file for ninety days, then reuses the disc." Turning to the computer on the counter behind him, he turned it on, speaking as he did so. "Anticipating your interest, we reviewed the video starting at dusk the night before this incident and reviewed it up until all the first responders began arriving. For the sake of your time, I'll not make you sit through the night." He chuckled. "Four deer and three javelina."

Scooting the chairs around to the front of the computer screen, they immersed themselves in the comings and goings at the national park starting at dawn on that fateful Thursday. A digital clock ticked off the date, hour, and minutes on the lower right-hand corner of the picture.

The first park visitors were two bicyclists at 6:49 a.m. This was before the park was officially open but also an acceptable routine for cyclists to enter for their early morning rides. The riders were a male and female, both wearing typical bike attire including a helmet, sunglasses, light-colored, skin-tight jerseys, black riding shorts, and biking gloves. Although not clear, it appeared the female may have been wearing a small fanny pack. Their ages were not determinable, but they appeared to be experienced riders—probably in their thirties or early forties.

The ranger opened the booth at 6:55 a.m., and the next visitor was a pickup occupied by a family of two adults and two children. Their vehicle was a Ford F-150 with the kids riding in the back seat. The truck bore an Arizona license plate.

The flow of visitors was sporadic with only four vehicles coming to the park before Mr. Krutoy. Two of them went only to the Visitor Center but didn't go into the park. A Kiddie-World van passed the booth but turned right to the picnic area and away from the loop at 8:18 a.m., and a mini-bus from Silver Fox Senior Center arrived at 9:02 a.m., but it, too, turned right to the picnic area.

Krutoy's Volvo passed through the security booth at 8:36 a.m. and went out of sight onto the loop.

The family apparently drove nonstop around the loop and departed at 7:50—just about right for someone to take their time and complete the loop after a casual ride.

It was not until 8:58 a.m. that a Chrysler Pacifica Touring Van bearing Wisconsin license plates entered. "This is the couple who had a memorable visit," Peoples said. "They found the body. They called 9-1-1 at 9:48 a.m. One of your deputies and I interviewed them," he said, glancing at Anaya. "They were shocked, but also exceptionally good witnesses. He was a retired cop from Madison, and she was a retired nurse from the V.A. Hospital. They drove around the loop on what is formally called Cactus Forest Loop Drive. They stopped at a couple of interest points before starting up the rise on the eastern portion of the loop. That's where they pulled off again to take in the view. They parked alongside Krutoy's car, but it didn't mean anything to them at the time. They assumed it was somebody hiking on one of the trails.

"They had been walking around enjoying the tranquility, and the husband looked down and saw Krutoy's legs and feet sticking out from under a cactus patch. He called his wife and they jumped over the wall and went down in the canyon. That's when they went over the wall to help whoever it was. Mrs. Kimble started to pull him out but realized he was dead."

Checking his notepad, he continued. "The man is Alan Kimble, and his wife is Patricia. They're in their early 60s and are here checking an item off their bucket list.

"Anyhow, Mr. Kimble tried his cell phone, but it wouldn't work down there, so he climbed back up to his car, made a connection, and called 9-1-1. We estimate they found the body at approximately 9:45, and it took three or four minutes to climb down, make a quick examination, then climb back up to make the phone call."

"What about the others?" Ricky asked.

"That just leaves the two cyclists. Keeping in mind they entered at 6:49, but they rode their bikes through the exit at 9:15. *Sooo*," he emphasized, "that raised a question in my mind. Assuming they were veteran riders, but not particularly in a racing mode, they would take about forty minutes to do the loop. That would put them back out here at roughly 7:30. Even giving them a few minutes to stop and take a blow, they would still be out by 7:45 or 8:00 at the very latest—but

9:15? So, let's do the math. Krutoy was approximately forty-five minutes behind them." Peoples gave the officers a sidelong glance. "Where were they and what were they doing for that long?"

Anaya responded. "Lying in wait." He looked pensively at the ceiling, then continued. "I don't think it will add anything to our case, but I'll run that Arizona plate and interview the parents, but my guess is they were oblivious to what happened."

Nodding his head, Ricky commented. "On the biker's exit, it does appear she has a fanny pack, but how are we going to track them down?"

Pepe answered. "This may be a shot in the dark, but there's a roadhouse about a mile further out the Spanish Trail. I've been there before for breakfast. I think they open at six o'clock." He gave a light-hearted chuckle. "Could we be that lucky?"

*

The two officers found an unoccupied table on the outdoor patio during the mid-day crowd at the Javelina Roadhouse. "Luck is on our side," Pepe commented. "Take a look up there."

Ricky looked up and saw the two outdoor security cameras covering the parking lot. He pursed his lips and spoke softly. "*Senora Justitia* sure is holding our hands today."

Pepe looked at him quizzically. "*¿Quién?*

"Roman mythology. She was the goddess of justice. We studied her in my Philosophy class when I was in the Marines and taking online classes at UC. But, by damn, somebody sure is pointing us in the right direction today."

75

An hour later, the two detectives sat in the office with Deborah Meyer, the owner of the roadhouse. "We put the cameras in a couple of years ago," she said. "There's just so much liability in this business, and they've paid for themselves more than once. Anyhow," she commented when she turned her computer on, "Let's take a look at last Thursday. What time span are you looking at?"

The officers glanced at each other before Anaya replied. "Six o'clock in the morning for starters and we'll see where it takes us."

*

They watched intently as the six o'clock hour began. "That's our cook's car," Deborah said, pointing out an old model VW bug parked in the northwest corner of the lot. "He usually is here around five o'clock." Then she pointed to a newer model yellow Camaro with black rally strips parked alongside the cook's car. "Ginger Bryson. Our property manager. She takes care of the real estate for my husband and me." Giving a sidelong glance to her visitors, she commented, "We've got this place and a few rental properties around the county. She does a hell of a job. If you want to talk to her or our cook Marty, just have at them." She waved a gesture down the narrow hall. "Ginger's in her office and Marty is in the kitchen." She looked beyond them toward the seating area. "Only one waitperson is on duty at that time. Thursday would have been Maggie McCorkle. She's here if you want to talk to her after the lunch crowd thins out."

"Yeah," Ricky said. "We'll need to speak to them, but let's move on with the video and see what we have."

The minutes slowly ticked away. At 6:31 a.m., a black Chevy Silverado pulled into the lot and came to a halt along the northern edge of the parking lot. The seconds passed slowly before the left front door opened and the driver stepped out—a man wearing biking attire identical to what the person on Park Loop Drive was wearing.

"Whoa," Pepe commanded.

Almost immediately, the passenger door opened, and a female alighted from the truck—one and the same—the female who rode her bike through the park.

As though choreographed like a ballet, they reached into the truck bed and lifted their bikes—both of them black with the TREK trademark emblazoned on the frame. Still choreographed, they leaned the bikes against the truck, removed their helmets from the back seat and adjusted them on their heads. At 6:34, the bicyclists pulled out of the parking lot and onto the paved Old Spanish Trail to the east.

Following Ricky's instructions, Deborah stopped the video and backed up to the start time, then progressed slowly, freezing it each time either of the pair was facially exposed; she printed a black and white copy of those freeze-frames.

After a ten-minute coffee break, the trio seated themselves at the computer and began the review process again, this time starting at 9:25. At 9:30, the pair returned to view, pulling off the shoulder of the road and into the parking lot. As expected, their movements were precise as though rehearsed. They pulled up to their respective side of the Silverado, tossed the bikes into the truck bed, and in one smooth motion, removed their helmets, opened their door, and tossed the helmets into the rear seat. At 9:33, they left the parking lot, outbound on Spanish Trail, going toward Interstate 10 and away from the scene of the crime.

The Texas license plate was visible when they pulled out.

Suspense is a hunter.

CHAPTER ELEVEN

After a good night's sleep and a breakfast of *huevos rancheros, frijoles,* and homemade *tortillas* compliments of *Tia* Elizabeth, Ricky drove his pickup truck onto the Old Spanish Trail en route to Saguaro National Park. He was one of the first visitors of the day, passing through the entry gate at 7:15 on a bright and clear morning. The sun had crested Tanque Verde Peak, throwing its long arms over the vast Tucson Valley. The desert was alive with the sweet scents from the overnight shower that pumped fresh life to the wildflowers and blessed the desert foothills with an abundance of beauty.

Twenty minutes later, he stopped at the viewpoint on the uphill grade of the Cactus Forest Loop Drive. His mind wandered. *It must have been just like this when Oleg pulled off that morning.* As Krutoy may have done, Ricky sat in his truck for a few minutes taking in the awe-inspiring view of the rugged mountains, the giant saguaro cactus, the chirping of the cactus wrens, and the cooing of the doves. He breathed deeply. Indeed, it was a place in which a person could revel in the wonder of Mother Nature's handiwork.

Or, be murdered.

Holding the still steaming cup of Starbuck's coffee, he climbed out. Then, unbeknownst to him, Ricky sat on the wall exactly as Oleg had done. He marveled at the solitude of the morning desert—so pure and innocent.

Turning his attention to the sound of the gurgling stream at the canyon bottom, he spied a covey of quail darting about. *It doesn't compute,* he thought. *Krutoy may have been a bastard, but this place is too perfect to be tarnished like that.*

Nevertheless, this is where it happened. One well-placed bullet and a man was dead and very likely, the female involved in his murder was dead at her own hand—another desert and hundreds of miles away, but dead by the same gun. They were two people with a lifestyle that foretold their demise. It was only a matter of when and where.

*

An hour later, Ricky was eastbound on I-10 climbing the steep grade of Texas Canyon. *They had to be going this way—exactly this way. I'm right behind them.* He laughed at himself, *Well, not exactly behind them, but this has to be what they did.* His mind raced ahead—I-10 to Route 146, then south toward Hachita, a little further south, and for whatever reason, he left her to go the remaining few miles into the desert afoot and alone.

Where did the male go? Why would she cut across the desert when they were almost to the Antelope Wells border crossing?

He smiled inwardly. Because they couldn't allow any record of them at the border. They traveled secretly and didn't intend to leave a trail to be discovered later. In fact, they weren't partners or friends. They were two people with an assignment. They did it. When it was over, they would return to whatever and wherever their lives took them.

*

It was nearing dinnertime when Ricky pulled into his driveway at home. He relaxed. Columbus never felt so good. Muncie's new car, a bright yellow VW was parked in the carport, and Lupe's big wheel and toys were strewn around the front porch and yard. It was a home as much as a home could be.

"Bienvenido a casa," Muncie shouted when she darted out the kitchen door with Lupe hanging around her neck, her tiny legs wrapped around her mamma's waist.

Ricky put his suitcase on the ground and scooped up Lupe who dropped down from her mommy and ran to daddy.

"Besame, Papa," she spat out when she was safely in his arms.

"My precious one," he whispered into her ear as they nuzzled one another.

"My turn," Muncie interjected when she joined the group hug. She and Ricky kissed lightly, then—holding hands with Lupe between them—they went inside.

Following a dinner of spaghetti and meatballs, it was bath and bedtime for Lupe.

For Mom and Dad, it was a strictly private time in the living room with Chihuahua Radio 99.9 streaming jazz tunes as they advertised from dusk to dawn: *Pedro Navaja, Fuxe, Café Tacvba, Tino Contreras*, and more . . . all night long.

It was a night of margaritas, moonlight, music, and passionate love.

*

Ricky was a good dad, a good husband and son, but also a good cop to the marrow of his bones. He was early to work when he passed through the security gates at the Task Force compound. Wiping his brow with his kerchief as he got out of his pickup, he realized the summer sun had already begun to scorch the desolate vistas of the southwest.

Entering the office building, he grabbed a cup of their infamous coffee machine muck and headed toward Miguel's office. He chuckled as he entered. "*Chingale, ese.* Do you have a home, or do you live here all the time?"

Miguel smirked. "Basurto, you're going to have to get up before the chickens if you're going to get here before me." Pushing his laptop aside and gesturing to a straight-back chair, he spoke. "*Siéntate.* Tell me about this Krutoy murder and our *cuerpo* down by Antelope Wells. How the hell did a man and a woman end up dead in the desert about four hundred miles apart, and both by the same gun?"

"In a nutshell, it was pretty easy. She killed Oleg and was going south to the border, got bitten by the rattlesnakes, then killed herself with the murder weapon. Case closed." He tilted his head like a dog listening to a siren. "Pretty simple, wouldn't you say?"

"Butthead," Miguel cracked. "Okay, I got the lay of the land, but where does it take you?"

Miguel and Ricky talked for an hour, taking time out only to refresh their cups from Miguel's new Keurig Coffee Maker.

Pushing his chair back and stretching with his hands behind his head, Miguel spoke. "I've got the big picture. We have a Russian Mafia gangster running a white slavery operation; he's killed by either a man or woman bicyclist with a unique Russian-made handgun; the woman is dead here in our desert with what likely is a self-inflicted gunshot, but also with multiple rattlesnake bites; we're working on identifying her; we have a license plate of the suspect vehicle from Tucson, and we've got a couple of names to run down from the female's cell phone." He paused in thought, screwing his lips. "I don't see what is so hard about this?" He looked Ricky in the eye, then broke out in laughter. "We've said it before. It's like writing a straight line with crooked letters."

"Seguro," Ricky said. "Here's my plan. Remember, we have Deputy Anaya in Tucson working on this. Actually, it's his murder case, but we're going to do most of the work. He'll locate the family in the pickup and interview them. Plus, he'll talk to the staff at the Javelina Roadhouse, but we don't have high expectations from any of them."

"Okay," O'Rourke replied. "You'll be the ball carrier, but I can still pull Anna Fernandez back from DEA to work with you again."

Shaking his head, Ricky replied. "She's good, but let me see which direction the investigation is going. If I start getting overwhelmed, I'd be glad to have her back."

Returning to his workstation, Ricky booted up his computer and ran a Texas registration check on the pickup that carried the two bikers. No sooner had he hit the Enter button than his reply popped up. It was registered to a 2017 Chevy Silverado belonging to Rio Lobo Outdoor Adventures, 417 Via Entrada, Alpine, Texas.

Tapping again into his computer, Ricky pulled up the Brewster County Texas Business License Department. As their website so proudly advertised, everything he wanted was there: Rio Lobo Outdoor Adventures was owned by Samuel Baca, Rural Route 170, Terlingua, Texas.

His next stop was down the hall to Acacia Rios in the Crime Analysis office. "I'm b-a-a-a-ck," he said, mimicking Jack Nicholson from *The Shining*.

"Oh my gosh," she blurted as she feigned a heart attack. Sitting up straight, she threw a don't-you-dare stare back at her interloper. "Be serious for a change Agent Basurto, and what the hell do you want this time?"

"In all seriousness," he said when he pulled up a chair and sat across from her, "I don't know if I'm chasing a Russian Mafia hit man or if I'm on a wild goose, but I've got a name to start with and hope you set me on the right path."

Acacia smiled. "You've come to the right place. Show me what you've got and let's see what we can find."

He showed her the computer printout about the Rio Lobo Outdoor Adventures and its purported owner. "This is about the sum total of what I have, but knowing you, I'll get more than what I bargained for."

She spun around facing her PC, "Give me thirty minutes and come back. We should have some feedback by then."

He replied, "10-4," shoved his chair back and went out her door.

Twenty-five minutes later, following a phone call to the Santa Fe Crime Lab about their findings on the blood sample from Jane Doe, he returned to Acacia's office. "*¿Qué Tal?*" he asked.

"You sure do know how to find 'em." She gave a wise-guy smirk and continued. "You might have a Grand Slam waiting for you." She laid her printouts on the desk and began reviewing them with him. "Let's start with the business. They've had a business license to operate in Alpine for twelve years, and always under the same ownership. They specialize in backcountry activities in Big Bend National Park with jeep tours, off-road bike outings, and hikes. Their events can be one-day or overnight, guided or self-guided, so it looks very legit thus far. However," she raised an eyebrow and tossed him a sidelong glance, "the El Paso Fusion Center documents Rio Lobo as being suspect or involved in immigration and/or drug smuggling." Giving another sidelong glance, she continued. "*But* they were always found on the fringe of an investigation and no one has been able to pin anything on them. No arrest. *Nada*. Technically, they are free and clear.

"Now, though," she commented when she laid out another data printout, "Samuel Baca individually may be a good place to start. The Fusion Center shows him to be the son of Manuel Baca, previously of Brewster County, but currently a resident of the Federal Corrections Institute La Tuna, just north of us in Anthony, Texas. He's in his late 70s and in poor health but serving a sentence for Importation of a Controlled Substance." She gave a light chuckle and continued. "He was arrested bringing in a plane load of heroin for the New Juarez Cartel. The report indicated a flight originated in Columbia, made a stop somewhere in Mexico where the load was divided into several small aircraft, and one landed on a desert airstrip near Jal, New Mexico, just off Highway 128."

"When was that?"

"In 2011. It was his first arrest. His name was highlighted several times in different investigations, but they never made a case on him until this one. He was guilty, sure as hell. They arrested five men when they were unloading the plane, and Manuel was the *patron*, overseeing the operation on the ground."

"But nothing on Samuel?"

"It's weak, but I'll go over it with you. You remember Nicolas Salinas from the Juarez cartel?"

"The son of a bitch. I'll never forget him. He runs the cartel business just across the border not more than a couple of miles south of this very spot." He emphasized his words with an exaggerated jab with his finger toward the floor.

Acacia smiled and nodded approval. "Your new best friend Samuel is Nicolas' cousin. Their mothers are sisters." Cracking a Cheshire cat grin, she continued. "It's just a little family business."

"Now," she said as she turned on her computer. "I'll pull up the Texas driver's license photo for Samuel. Maybe you can identify him from one of your Tucson freeze frames."

Moments later, it printed out.

"He's not the suspect from Tucson," Ricky remarked while the photo was printing. "How old is Samuel?" he asked.

"The driver's license gives his date of birth as November 6, 1963."

Ricky shook his head. "Our bike suspect from Tucson looks about thirty-five at the oldest. Samuel is much too old. Maybe our biker is his son or a *sicario*, a hitman."

"Good chance, but it's something you're going to have to chase down." Giving a deep exhale and leaning back in her chair, she asked, "Now, tell me about your *cuerpo*. Do you have any identification on her yet?"

Thumbing through the notes from his phone call to the crime lab, he read it off. "There was a DNA hit on her with a match from Kansas City two years ago. It was a case of forced prostitution—white slavery. KCPD arrested this woman named Olivia Camacho along with a Francisco Chacon and charged them with Felony Prostitution. I don't know why, but the charge against Olivia was dropped. Chacon bonded out after a few days, then skipped bond."

Ricky shrugged, then continued. "Neither of them has been heard from since then; that is until now and we've got her remains in cold storage in Santa Fe. Now, one more name, and I'll get out of your hair."

"*Digame*," she replied.

"It's a long shot, but let's give it a try: Pablo Gonzales in Boquillas del Carmen, Mexico."

Acacia brushed her dark hair from her brow and lifted an eyebrow. "You have to be kidding. Aren't you?"

Ricky shook his head, "Not in what looks like a very complicated international murder case, no."

She turned her back to him, returning to her keyboard. "Give me a few minutes and come back." She gave a half-hearted chuckle. "With the types of cases you work, who knows what we'll learn."

"Twenty-five minutes. I'll be back," he replied.

True to his word, he was on time. Acacia looked up from her desk with a smile creasing her lips. Shaking her head in amazement, she spoke. "Ricky Basurto, you're the luckiest man I've seen in many moons." Gesturing to her chair, she spoke in a soft tone, making a point of being very precise. "Pablo González of Boquillas del Carmen is the unelected but nevertheless *very* prominent village leader in his community. Boquillas, as it is normally called, is the northernmost village in Coahuila with about 150 residents. They've got a part-time border crossing into Texas by foot or rowboat five days a week depending on the river's current. Their economic base is strictly a handful of *turistas* on any day."

"I don't understand. His name is in the Fusion Center? Has he been tied to any criminal activity?"

"No," she replied with a barely perceptible shaking of her head. "I did a search on the Internet and found him, then went to Wikipedia on the village. Apparently, he's a nice old man. People hold him in high esteem, which causes me concern that his name would pop up in an international murder case. It doesn't jive."

"I'll find out," Ricky said.

Uncertainty is a hunter.

CHAPTER TWELVE

Ricky was in no hurry. He checked out of the Gage Hotel in Marathon, Texas, en route to the southern tip of the USA and Big Bend National Park. It was noon, and the scorching sun was overhead. Approaching the tiny border-crossing station on the hill above the river, he saw the thermometer over the entryway: 103 degrees. The heat of the day was yet to come.

He spoke briefly with the on-duty Border Patrol officer, Sandra Sensing, a stocky thirty-something, wearing her BP greens, gun belt, and a bullet-resistant vest beneath her shirt.

"Good day, sir," she said when he started through the exit leading down to the river. "Do you have a passport? You'll need it to come back."

Ricky slipped his undercover passport in the name of Sixto Bustamante from the breast pocket of his white western shirt, held up momentarily for her inspection, then passed through the door marked *Entrada a México*. Moments later, he was at the bottom of the hill where four brightly colored rowboats with their Mexican rowers awaited the day's fares to cross the river. Choosing the boat at the upstream end, a turquoise-colored dory and an obvious veteran of many river crossings, he stepped over the gunwale and offered a polite *"Buenos días,"* to the oarsman.

The muscular rower smiled, holding out his hand for payment of his services: a necessity in today's waist-deep, fast-flowing current. *"Me llama Sergio,"* he said, displaying his sparkling white teeth surrounded by a scraggly, unkempt salt and pepper beard. *"Bienvenido a mi pueblo."*

Ricky responded, *"Gracias, Sergio. Hace calor hoy."*

Sergio leaned into the oars against the current but smiled and nodded in agreement. "Hotter than hell," he laughed.

After a three-minute and five-dollar venture across the river, Ricky clambered up the steep, rocky incline to *Boquillas*. "Damn," he grunted when he was halfway up the rock-strewn incline. "I'm out of shape." He huffed his way up the trail, questioning his thought about not paying another five-dollar bill for the burro ride to the top. *Should have taken it,* he thought.

The town square, if you could call it that, consisted of a scattering of old but neatly trimmed shops: two cafes, three souvenir shops, a bar, a raspada stand where youngsters and dehydrated travelers bought snow cones, an aged but clean grocery store, and what passed for an outlet dubbed "The Falcon," which sold a variety of second-hand clothes, shoes, and tools. Choosing the grocery store, Ricky approached the lone employee, a young lady wearing a Mexican peasant dress with embroidered, multi-colored designs from the neck to the hemline. With her dark hair pulled into a ponytail and a minimum of lipstick, she was nothing less than elegant.

"Good day, sir," she said in impeccable English. "Can I help you?"

Removing his straw hat, he approached her at the checkout stand. "Yes, ma'am. I need to speak to Señor Pablo González. Do you know where I can find him?"

She tossed a relaxed, *c'mon* grin and tilted her head, "My grandfather?" She paused momentarily, then continued with a stifled laugh. "In Boquillas, everyone knows *Abuelo*. He is the grandfather to all of us. Come," she said, motioning him to the door. Outside on the clean and well-kept dirt sidewalk area, she pointed to a small adobe compound of a dozen or more single-story homes. "His is the last one on the right. This time of day you'll probably find him sitting in the shade under his ramada."

Ricky tipped his hat. "Many thanks, *señorita,*" he said when he turned toward the compound. She hollered as he stepped away, "Its *Señora . . . Señora Molina.*"

He stopped in mid-step and turned around, laughing at his error. *"Perdóname, Señora.* I promise I will not forget."

At the end of the equivalent of a long city block and with two mangy dogs yapping at his heels, Ricky reached Abuelos's house. He knocked on the door, and then, without waiting, rounded the corner and found the elderly man sitting in an old wooden chair, leaning back against one of the posts of the ramada. The elderly gentleman looked like a travel poster for the gringo turistas on their first trip south of the border . . . maybe the first time out of their neighborhood.

Dressed in loose-fitting, white, cotton trousers, a white cotton guayabera shirt, a straw hat pulled down over his eyes, and wearing a traditional pair of huaraches, Abuelo fit the mold.

Ricky smiled inwardly. *He's everybody's Abuelo.*

Calling out *"Ola,"* from a distance so as not to frighten him, Ricky extended his hand in friendship as he approached.

Mr. González lifted the brim of his hat and pushed it back, turned slightly to the sound of Ricky's voice, then allowed his chair to slam down on its front legs with a thud. Standing and extending his hand, the two men spoke in Spanish.

"Señor," Ricky said, then introduced himself as an officer from the United States. "I'm working on a series of crimes that may run across the border. One of the bits of evidence we uncovered was a cell phone in your name."

The elder statesman chuckled. "Mr. Bustamante, yes. That phone is in my name. You passed it on the way into our village." He smiled wryly, then offered Ricky a seat next to him in the shade. "Oh, sir, I am not laughing at you. It's the cell phone. You see, we do not have a regular telephone service in Boquillas. We're much too small for the phone company to provide service to this little out-of-the-way village." Clearing his throat, he paused to spit, wiped his lips on his sleeve, and continued, "A friend to all of us here in Boquillas pays for a satellite cell phone so we have access to the world. You walked right past it." Pointing back to the top of the trail where Ricky entered the village, he continued his story. "That phone booth. It's not a real phone booth, but our benefactor put the phone there along with a solar panel on the roof. Anyone," he paused, and gestured to the village, "Anyone can use it. Our only rule is we must limit ourselves to no more than three calls a week per person, and no more than three minutes for each call."

Ricky interjected. "What about in-bound calls?"

Smiling to his newly found friend, *El Abuelo* replied. "Whoever hears it, answers it. It's that simple."

"Okay," Ricky said. "What about on June 14th in the evening?"

Abuelo nodded affirmatively "Yes, that was my call. I was expecting it. It was my granddaughter, Maria—Maria Espinoza." Pablo paused to gather himself. Ricky noticed a sudden forlornness in his eyes. "She said she had a job but was scared and didn't want to do it. I told her, 'No, come home. Right now.' She was crying and said she loved me, then hung up." Leaning with his arms on his knees, he implored, "Is she okay? Is she alive?"

Ricky paused, leaned back in his chair, then produced a copy of Olivia's Camacho's mug shot from the Kansas City arrest. He handed it to El Abuelo. "Is this Maria?"

The old man held it frozen in his fingers. Tears dripped from his eyes onto the photo. "Tell me. I need to know. I have prayed every night and every day since that phone call."

Ricky reached out and placed his hands on Pablo's knees. "I'm sorry, sir. She is dead."

Grief is a hunter.

CHAPTER THIRTEEN

Ricky sat quietly while Abuelo González wept, his tears falling onto the dry soil of Boquillas del Carmen, Coahuila, Mexico, three-hundred miles from Hachita, New Mexico, and hundreds more from Saguaro National Park.

The sun beat mercilessly on the quaint village. The old man sat up and looked at Ricky with tired, red eyes. "I prayed constantly for her, but she joined hands with those jackals from Juarez." He paused, leaned back in his chair, and looked to the heavens above. "Father McGuire. You must talk to the good Father before you leave." Squinting against the sunlight, he looked deeply into Ricky's eyes. "You are a good man, Mr. Bustamante, to come so far with this terrible news." He shook his head, looked to the ground, and spit again. "I can go no further. The priest can tell you much more than I can." He offered a humble chuckle. "He's an Irishman but has been in Mexico for many years. He is very holy and will tell you how the hand of the devil came to our little village."

Rising from his chair, El Abuelo directed them around the house where he stopped and gave a light, self-deprecating laugh. "At our age, we get to pee a lot," then excused himself and hurried inside. Minutes later, he returned carrying his rosary beads. "Come now, let us go see Father McGuire." Holding Ricky's arm to keep his balance, the old man guided them back to the commercial area. They turned up a narrow side street, passed a scattering of modest adobe houses, a corral with half a dozen burros dozing under a ramada, and a schoolhouse: a simple, one story, whitewashed adobe building. A brightly painted green door had a window of either side. Walking with carefully guarded steps, Pablo spoke softly. "My granddaughter, Elena Molina, is the teacher for the little ones." He looked at Ricky and cracked a genuine smile. "Elena is precious. These children love her."

Ricky accepted the grandfather's accolades of the young woman. No doubt, he was correct.

Following a well-used footpath around a hillside abutment of cholla and prickly pear cactus, they came to the village church. Gesturing toward the adobe building, El Abuelo offered Ricky an introduction to their house of worship. "This is *El Santuario de San Isidore.*"

Ricky halted momentarily. It was a near replica of the famous *Santuario de Chimayó* in New Mexico with its surrounding wall, twin bell towers, and the modest adobe church and cemetery.

"We'll go around here to his rectory," the old man said, guiding his guest around the side toward the rear of the property. "He should be home, and I want him to tell you how the hand of the evil one swept over our village."

Turning at the sound of the church's rear door opening, they were greeted by the priest with his strong Irish brogue. Dressed in the traditional Franciscan attire of a brown ankle-length garment, a white cincture around his waist, and sandals, the diminutive priest offered a boisterous, "*Ola*, Pablo. You have a friend?" he jested.

"Father McGuire, yes. A nice gentleman I want you to meet." Gesturing to both of them, he continued. "Your two businesses are very different from each other, but I think you have much in common."

Pablo introduced the priest and the cop to each other, then offered to take his absence from their conversation. Lifting his rosary, he said, "My friends, I will be in the church to pray my rosary. If you will excuse me, I'll leave you to discuss your important matters."

The priest acknowledged Pablo with a shallow nod, then turned to Ricky. "Come, my son. Let's go to the rectory. *Juana*, my housekeeper, always makes *tortas* for me in the afternoon. Have you eaten your lunch yet?"

"No, Father. I haven't. A *torta* sounds perfect to me."

Inside, the two men sat at a small oak dining table in the kitchen, a gloomy but cool little room in a tired, old, adobe house. Ricky scrunched his neck when they passed through the door because of the low open beam ceiling. His footsteps thudded on the heavily worn, amber Saltillo tile floor which evidenced decades of use in the *Rectoría* after a century of service.

The men ate a simple lunch of a torta consisting of a homemade roll, lettuce and tomatoes from the garden, goat cheese from Juana's husband Manuel, and a tin cup of well water while they had busy-talk—the weather, the elections on the horizon, and the plight of the *Campesinos* trying to feed their families.

After Juana cleared the table, the priest scooted his chair back and crossed his leg over his knee. He offered a smile and a slight nod of his head. "Now, Officer Bustamante, let's get down to business. What exactly brings a man of your stature to Boquillas to see a couple of old men like El Abuelo and me?"

After providing the priest with an overview of the potential international murder case, Ricky came to the point. "Two questions jumped out at me, Father. The first is about the generous soul who is providing the cell phone—who and why?"

The priest gave a hearty belly laugh. "I hope all your questions are so easy." Scooting back up with his elbows resting on the table, he answered with a broad smile. "Jose de la Garza is our donor, and I don't believe you'll find him in any of your records. Little Jose was born right here in this house. His father had been killed in a farming accident a few months earlier, so his grandmother brought his mother, *Angelica*, into town from where they lived not many miles south of us.

"Right here on this floor," he emphasized jabbing a finger toward the floor, "she gave birth to Jose. That was long before I arrived, but the story has been passed down and I believe it to be true. Nevertheless, Angelica died in childbirth and the baby had only his widowed grandmother. She was much too old to care for the baby, and in poor health. So, the priest here at the time, Father Miguel Osuna, and his housekeeper cared for the child until they could find a family member somewhere." He stopped to take a deep breath and wet his lips. "An uncle in Saltillo eventually came and took Jose, and," he paused to shake his head, "the youngster didn't come back until

97

about five years ago—a grown man, an engineer in the automotive plant in Saltillo where they make cars and trucks. He's a very successful family man and he never forgot the people of Boquillas who cared for him. So, now we have phone service, bought and paid for by a little orphan boy named Jose."

"Thanks, Father. I hope my next question is as smooth and easy."

"Fire away, young man."

Ricky removed the Kansas City mug shot from his breast pocket and placed it on the table, face up. "Do you know this lady, Father?"

The elderly priest studied it for a moment, then nodded almost imperceptibly. "Maria Espinoza, not her most elegant photograph."

"She was arrested in Missouri along with a man a couple of years ago. The charges were dropped—what they called 'The Interest of Justice,' whatever that means. Her whereabouts until recently are unknown."

"Now," the priest interjected. "Where is she *now*? In jail?"

"She's not so lucky, Father. She's dead. We have her remains in Santa Fe, and that's what brings me to Boquillas. She called El Abuelo shortly before her body was found."

Father McGuire choked. "Her body was found?" Shaking his head, he stammered, "What do you mean, *found*?"

Ricky leaned forward, holding the old man's hands, and explained the how, where, and when of the death of Maria Espinoza. "Now, Father, tell me about what El Abuelo said regarding the hand of Satan coming to Boquillas."

The little priest went to the faucet for another cup of water, then faced Ricky. Leaning back against the counter with tears streaming down his cheeks, he began the story of the day the devil came to Boquillas del Carmen.

Wickedness is a hunter.

CHAPTER FOURTEEN

The old priest returned to the table and pulled up his chair. He wiped his tear-stained eyes with the cuff of his garment, took a deep breath, and composed himself. Leaning forward on the table, he told his story of Maria Espinoza.

"It was about four or five years ago. Maria lost her parents a couple of years earlier. They were migrant workers in the United States and died in a car wreck in Oregon. Fortunately," he paused, "or maybe not. Nevertheless, she didn't go apple picking with them but stayed here. It was a busy tourist season, and she ran the burro trips up and down the hill. On a good day, she could make sixty-dollars or more. She was pretty and had a personality to match, so she got terrific tips." Nodding and smiling, he continued. "There was an outdoor company up in Texas, and they always needed local guides to take the tourists on day hikes—sometimes even overnight into the mountains to go fishing. Maria fit the bill perfectly, so they hired her to work part-time. She was making excellent money compared to others living around here, and that started her new career. She was good at her job—too good."

The priest paused to fetch another drink of water for himself and Ricky, then returned to the table. "She was a precious girl but was trapped here with no future. Anyhow, the outfitters offered her a full-time job working for them." Shaking his head, he looked down at his feet. His voice was so soft Ricky strained to hear him. "I started to have doubts. She would be gone for a few days, then come home with money: plenty of it. I never asked and she never said what she was doing, but I'm not a fool. I knew something was afoot. Then, one day out of the blue, she told me she was leaving. She sold her house and her burros and was gone."

"'It's a good company,' she told me. "'I have a future there and won't be poor all my life.' Poof, she was gone. She'd come back every once in a while . . . always pretty and full of life.

"Oh yes, before I forget it, that man who would bring the tourists down and who gave her the job, his name was Humberto. A sharp dresser: nice shirts and jeans, expensive hiking boots, and a gold tooth. A flashy fellow, that's what I thought of him." Father Maguire chewed his lips, then spoke bluntly. "He was Satan personified. I haven't seen him in a long time. They've got a couple of other young men who bring the tourists down now."

The priest sat in his chair and looked coldly at Ricky. "I'm an old man, but I know how the world spins, so I did a little bit of inquiry myself." He chuckled modestly. "Maybe we're a bunch of gray-haired men, but we know what's going on in our world, and certainly we have our resources. We, maybe more than most, have a great deal of insight into the evil of this world. To make a long story short, I contacted a trustworthy friend in Juarez and told him what I have told you. My friend laughed, not at me, but that I was so late finding out how some people got things done, and it's usually not within the laws of man or God. 'White slavery,' he told me. The cartels work hand in hand with the Russian Mafia. They have their dirty hands into everything—guns, drugs, women, children—there is no limit about what they do for money, and they use the cartel contacts and muscle to make sure things happen."

"Did your source know about Maria or the outfitter company?"

"Not her or that company specifically, but what he told me matched what I was seeing here in Boquillas. It was a perfect fit. They find young innocents, treat them to the high dollar life, and suck them in until they are no longer of use.

"I must give you an observation—an introduction of the world that was revealed to me. I am not breaking the seal of confession of our church, but I am sharing with you my very last visit with Maria Espinoza. It was a couple of months ago. She came home for a few days and asked if she could talk to me. Of course, I accepted. She came here for dinner. I remember it well. We had *cerdo asado* which Juana had made, and Maria brought a pot of beans and fresh tortillas. But we only had my sweet, cold well water to drink—no Cerveza."

Ricky thought Father McGuire was steeling himself as the old man looked down at his feet, then up at the ceiling. "She had a terrible story—incredibly sad, and she was frightened. The poor child couldn't get out, and she couldn't go on. I was blunt with her. I said, 'Tell me exactly what you are doing for these people.' She cried, but I wouldn't let her off the hook. I screamed at her to tell me."

The old priest gave an embarrassed snicker at himself. "I think I scared her. She just blurted it out to me. 'Father, they make me do things when they want to kill someone. They're so mean I don't dare go against them. I just do it.' So, I put her on the spot and asked her if she killed anyone."

"'Oh, no Father,' she said. 'But I help them do it. I pick someone up or drop them off; I get rid of people or things they don't want the police to find. One time I helped a man get rid of a woman he'd killed. We buried her in the desert. Now they call me *La Dormida*—one who takes care of people who have gone to sleep. The worst is yet to come, I know. They're going to make me kill someone, and I don't want to do it.'"

"Did she ever say exactly who or what or where? Anything like that?"

Shaking his head, the priest's response was barely audible. "No. Nothing."

"How did your meeting end after such a tale?"

"It was very anticlimactic. She was extremely somber, then looked at her watch, and jumped up. 'Sorry, Father,' she said, 'for taking up so much of your time. I must go now. Someone is waiting for me.' Then she walked out the door and drove away. I haven't seen her since then." The old man stopped to wipe his tear-filled eyes with the cuff of his garment, then spoke solemnly, "She was terrified about talking to me, and terrified about leaving to go meet whoever it was or wherever it was." He shook his head. "Either way, she was going to lose. She knew it then, and you are here today to establish the truth. She was going to die long before her time."

"Your source, Father. Can I speak to him or her, whichever?"

The diminutive priest smiled and shook his head. "No, my son. I can't do that and endanger anyone's life. This is a very important person. The evil ones know of him—yes, it is a priest—but please do not ask me for this. Truly, I cannot help you any further."

"I understand, Father, and thank you for your assistance." Standing up from the table and turning for the door, Ricky commented. "El Abuelo will need you."

"I will pray for him, and for you, too, Officer Bustamante. Go in peace."

*

It was early evening when Ricky returned to the hotel in Marathon, too late to start the long ride home, but too early to call it a day. There was more work to be done. His next stop would be in Alpine, the home of Rio Lobo Outdoor Adventures. Forty minutes later, he found his target located in a clean but modest strip center on Via Entrada, just off the Sul Ross campus. A lone pickup truck was parked near the front door—a dark-colored Chevy Silverado.

Ricky parked his pickup and went to the front door. It was eight o'clock. The sign on the door gave their business hours from 8 a.m. – 8 p.m. They were closed. Pressing his nose to the window, he saw a man working behind the counter at the rear of the showroom. At that moment, the man looked up, saw Ricky, waved, and shouted out, "Closed."

The undercover officer was not so easily dissuaded. He hollered back, "Please, I came a long way. We need you."

Apparently considering the possibility of booking a trip, the employee came forward. Ricky recognized him when he approached the door—the same man who was on the bicycle at Saguaro National

Park. He juggled his keys for a moment, then unlocked and opened the door. "Sir, we're closed. Can you come back tomorrow?"

Stepping in, Ricky smiled and extended his hand to the murder suspect. They spoke in Spanish. "I'm Arturo Ochoa," Ricky said, utilizing one of his undercover names. "I'm sorry for keeping you, but I came a long way. I'm from New Mexico and my sister is getting married. Her husband to be is an outdoor guy." Taking a moment to remove his cowboy hat, he continued, "My buddies and I thought we'd give him a bachelor party—an overnight hike in Big Bend—no girls or anything wild. He's a cool guy and doesn't screw around," at which point he paused, allowing them to have a good laugh at the groom. "Anyhow," Ricky said, "I screwed up getting here so late, but I heard about Rio Lobo's reputation. I wanted to get here earlier but made a roundabout loop around Terlingua and Big Bend, so here I am—late. Can you help me, or do I have to wait until tomorrow?"

"No, no. You're fine. I'm Alberto Salinas, the assistant manager," he said when he shook hands with his potential customer.

Ricky couldn't help but notice his gold front tooth reflecting the overhead light when he spoke. *Humberto, he thought. Father McGuire had you pegged right.*

Alberto spoke as he walked back to the counter. "For sure, I can book your trip. Do you have your dates set?"

Following behind, Ricky replied. "Yes sir. Four weeks from Friday, whatever those dates are."

Alberto pulled up his tablet and scrolled down the dates. He smiled and looked at Ricky. "Excellent, we have an open date. Are you looking for an overnighter or just a day hike?"

"Overnight. There'll be four of us, including the groom. Three of us will share the cost so Armando will go free." He laughed and smiled. "It's the last time the fucker will get anything for free."

Alberto joined him in a good laugh. "It's $70.00 per day per person if you provide your own food and drink and $95.00 if we provide food and water. If you want any alcoholic beverages, you have to bring them, but we provide packable coolers you can carry."

"Perfect. That's exactly what we need. We'll bring our own drinks, so two days and one night for four of us with you doing the food will be—" He paused while he did the mental gymnastics, "$760.00. Right?"

"Almost. The tip for your guide is eighteen percent." Alberto pulled out his pocket calculator, tapped in the numbers and replied, "That's another $137.00 for Ronnie. He's a great guide. You'll be happy with him."

"We've got a deal," Ricky said. "Give me your card and tomorrow or the next day after I go over it with my buddies, I'll give you a call and pay the deposit."

Alberto pulled a business card from his pocket and wrote his cell number on the reverse side. He handed it to Ricky and shook his hand. "Call me when you have your friends lined up. We promise you a great overnighter."

Ricky accepted his DNA-laden business card and slipped it into his shirt pocket. "I'm looking forward to doing business with you, my friend. You'll be hearing from us."

Returning to the hotel, his mind raced back to another case a couple of years ago with Beavis and Butthead, two young men of

106

minimal skills who used their muscles on behalf of the cartel. They were apprehended by the Chihuahua State Police for drug dealing and kidnapping. The young ruffians took their orders from brothers Alberto and Federico Salinas and did their bidding. But Alberto and Federico took their orders from their father, Nicolas, who was with the New Juarez Cartel operations in Northern Chihuahua and into New Mexico. *Small world*, Ricky thought. *And we meet again.*

Corruption is a hunter.

CHAPTER FIFTEEN

Early the next morning, Ricky drove the 350 miles from Marathon to the task force headquarters on Hwy. 9, a five-hour drive, but only four considering the time change from Central to Mountain Time. Going to Miguel's office, they reviewed his meetings with El Abuelo and the priest in Boquillas del Carmen, then his good fortune at Rio Lobo Outdoor Adventures.

"Son of a bitch," Miguel bellowed. "I think you hit a walk-off homer. I remember that Salinas family from a couple of years ago. The father, Nicolas, was a lieutenant in the New Juarez Cartel." Leaning back and shaking his head in amazement, he said, "The friggin' Russian Mafia, the Juarez Cartel, a dead *sicaria* at Antelope Wells, a dead Russian in Tucson, and a KGB pistol. What's next for you to find?"

Ricky smiled and pushed his chair back to leave. "Nicolas Salinas is in my sights. I've just got to find a way to get him."

"How might that be?"

"Like any other cop—stick to it, see where the evidence goes, and be patient. It'll happen."

*

Returning to his workspace, he powered up the computer. His eyes fell on the first item in his email inbox. It was from the crime lab in Santa Fe. He took a deep breath as it printed out. The unique gun found with Maria Espinoza's dead body yielded a plethora of evidence. Each of the unfired bullets in the magazine, and the magazine itself, had numerous complete and partial fingerprints, plus a collection of DNA evidence. Additionally, DNA and fingerprints were found on the inner workings of the weapon, indicating it was handled by one or more people who had assembled and loaded the weapon.

There were three separate DNA profiles. The deceased's positive identification was on two of the unfired bullets and the magazine. Other trace evidence included partial and complete fingerprints and DNA which were on the trigger group, frame, slide, and barrel. Smaller bits of unreadable DNA were found on the spring.

An analysis of the profiles not belonging to the deceased was determined to be from two people. They were likely close relatives since one of the profiles contained one-half of the DNA as the other profile. Submission of those samples to regional and national databases failed to identify the people other than the deceased whose DNA was found on the interior and exterior of the weapon.

Ricky's mind wandered . . . the gun; her body snake-bitten and shot; the same gun responsible for Maria's and Oleg's deaths; the unique expended and sealed brass . . . then it hit him. Where was the expended brass from the Oleg murder?

A quick call to Anaya gave him an answer, but not the one he wanted. Investigators looked, but never found the expended brass from the shot that killed Krutoy. At the crime scene and not knowing the caliber of the bullet, they had assumed incorrectly that the murder weapon was a revolver; therefore, there would not be an expended shell.

Hmm, Ricky thought. *The pair must have recovered the expended shell and taken it with them.* He gave a self-deprecating smirk. *What would I do with it if I killed someone and didn't want to get caught with the spent shell? Throw it as far as I could.* Biting his lip, he continued his conjecture of how it occurred. *Pretty smart of them. One did the shooting. One watched the brass and snatched it up. The only evidence left behind was the bullet in Oleg's head.*

He looked on his desk at the sealed evidence envelope with Alberto's fingerprints and DNA. He smiled as he tucked it into the evidence bag that would make the trip to the Santa Fe crime lab. It was only a matter of time before the noose began to tighten around the Salinas family neck. The only question was which one of them would fall first and how far before they tried to talk their way into a lighter sentence.

Sitting in the chair with his boots on the desk, Ricky reminisced about his friend and colleague, Sergeant Sergio Mora of the Chihuahua State Police. He and his fiancé were murdered by the New Juarez Cartel, most likely at the direction of Nicolas Salinas.

"Vengeance is mine," says the Lord. But justice is mine, you cabrón.
Assassination is a hunter.

110

CHAPTER SIXTEEN

After eight days without a break, Ricky and his family enjoyed a three-day weekend in Albuquerque. Following an easy schedule of eating, relaxing by the pool, and taking a jaunt to Old Town, they left the grand prize for their last night—the tram ride to the top of 10,000-foot Sandia Peak with dinner overlooking the city lights and the vast Chihuahuan Desert.

For Ricky, it was a rib eye steak, the grilled salmon for Muncie, and the Kiddie Grilled Cheese for Lupe. Like all good things, the end comes too soon. For the Basutos, it was the last tram down the mountain with Lupe asleep in her stroller.

Sunday they drove to Mesilla and met Ricky's mother, Sophie, at the Basilica of San Albino, one of the architectural treasures of southern New Mexico. Following the five o'clock Mass, they adjourned to Lala's Café, a quaint family restaurant dating back to the days of Governor *Ezequiel Cabeza De Baca* almost one hundred years ago.

"I love to come here," Sophie said when they were seated in the cool, quiet dining room. "My papa would bring us here every Easter after Mass." She gave a light chuckle and blushed. "Of course, the village was so tiny we knew almost everyone." Looking at Lupe in her high chair, she continued. "My little brother, Arturo, was her age and he'd always go to sleep sitting there. It was nice and refreshing in here—not like our house where it was so hot." She paused again and wiped Lupe's slobber from her chin. "*Oh, Dios mío,* how Papa spoiled us." She looked at Ricky and smiled. "Just like you're doing to *Lupita.*"

After their meal and a dessert of cinnamon-sugar *churros* and chocolate sauce, Muncie reached out and held Sophie's hand. "Mamma let me tell you about my new job. I'm going back to the field. We're starting a new dig, and that's work I love to do. The site is about three miles west of Ricky's office, south of the highway, and almost to the border." A smile creased her lips when she looked at Ricky. "That way, he can keep an eye on us. The center-point of our site is exactly 1,681 yards north of the border fence—just about one mile." Looking back to Sophie, she continued, "From our center-point, we'll lay out our grid 220 yards in each direction, so we'll never get closer to the fence than roughly ¾ of a mile."

Sophie turned to Ricky "Will they be safe?"

Nodding his head, he took his wife's and mother's hands and cupped them in his own. "*Por supuesto. Todo el tiempo.* I always keep my ladies safe."

*

Monday morning began with military precision. Sophie rang the doorbell to babysit Guadalupe; Muncie joined Dr. Sara Gerber in her new SUV for the short ride to the new archeological digs; and Ricky was the last to leave, kissing his mamma and Lupe when he walked

112

out the door at 7:40. Everything and everybody was in tip-top shape. The day looked good.

Ricky and his former partner, DEA Agent Anna Fernandez, were sipping their break room coffee and discussing his current investigation and its relationship to their previous case with the Salinas family. His cell phone vibrated as he began to pour them another cup of coffee—fresh and tasty from their new coffee vendor. He looked at his phone and commented as he stepped into the hallway, "My wife. Give me a minute." Cupping the phone close to his lips, he spoke. "*Que tal*, Muncie?"

Her voice was harsh. "Ricky, we've got a problem and I didn't know who else to call. Somebody shot at us."

His voice was strong but compassionate, "Are you okay? Was anybody hit?"

He could hear her gasping to control her breath. "We're fine, but Ricky we're scared. Someone shot at us and hit Dr. Gerber's new car. It went right through the driver's window and out the other side."

"Okay," he replied. "I'm on my way. I'll get help there *pronto*. Get the hell out now. Meet me up on the highway."

Five minutes later, Ricky and two Border Patrol Agents arrived simultaneously. The BP helicopter, call-sign Oscar-Nine, swept low over the dig site and south toward the border. Dr. Gerber sat on the ground at the rear of one of the two New Mexico State University engineering department vans, her face buried in her hands, weeping. Muncie and the students from the engineering class and their instructor stood alongside her.

The students and the instructor, five men and three women were dressed for a day in the sun on a real work project. Instead, they found themselves thrown into a cauldron of violence, unprepared for their shattering experience. A single gunshot changed their day from a hands-on learning project to becoming another victim of the border wars.

Muncie ran to Ricky when he got out of his pickup. Wrapping her arms around him, she pressed herself tightly in his arms. She spoke in a calm but emphatic tone. "We never heard the gunshot, just the zing as it whipped past us and hit her car." He held her close, brushing her hair from her brow and comforting her while the officers spoke with the victims, questioning to assure there were no injuries other than a student who had fallen into a cactus in the melee.

Leaving his wife and the others after confirming no one was seriously hurt, Ricky and Felix, one of the BP agents, drove their vehicles to the site. Studying the location of Gerber's vehicle and the broken glass, they determined the shot came from the south/southeast. Relaying the information to the observer in the helicopter, they began a slow, steady walk along the assumed line of fire with the helicopter, Oscar-Nine, serving as their lookout.

Felix made a passing comment. "There's never enough money for the technology we need. If we had the Spot Shooter Triangulation System, we'd already know where the shot came from."

Ricky gave a disheartening smirk. "It's a big desert."

Twenty minutes later, they came to the fence marking the International Border where it was apparent the shooter or shooters stood on the south side of the fence and outside U.S. jurisdiction. The only evidence the suspects left behind were footprints and two crushed cigarette butts.

"Oscar, do you have an eyeball on anything?" Felix asked over his radio.

"There's a dirt road about a quarter-mile south of your position, and an old shack about one-half mile further south, but no activity."

"10-4. Thanks. Request you stay in the area while we scout around."

"10-4," Oscar responded.

"Screw it," Ricky mumbled when he found a foothold and lifted himself over the fence and into Mexican territory. He pulled a pocketknife from his Levi's and a handkerchief from his hip pocket. Getting down on his knees, he slipped the knifepoint into the burnt end of a Marlboro cigarette and placed it on the clean hanky he laid out in the dirt. Being equally careful, he picked up the second butt the same way—a filtered *Delicado*, and rolled it into his handkerchief, trying to keep them separate from each other.

Walking in a circle around the scuff marks, Ricky snapped a succession of photos on his cell phone. After a few moments, he leaned down and examined the footprints carefully. "*Nada*," he remarked. "They were wearing burlap and duct tape around their shoes, so there aren't any distinguishable footprints."

"Any brass from the gunshot?" Felix asked.

Ricky scanned the ground and probed into the creosote bushes. "They must have picked it up so we couldn't identify the weapon. We may never find these bastards, but if we do, they'll pay a hell of a price." Looking at Felix after he climbed back over the fence, he asked, "Can you conjecture why they would want to pop a cap at a bunch of innocent civilians?"

"You just answered it yourself . . . innocent civilians. They're an easy target. It's fun. Why not? They're *Los Ricos*." He gave Ricky a Cheshire cat grin. "They don't need a reason. The *Yanquis* are there, so let's scare the crap out of them."

"Assholes," Ricky said. Standing with his back to the fence, he extended his arm to the north. "Look at that. A straight line to where they were. Gerber's SUV was the ideal target." He glanced down at his boots then up toward the dig site. "My guess is we're about twenty-five feet in altitude above where the SUV is, so these guys had a perfect line of sight." He shook his head and spat on the ground. "I agree with you. They had no intention of hitting anyone. They wanted to scare them, and they did."

Starting back to the dig site, Felix looked up at the chopper. Speaking into his shoulder-mounted radio, he contacted them. "Oscar-Niner, we're clear here. Thanks for your help."

Ricky listened as the chopper unit responded with an abrupt "10-4" and made a hard turn and sped to the west. They were responding as the dispatcher gave them an assignment.

"Oscar-Nine, ground unit on Old Battalion Road west of Cloverdale has an adult male immigrant in poor condition. EMS is en route. The found person reports his group is somewhere south of his location. It is unknown how many people or when he last saw them."

Ricky shuddered as he listened. Life and death on the border respected no one—children, the elderly, the lost, and the poor. It was an equal opportunity situation in the vast Chihuahua Desert. "What are their chances?" he asked Felix.

The Border Patrol Agent spat into the dirt. "Not likely. The ground and air units will give it all they have, but if he had to leave his people behind, they may be dead by now. There's no water or shade within fifty miles of 'em." He shook his head. "They probably tried it on their own. An experienced *coyote* would never set out across this place in the middle of summer." He gave a disheartened smirk. "The guy had no idea what he was getting into. He threw the dice and lost."

*

All the university personnel had returned to the archaeological site by the time Ricky and Felix got there. A Doña Ana deputy and a New Mexico trooper were interviewing the students, Dr. Gerber, Muncie, and John Fitzgerald, the civil engineering instructor. Felix and his partner acknowledged their counterparts before returning to their van and starting back up the dirt road to the highway.

"Ricky," Muncie said, "Dr. Gerber and I think we're going to postpone this project. She'll run it up the administration, but our thoughts right now are we can't jeopardize anybody until we've made this place safe." Gesturing to their surroundings, she continued, "It might require around-the-clock protection—campus police or private security."

He chuckled. "Y'all must have a lot more money than we do."

*

Dinner time at the Basurto house was a quiet affair—Ricky at one end of the table, Sophie at the opposite end, and Muncie sitting alongside Lupe in her highchair. Sophie had made a heaping platter of Migas . . . scrambled eggs, cilantro, jalapeno, tortillas, avocado, salsa, and *cotija* cheese.

Wiping her hands on her apron and scooting up to the table, she spoke softly but directly to her son. "*Hijo*, we have an elephant in the room, and we need to discuss it."

He met her stare while helping himself to a plate of her homemade dinner, picked up his fork, sighed, and put it down. He looked at Muncie, then at his mother. His face was taut with anxiety. "Mamma, the border is a dangerous place." Shaking his head slowly, then pausing to take a bite, he continued. "In 1916, Pancho Villa invaded right here where we are sitting at this precise moment. He killed nineteen people and burned Columbus to the ground." Pausing to take a deep breath and to control his emotions, he continued. "Villa is dead and gone, but the army we're fighting now is one cartel after another—New Juarez and La Linea, the Sinaloa cartel, maybe even the Russians. Add to that the mishmash of individuals trying to make a living or make a name for themselves. One way or another, we're at war every day, twenty-four hours a day." He took another deep breath, leaned back in his chair, and gave a *real* Ricky smile. "Did I ever tell you about the Aspen groves?"

Musing is a hunter.

CHAPTER SEVENTEEN

Ricky had one consolation as he drove to work the next day, the archaeological dig was on hold. He wouldn't have to worry about Muncie and her colleagues being used for target practice, at least not now.

Driving west on Hwy. 9, he glanced to his right at the old El Paso and South West railroad trestle with the number 15 emblazoned on its timbers. This was where it had started and eventually led him to the Salinas family and the Mexican organized crime organizations.

He sighed and thought of what might have been but wasn't. The Salinas brothers and their father, the Juarez Cartel, La Linea—all of them were bigger, more powerful, and more evil now than they were a few short years ago.

Acacia greeted him when he arrived at the Task Force office, "Good morning, Mr. Lucky Investigator," she cracked. "I've got some fabulous news for you."

"What might that be?" he asked.

"The fingerprints from Mr. Salinas's business card. No sooner had I entered them into the Fusion system than I received a reply. It was a perfect match with Francisco Chacon, the man arrested in Kansas City with your deceased female victim. The same with his

DNA profile. Remember, the current policy on arrest such as the one in Kansas City mandates submission of the DNA into CODIS. Plus, his prints were on the Russian assassination weapon. So, Mr. Super-Agent, you hit a homerun."

"You're telling me Alfredo Salinas and Francisco Chacon are one and the same?"

Acacia smiled and nodded, "*Exactamente.*"

"I assume Kansas City has an outstanding warrant for him?"

She paused and brushed the hair from her brow, then continued. "10-4. Jackson County has a warrant for Failure to Appear and for the Class E felony charge of Prostitution. Of course, the female in their case identified herself as Olivia Camacho but in fact, is Maria Espinoza."

Ricky grinned wryly to Acacia. "What a tangled web we weave.'"

She gave a soft laugh and replied. "Sir Walter Scott beat you to the punch. The actual quote is, 'Oh, what a tangled web we weave when first we practice to deceive.'"

*

After a quick succession of phone calls to Jackson County and the Kansas City Police, Ricky had an answer. Once again, not the one he wanted. Yes, the warrant was outstanding and valid. However, for a Class E felony, they would not extradite him from Texas to Missouri. As the Warrant Division officer-in-charge said, "He's not worth the time and money it would take to bring him back to stand trial. Good luck. He's all yours."

120

*

It was midafternoon when Ricky, Miguel, Acacia, and Anna gathered in Miguel's conference room, a stark 10' x 10' space furnished with a six-foot walnut veneer table surrounded by six folding chairs. Border Patrol Supervisory Agent Miguel O'Rourke sat at the head with Ricky and Anna to his right and Acacia sat across from them. O'Rourke exuded command presence, a drastic overhaul from the early years as Supervisory Agent to the Task Force when he could pass for a derelict from the Salvation Army. He had grown professionally, and it was exhibited in his attire—a starched white western shirt tailored to his slim physique; his black hair neatly groomed; pressed and creased khaki trousers; and his silver-tipped cowboy boots. He wore his .40 Glock on his brown western belt. His voice was authoritative—clear and distinct, but not intimidating.

"Ricky has described this case as a tangled web, and I agree with him." Counting them off on his fingers, he began his monologue. "First are two unrelated deaths—an elderly Russian male in Arizona later identified as a former Russian mafioso involved in white slavery; a Hispanic female body found near Antelope Wells; a Russian-designed and built handgun used in both deaths; the same woman hired by an outdoor tour company but later arrested in Missouri for prostitution; her criminal charges were dropped, but she ends up dead in our desert; a Hispanic man with the name Chacon arrested with her, but who jumped bond; that same man later identified as Alfredo Salinas, the son of a major player in the New Juarez/La Linea Cartel and the operator of Rio Lobo Outdoor Adventures in Texas; and the same Salinas family involved in one of our drug importation cases a couple of years ago." He glanced at Ricky. "Am I missing anything?"

Ricky replied, "Fingerprints on the gun and Alfredo's business card tie him in with our deceased female, Maria Espinoza, aka Olivia Camacho. However," he emphasized when he leaned back and gave a cocksure smile, "We still have one unidentified DNA swab from the gun." He leaned back with his arms folded across his chest. "Somehow, someway, we have to identify who we've missed and get a sample of their DNA and/or fingerprints. Then, just maybe, we might bring this case to a close."

"I'm working on it," Acacia interjected. "I already went back to the old Beavis and Butthead case with the Salinas family. I haven't come up with anything yet, but I'll stay on it."

O'Rourke looked at DEA Agent Anna Fernandez. "Any ideas?"

She raised an eyebrow and smiled. "Yes, but I can't hurry it." Leaning forward with her arms on the table, she spoke softly, "I'm working on a confidential informant. I have every reason to believe my CI is well connected and if it comes together, that person might be our ticket." She shook her head. "These things take time. I'm confident he can do it, but the CI is extremely leery. We're talking about major players and major cartels. This is a game of keeps. You only lose once. There are no second chances."

Miguel turned to Ricky, "What's your next move?"

"I'm working on it, but like Anna, I've got to move slowly. If I blow it, there won't be any do-overs. One way or the other, I'll get into wherever Maria Espinoza lived and see what I can find . . . maybe a smoking gun, maybe nothing more than her laundry."

"I'm working on that with him," Acacia said. "So far, I have a copy of her Mexican driver's license, but it only shows her home as Boquillas del Carmen."

"Where else can you go to find something with her address?" Miguel asked.

Ricky paused momentarily, tossed a glance at Acacia, then responded very matter-of-factly to his supervisor. "We have a wildcard we're going to play. It could be a grand slam or a game-ending strikeout."

Impatience is a hunter.

CHAPTER EIGHTEEN

The investigation into the murder of Oleg Krutoy and the suspicious death of Maria Espinoza, along with the continuing criminal enterprise of the New Juarez cartel had reached a critical point. Ricky's mind was in turmoil. "It's for all the marbles," he mumbled when he parked his pickup and he and Anna started for the front door of the Federal Building. The time had come. They would meet with the Feds who would play a vital role in the outcome of his and Anna's investigation. And, of course, there was Deputy Anaya in Pima County who also had a vested interest in the case.

Entering the El Paso conference room, he wasn't surprised by the number of people who were stakeholders in the case. Besides Ricky and Anna there were the El Paso DEA Supervisory Agent Freddy Molina, their Legal Adviser Maria Padilla, and Patricia Ryan, the El Paso Fusion Center Technology Supervisor.

Following introductions and light, casual conversation, Ricky began with a review of the facts starting with the original Salinas case that centered around drug importation, human trafficking, and the New Juarez Cartel. He followed with the evidence into the deaths of Oleg Krutoy and Maria Espinoza; the Russian handgun and cartridge; Krutoy's background with the Russian Mafia; and the information he

124

gleaned from his visits to Boquillas del Carmen and Rio Lobo Outdoor Adventures.

Padilla cocked her head and smiled wryly. "I'd say you've been thorough so far. What's next on your agenda?"

"A search warrant."

"Pray tell, where, and for what?" she asked.

He nodded confidently. "I need to get into wherever Miss Espinoza lived, but I know of only one place where I might find her address . . . Rio Lobo."

Padilla sat back and smiled. "Go ahead. How do you intend to carry out a search warrant *if* a court will approve it?"

"Surreptitiously," he said. "I need a warrant that will authorize us to get into Rio Lobo personnel files electronically." Holding up his crossed fingers, he continued. "She worked several months for them so we should find payroll records, tax and banking information, and last but not least, her address."

Padilla nodded. "Assuming we get a warrant and you find everything you're looking for, then what?"

"Another search warrant." He took a deep breath, exhaled slowly, then spoke directly to Padilla. "With any luck, I'll get into her residence and find some history she may have left behind." He gave a half-hearted chuckle and shook his head. "Maybe she left some notes, letters, anything that could point us in the right direction to the who, what, and how behind Krutoy's and her death." He paused again and with hands in the air, gesturing as if surrendering said: "She's the key to all of this. Maybe she can speak to us from that cold slab she is lying on in the morgue."

*

It was almost eleven o'clock. Muncie had put Lupe down for the night. She and Ricky had scooted close together on the couch, and each nursed a chilled glass of Pinot Grigio when Ricky's cell phone buzzed. Snatching it from the coffee table, he looked at the caller ID. It was the El Paso DEA office. He pressed the *Talk* button. "This is Ricky."

"*Hola, amigo.* This is Agent Molina. Do you have a few minutes to talk?"

"I'm just sipping my adult beverage, but you've either got good news or bad. Which is it?"

"We threw the Hail Mary and scored. How's that sound?"

"Music to my ears. Fill me in."

"The Federal Magistrate approved our request for a search warrant, and we had it in hand at five o'clock. I assigned Agent Flannagan to work with IT, and they had it up and running at nine o'clock Central Time. The Rio Lobo computer worked on Word and Excel programs, so our people dove right in. No firewall or anything of significance to block them, so they were in and out in twenty minutes."

"You got everything we were looking for?" Ricky asked.

"Totally. It was a piece of cake. We'll return the completed warrant and inventory to the magistrate tomorrow morning: signed, sealed, and delivered."

"Any surprises in her files?"

"*Nada.* Everything was clear-cut. You'll have it in your office email when you get there in the morning."

"Thanks," Ricky said. "I appreciate your work."

"*De nada*, my friend. Maybe someday you can bail us out when we get in over our heads."

*

Sitting in the Task Force office, Ricky, Anna, Acacia, and Miguel each read the Fusion Center report Ricky had printed for them. It was clear and concise. Maria Espinoza, also known as Olivia Camacho, was a contract guide for Rio Lobo Outdoor Adventures. Her date of birth was November 28, 1994, and she lived at 1607 Allen Road, Apartment 204, in Alpine. There was no documentation of her cell phone or landline. Neither was there any documentation of her next of kin, banking, or education.

After reading it aloud, Ricky gave a disheartening shrug. "That's all we know about her, and now she's on a slab."

Miguel leaned forward with hands clasped on the table; he looked directly at Ricky. "You've got work to do, and there's no time to waste. Organize your travel papers, *pronto*. I want you and Anna to have a search warrant issued for her apartment." He turned to Anna. "Call ahead to your colleagues in El Paso so they can get started on the affidavit for the warrant. Tell them you and Ricky are on your way."

He glanced back at Ricky. "Get on the phone with Alpine Police. Have them get a photograph and description of her apartment for the affidavit. By the time you get to El Paso, everything should

127

come together to satisfy the magistrate on the scope and depth of the search. Once you've obtained the warrant, request the Alpine Police to station an officer outside the apartment to prohibit anyone going in or out. We want it as pristine as possible."

*

It was afternoon and another day without lunch before Ricky and Anna were eastbound on Interstate 10, and more than three hours until they could reach Alpine. It was going to be a long day.

The dying rays of the afternoon sun peeked over the mountaintop when they drove into the parking lot of the Beckwith Hills Apartments on Allen Road. It was a modest but clean complex of one- and two-story buildings, grassy areas with picnic tables and palm trees, a fenced-in swimming pool, and rows of covered parking slots.

Anna spotted the Alpine Police car backed into a shaded parking area midway down the row to their right.

Ricky slipped his pickup truck into the empty slot next to the police car, opened his window, and displayed his badge to the officer. "Thanks for holding down the fort until we could get here," he said while the female officer gave a cursory glance at his credentials.

After they exited their vehicles and introduced themselves to each other, the Alpine officer, Irene Luna, stepped back slightly with her hands on her hips. She was a petite but professional appearing officer with a pixie haircut, perfectly attired in her sharply pressed navy blue uniform and black leather Sam Browne belt.

The ideal image for a police recruiter, Ricky thought.

She shifted her weight to one foot as she looked quizzically at the two agents. "I'm extremely concerned." Her voice quaked. She paused to wet her lips and spoke softly, "Maria and I have been friends since she moved here from Mexico." Pointing up to the apartment, she continued. "I've been in her place dozens of times, and she has been in mine." She nodded at the next building over. "I live right there in 178. We're friends . . . the best of friends. I haven't seen her in a couple of weeks, but she travels a lot with her job. What's this all about? Is she in trouble?"

Ricky took a deep breath. "I can't say right now, but something came up since we got the warrant." Glancing at the apartment and back to the officer, he continued. "Without going into any details, we need to speak to a supervisor. Is your sergeant available?"

She shrugged and gave Ricky a caustic reply. "If you need someone higher up than me, sure. I've got a sergeant, Freida Gebhardt. I'll call her and she can be here in a few minutes."

"Thank you," Ricky said.

*

The unmarked, black Ford sedan wheeled into the parking lot and stopped in the driveway in front of Ricky and Officer Luna's vehicles. Ricky was immediately aware of the sergeant's demeanor. She was in a fighting mood—her lips pursed, brow furrowed, hands clasped into tight fists. Rounding the front of her car, Gebhardt's voice was commanding. "You have a problem with my officer?" Her eyes were glued on Ricky, then shifted to Anna.

Ricky stepped forward and offered his hand. He was firm but non-threatening, "I'm Trooper Basurto of the New Mexico State Police." Nodding over his shoulder at Anna, he resumed his introduction. "This is DEA Agent Anna Fernandez. We're assigned to the Joint Federal and State Task Force on Human and Drug Trafficking. We have a search warrant issued by the Federal Magistrate in El Paso for apartment 204, the home of Maria Espinoza. However, an unexpected issue has come up and we think we need to discuss it with you before we continue with the warrant."

The sergeant took a half step back with her fists on her waist. "Shoot. I'm listening." Fernandez moved toward a shaded parking slot several spots over. "May we speak privately, Sergeant?"

Gebhardt's eyes bounced from Anna to Ricky, then back to Anna. She exhaled with a disgusted blow. "Sure," she replied and followed Fernandez.

Anna offered a handshake that the sergeant accepted and immediately asked, "So, what the hell do you people have going that my officer can't handle?"

Anna spoke softly. "Our investigation has worked into a murder case with international implications. Unfortunately, Maria Espinoza and Officer Luna were friends, but we were not aware of that until a few minutes ago. However, our problem is rather awkward. Ms. Espinoza is dead, and she's right in the middle of our case."

"Damn," Gebhardt whispered. "How? When?"

"It's a long story, but we thought your officer shouldn't hear this like a cold slap in the face from total strangers. It'll be better if she has support when we give her the news."

The sergeant bit her lip, looked down at the ground, then back to Anna. "I'm sorry I came on so strong—my error." She looked at Ricky and Irene standing alongside the marked patrol car. "Let's do it," she mumbled when she turned toward Officer Luna.

Pain is a hunter.

CHAPTER NINETEEN

Ricky turned toward Anna and the sergeant when they came back. The young officer looked at her supervisor, then at Ricky and Anna. Her voice broke. "What's the matter? What's going on?" Steeling herself for whatever was coming, she stood erect, nervously adjusting the weight and alignment of her Sam Browne belt, then locked eyes with Agent Fernandez. "Give it to me," she barked.

"Irene," Anna said, "We started our day with one purpose—to serve the search warrant on Maria's apartment. But things changed when we got here . . . for you and us. Of course, we didn't know you and Ms. Espinoza were friends. Likewise, you couldn't have any idea about the extent of our case. I'll give you a little background—"

Irene stepped forward and snapped, "Stop it, damn it. Quit beating around the bush. I don't need the background or anything else. Just say what you've got to say and get it over with."

Anna was firm but gentle. "Maria is dead. The Border Patrol found her body in the desert near Hachita, New Mexico." Before she could continue, Irene lowered her head into her hands and wept bitterly, then leaned over her car with her back to the others. Sgt. Gebhardt put her arm around Irene's shoulders, whispering into the officer's ear.

The minutes slipped by before the young officer stood straight and breathed deeply, wiped her eyes with the back of her hand, and spoke calmly to Anna and Ricky. "Thank you for telling me." Shaking her head, she forced a smile. "Death notifications are a bitch, aren't they?"

Anna took Irene's hands in hers. "I'm so sorry. Now, what can we do for you?"

"Give it to me straight. She went crooked, didn't she?"

"Yes, she did," Anna said. "But what made you think that?"

Irene looked at the ground and kicked a small stone. Her eyes were downcast when she spoke. "It was just little things she said over the months that we knew each other. She was a good person but she got in over her head. I didn't know the details, but it was clear her job was more than she bargained for. She hated it but didn't want to go back to burro rides in Boquillas, so she put up with whatever was happening at work."

"Did she ever say what it was?" Gebhardt asked.

Irene shook her head. "*Nunca.* Not a peep. I only know she thought her boss, Mr. Salinas, was slimy. He kept trying to put the make on her. However," she paused and inhaled deeply, "there was more to it than just him, but I never knew what it was."

"What makes you say that?"

Irene shrugged. "There were a couple of times she was moody but wouldn't tell me what was happening."

"When did you last see her?" Ricky asked.

"About two weeks ago. She came to my place for dinner. She was having a downer. I told her to get it off her chest. She needed to

133

talk to someone. I'll always remember her face. It was so sad, but all she would say was she wished she'd never been born. I begged her to tell me what the hell was happening. I would help her or find someone who could."

Luna leaned back against her car. Her lips curled when she stifled her tears. "I didn't know what to do but knew things were horrible. We cried together." Shaking her head with tears pouring down her cheeks, the young officer vented her emotions. "I'm not stupid. I knew it was something big she was holding inside. I told her a dozen times, 'Get it out. I'll help, whatever it is.' She just shook her head and thanked me for being her friend, then said, 'I've got to go. Pray for me,' and she left. That was it. I never saw her again."

"Is there anything else?" Gebhardt asked.

Wiping her tears, Irene nodded. "There was a boyfriend, Phil Arnold."

Gebhardt fired a quick question. "Deputy Arnold?"

Irene and her sergeant locked eyes. "One and the same."

"Is he compromised?" Anna asked.

Luna nodded, turned her back to the others, and gazed at the distant mountains—barren and rocky outcroppings, cacti and rattlesnakes, perilous cliffs—an unyielding and unforgiving landscape. "I think so. He has too much money for a deputy, and his parents are blue-collar laborers at the golf course. He's getting money somewhere besides working for Aintry County and an occasional guide job for Rio Lobo."

"Was he part of her problem?" Ricky asked.

Luna took a deep breath, exhaled with a huff, and turned back to her fellow officers. "The poor girl. All she wanted to do was work outdoors—take people hiking, fishing, or trail riding—that sort of thing. But the deck was stacked against her. I don't have a shadow of a doubt that Rio Lobo and Phil are as crooked as a dog's hind leg. I don't know the facts, but putting two and two together, something stinks."

Anna interjected while Luna paused to compose herself: "Tell us about Arnold."

The young officer wiped her tear-stained face, brushed her trousers, and forced a smile. "They met at Rio Lobo. He was a full-time deputy but was an occasional guide for some off-duty income. He was gung-ho into outdoor activity, so he and Maria hit it off."

"What about his duties as a deputy?" Ricky asked.

Luna smirked. "Aintry County is about thirty miles west of us. It's massive, nearly 4,000 square miles of desert and mountains, but almost no population—maybe 500 people. The county seat is Colina Seca. Their population is about 250, and that leaves another 250 out on the ranches." She continued as she tilted her head and raised an eyebrow. "It has a reputation for being an access route for the dopers—marijuana, coke, you name it, and it comes through Aintry. Phil is on the regional task force—personnel from the small towns and the adjacent counties—there are about four or five cops and deputies assigned to it. None of them are full-time on the task force. They work together a few times a month, take down a load here and there, but don't have the resources to have a major impact on the drug flow."

Officer Luna paused, twisted her lips, then locked eyes with Anna. "But he's a crooked cop. He's got a $65,000 pickup truck, lives in a high-dollar apartment, goes to El Paso for his custom-made boots, and got a set of dental implants that set him back several thousand dollars. Match that with a deputy's pay with normal overtime and a few guide jobs, and he should be making about $45,000 a year." She shook her head. "It doesn't compute. He's doing more than a few hikes for Rio Lobo. Somebody is paying him for services rendered," she emphasized, symbolizing a quotation mark with her fingers.

Ricky stood alongside the young officer. "But Maria never discussed him or what he might be doing on the side to get all his money?"

She shook her head. "Never. Even when I was pressuring her to get it off her chest, she just clammed up and wouldn't say anything." Nervously wetting her lips, Luna glanced at her sergeant and stood tall. "Maybe I couldn't help her then, but let's see what we can do for her now." Gesturing toward the apartment, her voice was strong and emphatic. "Shall we serve your warrant? Maybe we can hang those bastards."

"Let's do it," Ricky said. "She needed a set of wheels. Is it here?"

Luna nodded toward a pickup. "That GMC parked in front of the apartment. I've been curious why she was gone but her truck was still here. Now I understand. She went with somebody, but who?"

"Does your warrant cover it?" Gebhardt asked.

Ricky nodded. "Her apartment and the curtilage, so we'll include it and have it towed in for safekeeping."

136

"I'll go to the office and get the apartment key, and you take the lead from there," she said.

*

Ricky wrote the time in his notebook—it was exactly five o'clock when Anna unlocked the door of Apartment 204, the residence of Maria Espinoza. Taking safeguards to minimize the introduction of a foreign object into the apartment, each of them wore a hairnet, latex gloves, and polypropylene disposable booties.

Anna entered, leaving her colleagues at the door. Using her cell phone video camera, she walked methodically through Maria's little domicile recording everything from wall to wall and ceiling to floor.

The living room furniture consisted of a sofa, two matching barrel chairs, an ottoman, and a glass-top coffee table. The walls were adorned with an inexpensive arrangement of paintings of the desert southwest.

The kitchen was spotless—granite countertops, a built-in microwave and glass top stove, a Mister Coffee, an apartment-sized refrigerator, and freshly painted cabinets. Anna opened the doors and videoed the contents—what little there was—a loaf of bread, some oatmeal, a box of Cheerios, a can of soup, and a roll of paper towels.

The refrigerator held an unopened quart of milk, a packet of tortillas, taco sauce, a two-pound pack of hamburger, and a six-pack of Corona.

The bedroom consisted of an unmade double bed, its pillows and sheets kicked back, a small oak desk and laptop computer, a wooden-framed cushioned chair, and a wall mirror.

137

Anna laughed to herself when she entered the bathroom—a typical girl's domain. Makeup, creams, oils, shampoo, conditioners, soap and body wash, tubes of lipstick, two hairbrushes, a curling iron, and female hygiene products, all of which were strewn about on the counter and in the open cabinets. A packet of twenty-one birth control pills was lying on the water tank lid of the commode. Three of the bubbles were empty.

Anna turned off her camera and returned to the door. "Ricky, go ahead with the coordinates of our search."

Starting with a quick walk-through, he returned to the living room. "I'm not anticipating any surprises, but let's take our time, be thorough, and see where it leads." He looked at Luna. "Does it look normal to you?"

She nodded. "Like she was here this morning. Tell me what you want me to do."

"Take your time and go through the living room. Look—not just on, under and behind—but also examine the stitches of the cushions. Be methodical. Don't take anything for granted. If it looks unusual, call me and we'll look together."

He turned his attention to the sergeant. "Do the kitchen—same instructions. Go slow and steady. Examine the cans and boxes to see if there might be any fake food containers that hold contraband."

"Got it," she replied.

He looked at Anna. "You've got the bathroom, and I'll do her bedroom." Glancing again around the apartment, he gave his final instruction. "If you find anything out of the ordinary, stop and we'll photograph it before we log it as evidence. Any questions?"

He made eye contact with his coworkers and smiled. "For Maria."

*

An hour later, they had searched, swapped positions, and searched again, bagged, and logged the laptop into evidence, and were finished. Maria's key ring was found in the dresser drawer with her door key, truck fob, and a small key marked A-223.

Hmm, he thought. *Bus station locker or safe deposit box?* He mumbled to himself, "To be determined."

The laptop would be submitted to the forensic staff at the crime lab. The door key would be returned to the apartment manager, and the fob would go to impound with the pickup truck. The *mystery* key would go into the evidence locker.

Ricky spoke as they closed the apartment and walked toward the parking lot. "One thing that makes me curious—no bank records of any type—monthly statements, a checkbook, mail, nothing." He shook his head. "*No comprendo.*"

Anna ran a registration check on the license. It came back to a 2017 Ford pickup truck, registered to Rio Lobo Outfitters. She and Ricky spent only a matter of minutes searching it. Nothing. No gas or repair receipts, no odds or ends, no trash. "*Nada,*" he exclaimed when they closed the doors. He glanced at Gebhardt. "Call your wrecker and we'll tow it in."

Thirty minutes later, Maria's pickup was on the back of the tow truck and on its way to storage.

Ricky turned to the Alpine cops and offered his gratitude. "Irene, I'm as sorry as I can be about what you had to deal with today. Agent Fernandez and I thank you for your strength and courage in dealing with this disaster and for helping us with the warrant. And Sergeant, we also want to thank you for being there for all of us." He gave a half-hearted smile. "Some days aren't worth a damn, but we want you to know you've been a tremendous help. We're very grateful for your assistance."

"Thank you," Gebhardt replied, "We appreciate the way you handled things here today." Cocking her head slightly, she continued. "What about the deputy?"

"Let everything ride," Ricky answered. "Don't say anything to anybody. We need to do some background investigation. When the time is right, we'll deal with him."

Ricky, too, cocked his head. "He's in for a hard fall."

Anna, Ricky, Acacia, and Miguel met for coffee and to review the previous day's productivity. Ricky started the commentary. "The lab has her laptop, and we've started running Deputy Arnold through the system."

Acacia interjected, reading from her notes: "Deputy Lester Phillip Arnold, but he goes by Phil. He's twenty-six years old, has an Associate Degree in Criminal Justice from Waymond Junior College in Corpus Christi, and has never been married," She gave a quick chortle, "At least that we know of." She paused to sip her coffee, then continued. "He received his Basic Law Enforcement Certification from the college four years ago; started with Aintry County when he graduated; and has kept his nose clean—*officially*, but maybe not so

140

much unofficially. We have an address of 2114 Bend Highway, Apartment 274. That's the Desert View Apartments—about one mile from where Maria lived."

"Any fingerprints on file?" Miguel asked.

"Certainly. He graduated, received his certification, and started with Aintry the following Monday." She smiled, "Before you can ask, I checked and double-checked—no match of his prints on the gun."

Miguel turned to Ricky. "Your thoughts?"

"I've already made contact with a friend at the IRS." He tossed a caustic smile. "Scratch my back, and I'll scratch yours. I worked one of my informants for them last year, so now I need a little favor from them." He smiled broadly. "The deputy is about to have an IRS audit. We're confident he'll have some tough decisions to make. Then we'll have a 'Come to Jesus' talk and help him see the light of day."

Miguel gave Ricky a Cheshire cat grin, "You're a heartless bastard when you go after a guy."

*

It was late afternoon. Ricky was at his desk completing travel expenses, mileage reports, and reviewing a stack of bureaucratic forms when his cell phone buzzed. He hit the *talk* button. "This is Basurto."

"Agent Basurto, my name is Marta Bravo. I'm one of the Forensic Supervisors in the Las Cruces lab, and I've got some urgent information for you. It's about the Acorn laptop you submitted. I just wanted to be sure you were in your office, so I'm sending it right now.

You'll see how critical it appeared to us, and we assumed you would want to have our findings ASAP."

Ricky nodded his head to the phone as he replied. "I'm at my desk now, so hit that *send* button, and I'll be right on it. Thanks for the heads-up. I was just getting ready to call it a day."

Marta gave a soft chuckle. "I don't think you'll be heading home any time soon."

Determination is a hunter

CHAPTER TWENTY

Ricky sat quietly at his desk, listening to the end-of-the-day chatter and commotion of his colleagues while the Task Force office closed for the day. Only a skeleton crew of radio and video technicians would remain in the building overnight.

The minutes ticked away. He looked at his watch. It was 5:28 when the halls fell silent. He listened to his own heartbeat, then braced himself for what awaited him on the computer. Taking a deep breath, he opened Marta's email, giving a casual scan of the bureaucratic legalese before scrolling down to the body of the report. He read it slowly.

Summary

The Acorn laptop computer contained minimal data, but the contents were unforgiving. The owner of the laptop listed an inventory of her physical property. It consisted of the clothing and personal items located in her apartment, #214 at the Beckwith Apartments in Alpine, Texas. She listed ninety-five dollars cash in her locker at Rio Lobo Outdoor Adventures in Alpine.

Additionally, she stored some items in a lockbox at Marfa Peak National Bank in Marfa, Texas. The only other document the forensic staff found in the laptop was a memo or letter to be read in case of her death. It was dated June 10th of this year. The memo directs law enforcement to a smuggling operation coordinated by the owners of Rio Lobo Outdoor Adventures and their family. The letter closes with an allegation of several murders in which the computer owner was involved. Staff also found numerous fingerprints on the computer case and the keys. They were consistent with fingerprints on file under the names of Maria Espinoza a.k.a. Olivia Camacho. No other fingerprints were found.

End of Summary

Ricky read it a second time and stopped to picture the first time he saw Maria—dead and decomposed at the bottom of a ravine. Pausing to take a deep breath, he printed the entire email and attachment, then read what was purported to be a dying declaration from Maria Espinoza.

I probably do not know you and never will. I am dead.

My name is Maria Espinoza. I was born and lived in Mexico until recently. I accepted a job with Rio Lobo Outdoor Adventures as a guide for bikers, hikers, and fishermen. What I didn't know were all the other jobs Alberto Salinas planned for me.

I love the outdoors but have always given my life to my village and friends. I never wanted to hurt people. I made a bad mistake when I gave my body and soul to Alberto Salinas. I became who I wasn't. He gave me money and one of his trucks to take home and drive for personal use. I had fun. I didn't want to go back to the burro rides for tourists. That was behind me. I wanted people to wait on me for a change. I didn't want to be anybody's servant. I wanted to be rich and have a real life.

Oh, God. I sinned against you. I was selfish and did bad things I can't take back. I wanted to be free. Now I know that won't ever happen. I would give anything to be home with my burros, my people, Father McGuire, and Abuelo. They will never again be in my life. I let Alberto Salinas and his father take me, but the worst was yet to come.

This is what the police need to know, but I cannot tell them in person because the hand of the devil took me. Alberto forced me into his bed. Later, he forced me to take him to *my* bed. I hate him and all he stands for. He videoed me in his bedroom without telling me. Then he told me he would do things with it if I didn't follow his orders. He gave me to his father. If only I could have died.

They told me I was going to have a lot of money and a nice time, to just keep my mouth shut. Enjoy your new life, they said—everybody should have a good time. I had to run errands for them. Sometimes I delivered letters or a package. Other times, I picked up packages from homes or at businesses. I never knew what they were, but I think they were money since Alberto would get so uptight about it. He worried a lot. Later, I had to meet people—sometimes men, sometimes women. I would take them wherever Alfredo told me. I would pick up the same people later and take them back to where I first picked them up. Sometimes I didn't. I always had doubts about what that meant.

I started making a lot of money after I drove the people where I was ordered. One evening in November, Alfredo told me to go to an address on Cholla Street in Ft. Stockton. I had to get there after ten o'clock. The place was a craphole with a long driveway. I followed it behind the shanty. Two men put a body in the bed of the truck. I was terrified. The dead person was wrapped in cardboard. They got in and told me where to drive. We went maybe ten miles into the desert on a little dirt path. They had their shovels and I stayed in the truck while they buried whoever it was. They never said and I didn't ask. I did it three more times from different places. Once in Ft. Stockton and twice in Pecos. Alberto was always the one who gave me the orders. The place in Pecos looked like an old garage or tire shop. It was close to the freeway. I never saw the men from Ft. Stockton in Pecos.

For those three trips, they always told me exactly where to drive, but I never got out and helped with any of what they did. Alberto always paid me well when I ran those errands. I'm not stupid. I knew the worst was coming. It did. I was sent to a house on a dirt road south of Pecos. A gringo met me when I parked, and he told me to come in. I didn't want to but was afraid not to, so I did. There was a lady about my age and she and two other gringos were talking and drinking beer. The woman spoke to me, then followed one of the men to the back of the house. A couple of minutes later I heard a shot. I was scared and started to cry, but they were nice to me. It didn't make sense. I watched them wrap her in a canvas and dump her in my truck. I followed their directions, but only one guy came with me. He told me where to go—up to an oil field north of I-10. I was too afraid. He made me help bury her, then slapped me on the back and called me *La Dormida*. Alberto gave me $500 for the job and said how good I was.

Then I didn't do much for a while before he told me he had a job in Tucson, and we would do it together. We're going to kill an old man. A Russian. He was supposed to be a Mafia hitman. I'm going to learn to shoot Phil's gun. We will go to a range in Odessa so I can learn to shoot his Glock. He knows the guy and we won't have to pay. I don't want any of this but can't do anything about it. Alfredo has a gun he got from his dad in Mexico. It's a special kind of gun we will use on the Russian. After we have done it, he will take me close to Antelope Wells. He will drop me off not too far from the crossing. I will hike cross country a little and get to the fence. Somebody will meet me there and take the gun. I will go with them for a few days to relax. That's a joke. Relax? What I'm going to do is a sin, but I'll do it anyway. I'm sorry, but it's too late. I made bad decisions and I'm going to hell.

I hope this helps you. More than anyone else, I hate Alberto's father the most. What he did to me. But I'm not stupid. We were at the Tropical Hotel in El Paso the night of February 15th. I saw his passport. He used the name Gilbert Henke. After he did his thing to me, I saved my panties and the washcloth he used to clean himself and me. He is so evil. The bastard. I'll put them in a safe deposit box. I know bad things are happening to me, but if I do this it may help somebody.

God, please forgive me of my sins. I wasn't raised this way. Abuelo, I love you. I want my burros back. I loved them. I want to go to Boquillas. I want to go home.

Ricky bit his lip as tears roiled in his eyes, then trickled down his cheeks. *She never took report writing,* he mused, *but she spilled out her life in vivid color.*

Truth is a hunter.

CHAPTER TWENTY-ONE

Once again, Ricky started his day in Miguel's office, this time accompanied by Acacia and Anna. He gave them copies of Marta's email and attachments, then watched in silence, reading their body language while they perused the lurid details of Maria Espinoza's life. He was not surprised that all of them continually shifted around in their chairs and sipped coffee in obvious discomfort while they digested the horrors of Maria's life and death.

Miguel leaned back with a disgusting huff and tossed the report on his desk. "It has to be true," he muttered. "You couldn't make this stuff up."

Acacia scooted her chair back and wiped her eyes when she walked out of the office.

Anna gently placed her copy on the desk, glanced at Miguel, then turned to Ricky with her arms folded across her chest. "We're doing the right thing. You and me. We'll hang those bastards from the yardarm and let the buzzards pick their bones clean. A slow death will be too good for them."

Miguel, too, folded his arms over his chest. His eyes bore into Ricky's, then toward Anna. "You better have one hell of a game plan, 'cause these contemptible bastards need to go . . . big time."

Ricky gave a caustic smile. "They'll go. Our first stop will be to Federal Court for a search warrant for her safe deposit box. Anything of evidentiary value will go to the crime lab and see what we can tie to Alberto, Nicolas, or anyone else. Then we'll invite the deputy to have a *Come to Jesus* talk with us. Depending on what we learn from him and the crime lab's findings, we'll go after the people behind our deceased suspect and victim, since they were one and the same person. At some point, we'll stop and take a deep breath, evaluate what and where we are, then go in for the kill."

*

Forty-eight hours later, Ricky and Anna were at Marfa Peak National Bank. They approached the Operations Officer at her desk, identified themselves, and were directed to the manager's office. Following an inspection of their credentials and with a copy of the warrant in hand, the manager, Marta Moreno, escorted them to the safe deposit vault, a windowless room lined with individual lockboxes ranging from letter sized to hatbox sized with a mahogany table in the center of the room.

Key A-223 fit a shoebox-sized vault along the left wall. "Mrs. Moreno," Anna said, "we'd appreciate it if you would remain while we inventory its contents. If we find any item we consider to be of evidentiary value, we'll take it with us and provide you with a receipt. Of course, if we don't find anything of value to our investigation, we will leave the contents here and the bank can follow protocols with the final determination of those items."

Mrs. Moreno nodded, then handed her key to Ricky, who inserted both keys into their respective slots, turned them, and pulled Maria Espinoza's box from its secure nook. Almost ceremoniously, he placed it on the table and stepped back for Anna to begin her photography.

Using her cell phone, Anna zoomed in on the lockbox, then began videoing the process of Ricky opening it with Mrs. Moreno pictured in the background. He opened the lid, then gestured for Anna to video the contents as they were found—a sandwich bag containing a pair of ladies pink panties; another bag with a cream-colored washcloth in it; a collection of six pictures of a girl, presumably Maria—a baby picture, two that may have been from her elementary years, one standing alongside her burros, another helping a tourist climb up on a burro, and one that may have been a high school graduation picture.

A single, yellow sheet of folded tablet paper was lying at the bottom of the box. Ricky unfolded it and laid it on the table for Anna's camera view. The note was short and tense:

Nicolas Salinas uses the name of Gilbert Henke. He made me have sex with him twice at the Tropical Hotel. He used this washcloth to wash his privates and mine. He would not allow me to spit but didn't see me when I wiped my mouth with this washcloth. My panties should have his trash on them too. Kill him for me.

M.E.

"That's it," Ricky said when he glanced at Mrs. Moreno. "We'll take everything with us and give you a receipt." He took a deep breath and looked down at Maria's effort to bring a sense of justice to the

Salinas cartel. He gave a timid smile and gestured to Moreno. "Thank you, and we'll be in touch if the U.S. Attorney needs to get a statement from you."

Mrs. Moreno dabbed her eyes with a tissue. "I'm so sorry all this happened. I was working the day this young lady contracted for her safe deposit box. She was so sweet. So pretty. But now, can you tell me about her? Is she okay?"

Anna reached for Moreno's hands and held them firmly. "I'm sorry, Mrs. Moreno. Ms. Espinoza is dead."

The professional, elegant bank manager caught herself when her knees sagged momentarily, leaned forward on the table, and wept.

Sorrow is a hunter.

Chapter Twenty-Two

Ricky felt a tinge of relief. With the laptop, the sandwich bags, and their contents in the hands of the crime lab staff, they were making headway in their far-flung investigation. From Oleg Krutoy in Arizona to the Salinas family in Texas and Chihuahua, and with the body of Maria Espinoza in New Mexico, the evidence was gathering like a monsoon over the heads of the New Juarez/La Linea Cartel and the Salinases.

Now, though, the time came to take a break, so he joined his colleagues for lunch—the first such occasion in a long time. It was Miguel's birthday—forty-two years old with nineteen years on the Border Patrol. They were joined by Miguel's wife, Milagros, three staff technicians, half a dozen BP agents along with Senior Agent Rudy Cifuentes from Las Cruces, plus Anna and Acacia. They filled the small private dining room at Duffy's Tavern, a quaint Irish/Mexican eatery off the beaten path near the Columbus/Palomas border crossing.

Considering everyone's duty status, the Irish stew, vegetables, soda bread, and Irish cream Tiramisu were accompanied by Assam tea—no Guinness Ale this time. With the backslapping and "Happy birthdays" behind them, Ricky scooted his chair back, ready to return to work when his cell phone buzzed. It was Marta. Rather than answer, he sent it to *message,* bade his good wishes to Miguel, and went to the parking lot. Minutes later and with Marta on the phone, he sat behind the wheel of his pickup, mesmerized by what she was telling him. "We have a complete match on the Chacon/Espinoza DNA from the weapon, the washcloth, and the pair of panties. Additionally, there was a match with two DNA locations on the handgun and several more on the panties and the washcloth as being someone other than Ms. Espinoza. We assume *they* belong to Nicolas Salinas but need a reliable and valid positive on him to call this profile his. Right now, we only have her accusation which may be correct, but we lack the necessary level of positivity before we can declare it to be him." She paused for a moment, then continued. "Following up with the Henke name mentioned in the letter, we pulled up his Mexican passport, so I'm emailing his picture to you along with his travels since he obtained it last year. You will find this interesting. He crossed the Nogales border on June 1st and returned on June 3rd. The first time he crossed was at El Paso on February 12th with a return to Mexico on the 16th."

After a long silence, she spoke again. "Agent Basurto, those of us in the lab who have had any interaction with this case have become a cheering section for you and Agent Fernandez. Those guys deserve whatever you can dish out to them." She offered a self-embarrassed chuckle before she continued. "I know we're not to become personally involved in our cases, but by damn, sometimes we just have to say to the good guys, 'Go get 'em.' As for that young lady, she made some bad decisions but paid one hell of a price for it."

"Thanks, Ms. Bravo. I couldn't agree more. Sometimes it seems the good *really* do die young. And we agree with you. Ms. Espinoza screwed up big time, but more than paid for her decisions."

"Before I go," Marta added, "I'm sending a separate email to you. Maybe it can apply to the Salinas men in this case."

"Thank you. I'm looking forward to our continued work together."

*

Back in his office and with the birthday party a distant memory, Ricky opened his inbox. At the top were Marta Bravo's emails—one marked *Evidence Summary* and the other an email addressed to him. They were long, so he printed them out and sat back to read them:

"*DEATH SENTENCE 1881*

The following is a verbatim transcript of a sentence imposed upon a defendant convicted of murder in the Federal District Court of the Territory of New Mexico many years ago by a United States Judge, sitting at Taos in an adobe stable used as a temporary courtroom:

'JOSE MANUEL MIGUEL XAVIER GONZALES, in a few short weeks, it will be Spring. The snows of Winter will flee away, the ice will vanish, and the air will become soft and balmy. In short, JOSE MANUEL MIGUEL XAVIER GONZALES, the annual miracle of the years will awaken and come to pass, but you won't be there.'

'The rivulet will run its soaring course to the sea, the timid desert flowers will put forth their tender shoots, the glorious valleys of this imperial domain will blossom as the rose. Still, you won't be here to see.'

'From every treetop, some wild woods songster will carol his mating song, butterflies will sport in the sunshine, the bee will hum happy as it pursues its accustomed vocation, the gentle breeze will tease the tassels of the wild grasses, and all nature, JOSE MANUEL MIGUEL XAVIER GONZALES, will be glad, but you. You won't be here to enjoy it because I command the sheriff or some other officers of the country to lead you out to some remote spot, swing you by the neck from a knotting bough of some sturdy oak, and let you hang until you are dead.'

'And then, JOSE MANUEL MIGUEL XAVIER GONZALES, I further command that such officer or officers retire quickly from your dangling corpse, that vultures may descend from the heavens upon your filthy body until nothing shall remain but bare, bleached bones of a cold-blooded, copper-colored, blood-thirsty, throat-cutting, chili-eating, sheep-herding, murdering son-of-a-bitch.'"

UNITED STATES OF AMERICA vs. GONZALES (1881) UNITED STATES DISTRICT COURT, NEW MEXICO TERRITORY SESSIONS."

History is a hunter.

CHAPTER TWENTY-THREE

Not wanting to leave loose ends or arouse suspicion, Ricky emailed Alberto at Rio Lobo canceling the proposed overnight hike. Simultaneous to hitting the *enter* key on his computer, his cell phone buzzed a message. It was from Anna. "Big news. See you pronto."

Twenty minutes later, Ricky was reviewing the documents from the crime lab when Anna zipped through the entryway to his cubicle. Dressed in a starched, white western blouse, tan khakis, cowboy boots, and with her silky black hair in a ponytail, she unceremoniously pulled up a chair and flopped down.

Incongruent, he mused, then gave her a soft smile. "It must be big for you to come running in here like that."

Anna's voice was filled with excitement. "You'll never guess what I have." She paused, then spoke before he could respond. "I've been working my confidential informant hard for two months and he came through." She took a moment to remove the lid from her Styrofoam cup and enjoy the sweet scent of her hot chocolate, then leaned forward and rested her elbows on her legs.

She looked intently at Ricky. "We've got an inside source to the New Juarez/La Linea/Salinas cartel. His 'handle' is Chico, and he's the *real* deal—trustworthy, and reliable. This man has done everything I asked for, did it on time, didn't try to cheat us on anything, and came through perfectly. It's all high risk, high rewards, or doomsday—nothing in between. We have to be careful, but we pay him top scale. Caution is the byword. He can't go too far too fast and get smoked, but we think the time is right. He can do it, and if we pull it off, Nicolas Salinas is going down."

Ricky smiled and leaned back in his chair. "What do you mean by 'do it'?"

Anna's voice turned icy cold. "First-degree Murder." She paused to place her cup on his desk. Her eyes bore into Ricky's. "It's dangerous for all of us, but we can make it happen. Maria Espinoza will get justice."

*

Ricky's warmed-over dinner was on the table when he got home. "It's eight o'clock," Muncie snapped when he came in. "You could have at least called so I would know when to expect you."

"*Lo siento.* I'm sorry," he murmured. "I've had a full day." He gave a half-hearted chuckle and wrapped his arms around her waist. "The day turned out to be far beyond my expectations. As the old saying goes, 'What's meant to be will always find a way.'"

Muncie draped her arms around his neck and pulled him close to her. They kissed lightly before she leaned back, his arms still wrapped around her waist. "*Digame,*" she said. "What could possibly catch the world's best undercover narc by surprise?"

He kissed her nose and looked into her eyes. "We're going to make our case. I'm certain of it, but it's going to be a challenge."

"So, what's the big deal? Why is this so different from the challenges you've overcome all your life?"

"Culiacán. Do you know where it is?"

She shrugged and tilted her head with a *who cares* smile. "Sinaloa?" she replied.

Ricky released his grip from her waist, and they sat down to the lukewarm dinner while Lupe crawled between their feet. Between slurps of chicken stew and bites of her homemade tortillas, he laid out what Anna and he would be doing in Culiacán. His explanation as to the *where* was simple, yet complex. He laid his fork on the napkin and cupped her hands in his.

"Culiacán serves as the heart and soul of language centers in Mexico. It's the focal point for business people, politicians, and bureaucrats to assimilate the language and culture of the country where they'll be working. But what we've learned is it provides excellent cover for the underworld to exist openly." He gave her hands a gentle squeeze and smiled before he continued. "The Spanish/Russian language school is one of the busiest in the city. It's given perfect cover where the Russian Mafia and the Mexican cartels can have a warm and cozy relationship, and they've taken advantage of it." Shaking his head, he inhaled deeply and gave a hapless grin. "They're a power to be reckoned with, but we'll give' em the fight of their life."

*

159

Anna traveled with her undercover passport and documents under the name of Isabel Montez. Ricky's documents were in the name of Rene Norzagaray. To fully develop their undercover scheme in case Salinas investigated their trip, they traveled on Thursday from El Paso to Los Angeles on Southwest Airlines. After an overnight stay, their next leg from Los Angeles to Culiacán on *VivaAerobus* put them at their destination mid-afternoon Friday. By cocktail time, they had checked into their rooms in *La Plaza del Rey,* a suspected cartel property owned by Hector Silva, a probable Class-One heroin trafficker between Mexico and the United States.

They met Chico at a nearby coffee shop at five o'clock. He was convinced Nicolas would take the bait, and Anna shared his confidence. The informant's brother, Arturo Sepulveda, was a driver for Nicolas but was killed in a shoot-out with a rival cartel in Juarez a year earlier. It was at his funeral that Chico and Nicolas met. From then on, Chico served as a conduit locating upcoming markets and friendly financial institutions in the United States for the New Juarez/Linea cartel.

*

For his role in this undercover operation, Ricky would be a bystander until the deal was done, but he wouldn't be alone. The three couples enjoying a dinner party at another table were agents from the DEA offices in Mexico City, Tepic, Durango, and Zacatecas.

The Talavera clock above the entryway struck eight o'clock—the precise moment the plan was scheduled to begin. Carrying a valise and wearing a sports jacket, white shirt, and a Kachina bolo tie, Ricky would only 'get in the game' if the scheme worked as planned. If things turned dangerously sour, the six DEA agents were heavily armed.

Anna dressed for the occasion. Wearing a short-sleeved, floral, embroidered Mexican dress and a squash blossom necklace, her ponytail was held in place by a turquoise holder, and her boots were from her favorite bootmaker, Old Gringo. She was an *elégante belleza*. Her dangling silver earrings served a dual purpose. Not only were they stylish, but a microphone was embedded in the jeweled centerpiece.

Two of the agents across the room wore recorders and earpieces to monitor and record the pair's conversation.

The maître d' greeted Anna and Ricky in the *Azteca* dining room. All the conversations were in Spanish. The tuxedoed gentleman escorted them to the table occupied by Nicolas Salinas and Chico, whose operative name was Francisco Medina. The men stood when their guests approached the table. Ricky was caught unawares— Nicolas towered over him by several inches.

Chico introduced Anna as the CEO of Golden State Finance Corp in Los Angeles, and Ricky as one of her account executives. Following casual chit-chat, Ricky and Francisco excused themselves with the informant leaving the hotel restaurant and Ricky taking a table in the corner opposite Anna and Nicolas.

The couple sipped Chateau Talbot St. Julien wine with their slow-paced dinner. The conversation lagged as they spoke in vague terms about *product* markets, transportation systems, the volatile investment market, and the inevitable negative impact from

161

unanticipated influences. Otherwise, they had an expensive business meal of a quail appetizer, chicken/avocado soup, a filet mignon for her, and a T-bone for him. Dessert was a Mexican bread pudding.

Nicolas nibbled the last bite of pudding, slowly placed his spoon on the napkin, then looked deeply into Anna's eyes. His voice was soft but distinct. "Our mutual associate speaks highly of you, Ms. Montez, and I stake my life on his word." He paused momentarily, then resumed, "But also, your life and his." He gave a light, sour sneer. "There is no allowance for error in our business. Everything and everyone must be beyond reproach. When I give a command, it must be followed explicitly. No one is to question my directions, and that includes you and your little minion over there." He nodded toward Ricky and threw a surprising question to Anna. "Is he your little boy-toy, or does he actually do a man's work?"

Anna didn't hesitate. "Never judge a book by its cover. Mr. Norzagaray is and has been an outstanding member of our organization." She shook her head and took on a subtle cynicism in the tone of her voice. "He is no *sicario* but is a genius on money matters." She paused briefly and stared at Nicolas. "That man over there can make millions of dollars for both of us. He knows how to clean otherwise soiled money of any denomination—dollars, euros, pesos, yuan, shekel—any of them. On top of that, he is uncanny at putting together real estate transactions." A sudden smile lit her face. "I can see you this minute resting on your patio above the cove at La Jolla. It's a ten-million-dollar estate, but you will be able to afford it, live in style, and enjoy a Permanent Residence Visa. We have a fine person who, for the right price, can arrange it for you." She tossed a glance at Ricky. "My colleague might look like a little shit to you, but he is worth gold to both of us." She sat back and sipped the last of her wine. "Are we in business? There is nothing in writing because it might be traced. It's our word to each other."

"Summarize your rates," he said.

"You deposit the cash in our office, and we guarantee it at eighty percent within forty-five days. The other twenty is our cost of doing business. We also understand emergencies happen, so we can compensate your investment at seventy percent in twenty days. Furthermore," she added with a polite smile, "absolutely nothing is ever documented on a computer. We're cautious—paper and pencil. No meddler can hack into our system. Plus, we sweep our facilities for electronic audio and video devices at least twice a week. We don't take chances. If anyone in our organization is leery of a deal, we back off immediately."

Nicolas offered a condescending smile with a raised eyebrow. "Frankly, Ms. Montez, I don't give a damn about anything except making money. How you do it is up to you. If you're late returning my investment, somebody is going to pay one hell of a price, and I might start with the little shit across the room."

Anna sat up straight and glared coldly at him. "It's a two-way street, Mr. Salinas—two-way."

He sat back and gave a Cheshire cat grin. "We have a deal. How soon can we start?"

Anna turned to Ricky and gestured. He rose from his seat, and with valise in hand, approached their table. The observant maître d' hurriedly went to an empty table, grabbed a chair, and had it in place when Ricky was ready to be seated.

"We're in business," Anna said to Ricky. On cue, her beautiful, red lips curled into a smile—first for Nicolas, then for Ricky.

Ricky opened the valise and, with a subservient nod, held up a bottle of Dalmore twenty-five-year-old Single Malt Scotch Whiskey. His voice was firm but polite. "As a testament of faith in our mutual interest, we would like to share this rare bottle of Scotch with you." Without hesitating, he removed from the valise a Faberge crystal glass holder that held three gold-trimmed Glencairn Scotch glasses. He passed a glass to Nicolas, one to Anna, and set one on the table for himself. He turned the bottle label to Nicolas to verify its quality, then took a small pocketknife from his jacket and cut the seal. Slowly, almost religiously, he opened the bottle and poured the glasses.

Nodding again to Salinas, he offered a toast. "I don't know who said it first, but 'We were born to succeed, not to fail.' And you, sir, will succeed."

They touched glasses and each paused briefly to take a whiff of their drink. They sipped slowly and finally placed the empties on the table. Anna kept Nicolas occupied in conversation while Ricky wiped two of the glasses clean; then he nonchalantly slipped the three back into the Faberge holder. Nicolas Salinas's DNA was as solid as the gold trim of the Faberge holder.

Holding up the bottle, he smiled and handed it to Salinas. "For your pleasure, sir."

Vanity is a hunter.

CHAPTER TWENTY-FOUR

It was four o'clock in the morning when Ricky and Anna walked out the front door of the hotel and climbed into the back seat of a black SUV. Kirby and Marcella, two of last night's dinner guests, were in the front seat with Marcella at the wheel.

"Good timing," Kirby said. Ricky and Anna fastened their seatbelts as Marcella accelerated into the dark exurban street—an eerily quiet neighborhood devoid of streetlights, traffic, or any other signs of life.

"Is it always like this?" Anna asked.

Marcella caught Anna's eyes in the mirror and offered a hapless explanation. "It's prime time," she smirked. "Nobody's out except kidnappers, *sicarios*, narcos, and us. As soon as we get you on your plane, we'll get somewhere safe—maybe even home." She gave a disheartened sneer. "Pardon my grammar, but there ain't nobody safe here anymore."

While Marcella zipped her way through the city streets, Ricky commented as he returned the Faberge set to Kirby, "I've kept the glass with our suspect's DNA, but everything else is washed and snug in the holder." Handing the valise over the back of the front seat, he tilted his head and proposed a question to Kirby. "So how the hell did you ever come up with this prop? It looks real."

Kirby and Marcella chuckled. "It isn't a prop," Kirby replied. "It's the real thing—part of a racketeering case we did in Tucson a few years ago. It was a major RICO investigation. We confiscated about $4 million worth of real estate and jewelry from the arrestees— a husband/wife team from Afghanistan. They were Class-One heroin violators and had been doing it for years before we made a case on them. But when they *fell*, they fell hard."

*

Twenty minutes later, Marcella pulled into the Charter Terminal at *Aeropuerto Internacional de Culiacán* and the Green Mountain Airlines gate. They were the last passengers to board the old, unmarked Boeing 737. A casually dressed woman in her fifties, wearing a white blouse and blue denim slacks greeted them at the top of the stairway. She tossed a caustic smile with an equally caustic, "Glad to have you. Grab a seat and you'll be on your way."

They squirmed through the nearly full aircraft that had begun the flight in Honduras with a stop in Belize before reaching Culiacán. Even with his experience in the Middle East and his work along the border, Ricky was surprised at the collection of nefarious-looking characters aboard—agents from the DEA, CIA, mercenaries, cold-eyed women looking like the cast of *Apocalypse Now,* and a scattering of laid-back, business-type executives.

It was nine o'clock when the Green Mountain plane landed at the Marana Air Park midway between Tucson and Phoenix. It had

166

been a flight with no chitchat among passengers or interaction with flight attendants—since there were none. The crabby witch who greeted them departed along with the set of steps. This was a quiet business flight—you mind yours, and I'll mind mine.

Walking down the stairs onto the Marana tarmac, Anna glimpsed one of her colleagues, Nita Barnes, standing alongside another of the standard nondescript black SUVs. Following brief introductions, Nita escorted them to Phoenix Sky Harbor Airport where they boarded the noon flight to El Paso.

*

After an exhausting 1,200-mile trip on a relic of an airplane followed by the drive from El Paso, Ricky stood at the reception counter at the Las Cruces Crime Lab. It was four o'clock. They would accept the DNA evidence and forward it to the Santa Fe lab for processing.

His mind was in a fog. It had been a long day, but with Nicolas Salinas's DNA in the lab, it was a worthwhile venture. The wheels of justice were grinding forward ever so slowly . . . but forward, nonetheless.

*

Ricky, Muncie, and Lupe had Sunday to themselves. After attending church with his family, Ricky spent the early afternoon mowing the lawn and weeding the flower beds. After a midafternoon snack of homemade tamales and a cold beer, the little family adjourned to the backyard. Ricky stretched out beneath the ramada on a chaise lounge while Muncie catnapped in the hammock. Lupe went into never-never land on her daddy's lap. Even Boots, their adopted alley cat

167

with snow-white paws and smooth black coat, found time to snooze curled into a little ball on Muncie's chest. It was a perfect day—similar to the way millions of others lived the American dream.

*

The weekend had zipped by before he knew it. At eight o'clock Monday morning, Ricky was in his cubicle at the Task Force office documenting the progress of their investigation. As he had said before, "It's like writing a straight line with crooked letters." It started with the murder of the Russian Mafioso in Arizona; then the mysterious death of Maria Espinoza south of Hachita; the unique Russian handgun and ammunition; *Rio Lobo* Outdoor Adventures and the Salinas family; the undercover operation netting the DNA sample from Nicolas Salinas; and suggesting the next chapter—an interview with the Aintry County Deputy, Lester Phillip Arnold.

It was not in Ricky's moral fiber, but he thought it anyway; *I want to see that son-of-a-bitch squirm.*

Retribution is a hunter.

CHAPTER TWENTY-FIVE

It was late afternoon. Ricky's updated documentation of the investigation lay on Miguel's desk for review. He had eased himself into his chair and taken the first sip of a cold Dr Pepper when his cell phone buzzed. He smiled when he saw the caller ID. It was Paul Hamilton, his IRS contact. *"Que tal, Pablo?"* he inquired.

Hamilton chuckled. "We're ready on this end whenever you are. We analyzed the deputy's lifestyle, and he's coming out on the short end of the stick. Our analysts verified his expenditures as exceeding $100,000 over each of the previous two years with a *net* income over the same period of a bit over $86,000. He's got money coming from somewhere, but he doesn't show it on his W-2s." The IRS agent gave a light-hearted comment, "It's time to pay the piper."

*

In response to a letter from the Internal Revenue Service, Deputy Lester Phillip Arnold appeared in casual attire at ten o'clock the following Tuesday at the IRS El Paso office. A middle-aged woman wearing a comfortable housedress and black lace-up granny shoes met him at the reception area. She reminded him of the Wicked Witch of the West with her graying hair pulled into a bun and her facial skin stretched taut. He struggled against his spontaneous reaction, swallowed his laughter, and dutifully followed her directions.

With minimal professional courtesy, she led him into a hallway where she opened the door to a sparse meeting room furnished with a six-foot, walnut veneer table, six old wooden straight-backed chairs, and an American flag in the far corner. "Have a seat," she snapped.

Lester scanned the room when Ms. Personality slammed the door and left him alone. There wasn't much to decide, so he took a seat, squirmed slightly in anticipation of what was about to happen, but remained confident. He was prepared for what he considered clever responses to questions they were likely to ask. Certainly, his W-2s might arouse the interest of less knowledgeable people, but they would meet their match with the good and honorable deputy. He was ready for them.

He turned at the sound of the door opening and saw a casually dressed middle-aged man enter the room. The deputy judged him to be his sparring partner for this adversarial joust—an IRS bureaucrat. But, to his surprise, a second man followed the first—this one a cowboyish-looking Chicano in his early thirties wearing a white western shirt, jeans, cowboy boots, and carrying a briefcase. He wore a badge and semi-automatic in a holster on his belt.

Lester stood when the first man stepped forward and extended a hand. "Deputy, thanks for coming in. I'm Paul Hamilton with the IRS." Turning slightly and looking over his shoulder, he continued the introduction. "This is Mr. Basurto. He will assist me with our interview."

Deputy Arnold took a seat on one side, and his adversaries sat on the other side.

Hamilton began the conversation informally while he placed his portfolio on the table and began removing various documents. He held a worn and tattered 3 x 5 card in his hand and read it verbatim to Lester. It was his Constitutional Right to remain silent and to have an attorney.

"No need to read that crap to me," Lester barked, "I've read it hundreds of times to the assholes I arrested. I know my rights, and I'm telling you right now, you tagged the wrong guy when you brought me in. I know my business, and maybe even yours better than you do."

Hamilton slipped the card back into the portfolio and smiled. Ignoring Phil's arrogance, he spoke politely to Lester. "Deputy, in reviewing your income tax status, it appears you have an outflow that is considerably more significant than your reported income."

"Not a problem," Lester interjected. "You see, I've been gifted by relatives who are glad to help me with my living expenses . . ." Hamilton held up the palm of his hand, cutting Lester off in mid-sentence.

"Any gift is taxable, sir. We're taking this opportunity for you to be open and above board with us." He gestured slightly with a tilt of his head toward Ricky, then continued. "Frankly, Deputy, you're in deep shit. Maybe I should have introduced Mr. Basurto in greater detail. He is with the Joint Federal-State Task Force on Human and Drug Trafficking."

A broad smile swept across Lester's face. "Now, we're talking. So, you need my help busting the dopers, eh?" He gave a cocky chuckle before continuing, "Yes sir. I know that desert like the back of my hand—be glad to help." He leaned forward with his elbows on the table and cocked his head, then gave his pitch. "You know this tax thing is just a crock of crap. Somebody is out to get me. They know I'm dangerous and I'll kick their ass if they try anything in my county."

Ricky's eyes latched onto Lester's when he spoke. "Do you know Maria Espinoza?"

The deputy was caught off-guard by the question. He returned the stare, then leaned back, crossed his arms over his chest, and gave a pouting whine, "It's none of your business, but she's my girlfriend."

"How good of a girlfriend?"

Deputy Arnold curled his lips. His brow furrowed as he spewed his anger. "That's none of your damn business. It's my private life and doesn't have anything to do with whatever you might be talking about."

Ricky ignored his little temper tantrum and continued. "When was the last time you saw her?"

"What difference does that make? She loves me, and I love her. You might say we're the best of friends, but it's still none of your friggin' business."

"Did you ever take her shooting?"

Perspiration dotted the deputy's brow, and his eyes bulged when he leaned across the table toward Ricky. "Leave her out of this. She's none of your concern. She has nothing to do with my business or I

172

with hers." He sat back and crossed his arms over his chest. "I don't have a tax problem; Maria is none of your business; and, if you need me to take down some dopers out in the desert, you need to speak up or I'm out of here."

Hamilton interjected, "I don't think so, Deputy. Let me spell it out for you. You bought a new Ford pickup in Odessa and paid $58,416.00 cash. On top of that and only two months later, you charged $8,212.00 on your Visa card to Dr. Manheim Berger for dental work. You paid off your credit card the following month. You took an Alaskan cruise for $7,204.00. You pay your landlord $717.00 a month for rent and utilities, and you do all of this with a job that pays you $34,800 a year before deductions." He smiled politely and nodded to Lester. "We know you're not a lazy man. You do some part-time guide work for Rio Lobo Adventures, and that gives you a little spending money. However, none of this adds up to what your cash outflow amounts to." He frowned, then sat back and allowed a cocky smirk to sweep across his face. "Deputy, we have a strong tax evasion case on you. You're dead in the water."

"You can't be serious," Lester said.

"We are," Ricky intoned. "Deadly serious. As we sit here, an IRS agent is securing your apartment with a lien for unpaid taxes, and we have already put a boot on your pickup with a lien on it, too."

Lester sat back and gasped. Shaking his head and with his mouth as dry as the desert he supposedly protected, he choked out his miserable plea, "This can't be. I need that stuff. I'm a good deputy. The people love me . . . the way I work to protect them. You can't do this to them. You and me. We have to work together." He stammered as he continued to speak. "Let's try . . . to work to . . . together on this. I can . . . can help. I'm sure."

Hamilton excused himself, then returned moments later with a bottle of water and handed it to the deputy. Taking his seat, he gave the deputy a broad smile and spoke in a friendly, casual manner. "Phil. Do you mind if I call you Phil?"

The once arrogant deputy nodded with a timid smile. "Yes, that's fine. My friends call me Phil." He paused for a moment before turning his head like a puppy hearing a distant siren. "How'd you know that?"

Ricky responded. "Phil, we know everything there is to know about you. You're dead in the water, so don't try to screw us around."

Phil's eyes darted back and forth between Hamilton to Ricky. "What do you want?"

"Everything," Ricky said.

Deputy Arnold stopped and took a deep breath, offered a modest shrug, and forced a smile. "I'm in all the way. What can I do for you?"

"Not for us," Ricky said. "It's your life that's at stake." He paused for a moment and looked deeply into Phil's eyes. "You can start with Maria."

The deputy shrugged again. "There's nothing to tell. We're lovers, Maria and me. We hit it off. She loves me and I love her. I think we're going to get married."

"Don't play word games with us," Hamilton said. "There's more."

Phil curled his lips and shook his head. "Okay, so she screwed me a bunch of times. Is that what you want? Do you want to hear sex stories? She was full of them. She was a wildcat in bed."

Ricky lifted his briefcase from the floor, removed an 8 x 10 color photo from an envelope, and slid it across the table, face up.

Phil shifted around for a better viewpoint and spoke softly. "What's this?" Without waiting for a reply, he continued to examine the photo. "A decomposed body, but what of it? I don't know anything about some *cuerpo*. I didn't have anything to do with this," he said as he flipped the picture back to Ricky.

"It's the woman you love so much. It's Maria."

"What?" Phil lurched forward and belched, jumped to his feet, coughed, vomited on the table, and did it again until there was nothing left in him. Tears poured from his eyes. He gasped for breath, then slowly lowered himself back into his seat, drained of every ounce of energy in his once arrogant body.

*

Twenty minutes elapsed while Hamilton escorted Phil to the lavatory, and the custodian cleaned the conference room. The deputy sat stoically when they gathered again at the table. The forlorn young man could only look down at his feet. His $1,600 Lucchese Ostrich boots meant nothing to him.

Meanwhile, Hamilton and Ricky sat quietly, allowing adequate time for him to gather himself psychologically. Ricky finally broke the silence. "We need to talk—three professionals on a matter you *now* understand is something much worse than tax evasion."

Phil nodded without looking up. His voice was barely audible. "What do you need?"

Ricky's voice was soft but authoritative. "Maria, the cartels, the shooting lessons, her trip. The entire story. Now isn't the time for you to mince your words. You can't save her, but you can save yourself."

The now mentally and physically destroyed deputy leaned back in his chair. Taking a deep breath, he began his tale.

Humility is a hunter.

CHAPTER TWENTY-SIX

P hil looked at the two agents through his watery and bloodshot eyes, then leaned forward and rested his arms on the table. He bowed his head and didn't make eye contact with them for the next hour. He spoke softly and soberly, pausing his monotone speech only to drink from the water bottles Hamilton placed before him.

"I never had a damn thing given to me in my entire life. My folks were as poor as piss ants, so I lived with my grandmother in Marfa most of the time. We didn't have much, but that was okay. I'm not complaining. I wasn't a very big guy, so the coaches never let me play on the football or basketball teams, but," he paused and gave a simple little chuckle. "I was the school mascot—the Shorthorn—had a costume head and gloves. They made me up fairly well, so I was all over the place during games. I got folks laughing and having a good time even though we lost almost every game—except Big Bend Christian. We kicked their butts in everything.

"There isn't much to tell. I was a nobody—didn't have a car, any money, a girlfriend, no real buddies to hang with. I tried to get in the Marines when I turned seventeen and still in high school, but they turned me down—told me to come back when I grew up, the bastards." He shrugged, rubbed his eyes, and wiped his nose. "I didn't like always being broke, so I started picking up odd jobs for a little cash. After high school, I figured the Marines could go screw themselves, so I took a few criminology classes on the Internet. It wasn't easy, but with some hard work, I got pretty decent grades. When I was twenty, I went down to Waymond Junior College in Corpus Christi. The Big Bend Regional Business Alliance gave me a scholarship if I agreed to work in law enforcement for at least two years in our area, so I did and here I am—up to my ass in alligators and can't swim.

"Aintry County Sheriff Ruben Acosta hired me when I got out of school. It was a real honest-to-God job. The pay wasn't so hot, but it was the first actual paycheck I ever had. My life was the best it had been from the day I was born. I bought a used car—a 2010 VW, had life insurance, health insurance, and rented my own place. It was a studio apartment a couple of blocks from Sul Ross, so there were lots of girls." He leaned back on the rear legs of his chair, looked at the ceiling, and smiled. The two agents didn't press him.

Let him enjoy the moment, Ricky thought. *He's going to need it.*

The now-humble deputy leaned forward and allowed his chair to slam down on the floor. Once again, he stared at his feet. "I caught Alberto Salinas speeding one night on Highway 90. He was driving his pickup—85 in a 55. I caught him cold. He didn't give me any static, just took his ticket and was polite about it. We stayed on the shoulder of the road for a while and shot the shit. He was a nice guy, and before it was over, he offered me a part-time job at Rio Lobo Outdoor Adventures.

"I was always an outdoor type of guy, and he wanted me to be a guide for some tourists down in the Big Bend. I did it a couple of times. Then he started having me take some of them across the river at Boquillas to hike in Mexico. Of course, I did, and that's where I met Maria. I told Alberto about her, so he started taking the tourists down and left me with the people who wanted to stay on this side of the border." He paused to take a deep breath and drink again from his water bottle, then resumed his monologue. "He paid me fifty dollars a day to be a guide. That was good money for me—but is it ever enough? I started getting an appetite for some of the good things in life—a new car, a girlfriend, maybe even get married. Finally, one day I asked for a pay raise. Alberto looked at me like I was crazy and asked me if I was man enough to do a real job."

*

The deputy paused, and with his head still bowed, sniffled, and wiped the tears from his eyes. "It was like I was a runt in high school again. 'Sure,' I told him. 'I'm man enough to do anything you can hand out.'

So, the bastard looked me dead in the eye, then reached in his pocket and pulled out a wad of money. It was so big you could choke a horse on it. He peeled off two hundred bucks, handed it to me, and said, "Okay, bigshot. Take the money and when I tell you something has to happen, you'll make sure it does."

"Maybe I am a runt, but I'm not a fool. I got the drift. He was into something big, and if I wanted to run with the big dogs, I'd have to learn to howl. I looked that skinny bastard in the eye and told him

I could handle whatever he wanted, and I really emphasized it. I stood straight in his face and told him so.

*

The afternoon hours ticked away. Deputy Lester Phillip Arnold's spirit fizzled like spit on a hot rock. Sitting in his chair with his shoulders slumped and head down, he ran his hands through his hair and bawled. He had gambled and lost.

Ricky suggested they take a break to which Phil solemnly nodded his approval. Hamilton escorted him to the men's room, then to the break room where they each got a cup of fresh coffee. As they walked back, Hamilton put his arm over the deputy's shoulder and spoke sympathetically, "I know you're going through hell, but you'll get through this. We'll work with you and do whatever we can. I know it looks like the end of the world right now, but the sun will come up tomorrow. You're strong and you can make it. Sure, you screwed up. You'll get some bumps and bruises, but I talked to the federal prosecutor ahead of time. She'll do what legally and ethically needs to be done. You'll have to testify, but you're a little fish in a big pond. You thought you knew what you were getting into, but it was far beyond anything you imagined. You didn't know it, but you had joined forces with the New Juarez Cartel."

*

As inhumane as it was, showing Phil the picture of his one true love dead and decomposing in the desert had accomplished the agents' purpose. Now they needed to help him recover, refocus his mindset, tell the inside story of Oleg Krutoy's murder, his involvement with

180

Maria Espinoza, and the trip that culminated with her death in the desert.

Hamilton reached for the door, then stopped abruptly. "Take a deep breath, stiffen your backbone, and let it fly. It's now or never and you don't want to go through something like this again."

Phil stood tall, inhaled deeply, and looked directly at Hamilton. His voice was firm. "Let's do those bastards."

Composure is a hunter.

CHAPTER TWENTY-SEVEN

P urple shadows of the setting sun swept over Las Sierras de Los
Mansos Mountains, heralding a gentle respite for the people of
the Chihuahuan Desert. With it came the close of an interminable day
for the three men ensconced in the Internal Revenue Office. They
had completed what they set out to do—resolve questions about the
deaths of Oleg Krutoy and Maria Espinoza; tighten the noose on the
Salinas family; and, for the deputy—provide him with the
opportunity to free his conscience.

For Ricky, so much had happened since his venture to Arizona
and the Krutoy death that he occasionally had to stop to recalibrate
his mind and reset the priorities. It was the Russians' murder in
Sahuaro National Park that brought together all the other issues—
Maria Espinoza's death at Antelope Wells, Alberto Salinas, and Rio
Lobo, and extended to his father and the New Juarez/La Linea Cartel.

The evening traffic had been vanquished from the man-made
canyons of downtown El Paso. Other than the custodial staff,
everyone in the Federal Building was gone except the two federal
agents and the demoralized Deputy Lester Phillip Arnold. He had
given three written, signed, and notarized statements to support the
charges of Murder, Importation of a Controlled Substance, and

Income Tax Evasion, albeit the final offense was a relatively minor matter.

The agents considered him to be truthful but also careful to exclude himself from culpability in Krutoy's murder. At the same time, he accused Alberto Salinas of culpability in all of it. Phil had obeyed Alberto's orders to teach Maria how to shoot—allegedly for self-protection in her daily routines, or when she was escorting people into the wilderness. Also, at Alberto's insistence and using data he learned from the Internet, most shootings happened within three yards between the shooter and the target. Therefore, she should be accurate at that distance but not be concerned with anything further.

From personal experience, Phil accepted Alberto's information as being accurate because he too was aware of that information. It also was reasonable that a .40 semi-automatic was appropriate for instruction since it was his duty weapon, and he was skilled in its operation and maintenance. Another advantage of the .40 was that it was readily available on the market and it would be easy to purchase one for her when she was ready.

Phil eagerly accepted the responsibility for teaching Maria the mechanics and safety protocols of carrying a gun, and he received an extra fifty dollars for each lesson he gave her. Not only did he like the money, but he was able to spend time with the most beautiful woman he had ever met. He also believed she would be drawn to him by his warm personality. These things, he surmised, would have a way of working out—life was going to get better every day.

He and Maria made six, half-day trips to Odessa and the Rusty Derrick Shooting Range where he taught her the art and science of shooting. Although she was inexperienced, she readily learned the lessons he copied from the Texas Law Enforcement Firearms Curriculum on Training and Qualification. That, along with his knowledge and personality, and with *her* inherent life skills, the way would be paved for both of them—a new skill for her, and a wonderful relationship each of them would enjoy. As he had anticipated, she quickly became adept at a high level of proficiency. She was good at everything she did.

On the personal side of his equation, he believed Maria not only enjoyed his company but looked forward to their time together. Neither of them was satisfied with where their lives were going. In their own words, "They felt alone." There was no one with whom they could laugh and talk, go to a movie, or have a party. She had a female cop friend in Alpine, but they were not confidantes to each other—just two single women without any prospects.

At that point, Lester broke from his commentary, looked at the agents, and smiled. "She missed those damn burros."

Although Maria and he never spoke in detail about the Salinases or Rio Lobo, they found an escape in each other's company, in casual conversation, and eventually, in each other's arms. After her shooting lessons began, Phil concluded that each of them was socially isolated from anyone who genuinely cared about them. It was this determination that led them to develop a personal relationship with one another—one that graduated from hamburgers at Sonic to her home-cooked meals, to holding hands when they went to the desert to observe the Marfa Lights, to having intimate dinner parties, and finally to lovemaking.

Phil knew his life was coming together. They would get married. That was certain.

The Russian gun? He never saw nor heard anything about it. Hearing of it now, he assumed that was only a fraction of her personal life of which he knew nothing. Maybe he would have learned more after they were married. At least, that was his hope.

What about when she left town and didn't tell him anything about it? Again, one of those secrets in her life. Maybe he would have learned later where she went and what was happening in her life. Or maybe not.

At that point in his monologue, he commented sheepishly, "There was a lot I didn't know."

*

His second written statement focused on the Importation of a Controlled Substance—marijuana, cocaine, and heroin. Secondary to that was the illegal transport of firearms into Mexico. His role was simple enough. Alberto showed him a dirt runway deep in Aintry County and far away from any semblance of civilization—at least thirty miles from the nearest FAA-approved runway. A must for the movement of their 'product.'

Phil went into detail about how Alberto had laughed when he explained the location of the runway. "Son-of-a-bitch," he had exclaimed. Alberto, the son of one of the leaders of the New Juarez/La Linea Cartel, described how he had just finished an exchange of 'product,' and was going home with nearly a quarter-million dollars in his truck. He further told the deputy that he had a gun tucked in his belt beneath his shirt. If getting ticketed wasn't bad enough, he was prepared to do what he had to do if the cop got too nosy. He'd kill the worthless *cuico* and be glad he did it.

Phil looked up briefly from his monologue, and with his tear-stained eyes made a damning admission. "I wish he'd killed me on the spot. At least I would have died a hero and people would think respectfully of me." Then he lowered his eyes and continued his sad story.

The cartel had taken strong measures to locate the ideal spot for their rendezvous point. With their unlimited cash flow, they were able to buy almost anything and anybody. Their geologist and meteorologist—with the help of USGS topographic maps and the never-ending flow of weather data provided by the National Weather Service—helped them find what they considered to be an ideal location for a landing strip. They identified five low mountain ranges starting sixty-five miles south of the border and reaching into west Texas. Traversing a series of canyons and valleys, a low flying plane could swoop around and through each mountain range and land in an isolated area unseen by FAA radar or Border Patrol cameras.

Using their soldiers, the New Juarez Cartel cleared a one-thousand-foot dirt runway and scratched out a path that a four-wheel-drive vehicle could maneuver from the airstrip to Highway 90. From there, the entire United States was their market.

The deputy's job was two fold. One project involved his ready access to the entire law enforcement database—people, places, and things. These were open highways of confidential information he could access on the Texas Law Enforcement Telecommunications

System, known as TLETS; the Texas Crime Information System (TCIC); the National Crime Information System (NCIC); plus, what was considered run-of-the-mill data such as license plate information, tax records, wanted persons, and any other information he could find through public access records.

Phil wasn't a runt anymore. He was a big shot. Alberto paid him a flat fee of $1,000 a month for his TLETS services. Sometimes, when the prize was big enough for Alberto, he threw in another $500.

With his assignment to the Drug Task Force, once again, he became a valuable participant in Alberto's endeavors. He kept Alberto informed when and where the officers and deputies were on assignment in the desert. Or, in the alternative, he assured no law enforcement personnel were anywhere nearby if a flight was scheduled.

Nevertheless, on several different dates, Alberto gave Phil valid information for the Regional Drug Task Force to use. It was simple enough. When he knew someone other than a New Juarez group was bringing in a load, he would give Phil the information. Phil would provide the information to the Task Force and they would intercept the load—usually a relatively small one of twenty or thirty kilos of marijuana, but still enough to keep the Task Force held in high esteem.

For Phil, this was a double bonus. Because of his supposedly talented investigative techniques, the Task Force would log another successful venture. Others in law enforcement and some elected officials soon took notice of the success, and Phil was hailed as the dedicated officer who provided exemplary leadership to others. His alleged investigative skills lifted his status which led to him receive a commendation from the Texas House of Representatives, plus a letter of commendation from the Aintry County Judge.

*

For each of his endeavors, he was paid 3,000 dollars in cash for either intercepting a load or assuring no one interfered with a New Juarez Cartel load. His pay never included more than two fifty-dollar bills. The rest was in ten- and twenty-dollar bills. As it was explained to him, one of the basic rules of their business was to always use cash and almost always to pay with less than a fifty-dollar bill. Alberto chuckled when he explained it to his unbelievably valuable employee, "We may have to use a wheelbarrow to carry our money, but hundred-dollar bills attract too much attention."

His orders were clear and straightforward—do what you're told, and don't do anything without permission.

*

After many months of being Alberto's obedient employee, Phil allowed his curiosity to cloud his judgment. It was a full moon on a Thursday night. The weather was perfect. Following a late afternoon shower, the sweet scents of the night-blooming cactus, creosote bushes, and desert mimosa trees floated on the most delicate of breezes. It was as though the world was at peace.

Alberto had told him that late that night or early in the dark hours of the next morning, a shipment would arrive. However, it would be different than most others—it was going to be a two-way trip. There would be an exchange of 'product.'

188

"Make damn sure there ain't no friggin' people anywhere around," Alberto had commanded. Phil wasn't stupid. He knew that meant drugs coming in, but, he paused. His James Bond imagination went into fast-forward: *There's always a black market for Levi's and computers. Guns? Sure, it might be guns. The cartel always needs more firepower.* It was too much excitement to pass up. Besides, he argued with himself, *I'm on their side. They'll be glad to see I have everything under control.*

Not knowing when the aircraft would arrive, but not wanting to miss the thrill, Phil drove his Sheriff's Department marked GMC Yukon toward the airstrip. As sunset approached, he drove five miles south from Highway 90 on the rudimentary road the cartel had built. He was about one-fourth of a mile north of the strip when he pulled off the road and went cross country up a mesquite-shrouded knoll with a good view of the airstrip. It was dark, and he was alone—he thought.

Ignorance is a hunter.

CHAPTER TWENTY-EIGHT

Phil packed two fried bologna sandwiches, three Dr Peppers, and a thermos of coffee. He was ready for a long evening. The night was beautiful—a tour guide's delight with a full Texas moon bathed the desert with an angelic blue swath. Coyotes—first here, then there—serenaded with their lonesome cries. Somewhere close by an owl hooted, then another one somewhere behind him. It was creepy but exhilarating—doing something he had never done. This would be a night to remember.

Seated behind the wheel with the windows open, he stretched out his legs with his fingers interlocked behind his head, yawned, and took a deep breath. He cocked his head and strained to listen. The soothing sounds of moments ago had stopped. The desert was deathly quiet. Nothing. There was the slightest touch of a breeze, but it was stale. The coyotes were silent. The owls surrendered their lonesome hoots to the dead of night. It was as if he were alone in the world. Even the sweet scents of God's handiwork evaporated. Now there was a putrid odor . . . like someone's bad breath.

*

It happened faster than lightning. A gloved hand reached through the window and grasped his face, covering his mouth and eyes. More hands than he could count grabbed him when someone opened the doors. They threw him on the ground, bellowing orders in Spanish, which he marginally understood. He lay helpless when they took his service weapon from the holster while other hands rolled him over and taped his hands behind his back. Someone pulled his boots off and wrapped tape around his ankles. It was over in seconds. He was hog-tied, blindfolded, and gagged, lying on the desert floor. He heard them rummaging through his Yukon, then he heard their laughter when they ate his food and downed his drinks.

Having spent his life in a predominantly Hispanic culture, Phil never mastered Spanish but was exposed to it enough to understand some words and phrases. *"Mata la mierda flaca,"* one of his captors said. He understood it: "Kill the skinny shit," a description he had heard many times growing up—*a skinny shit.*

He heard a cell phone buzz, then a man talking with someone who may have been above him in the hierarchy. Then his captors began arguing with each other. Trying to remain calm while aware they might kill him, Phil struggled to understand exactly what was happening. There were four voices—three male and one female, but one male was more dominant than the others. *The Jefe,* Phil decided. *One guy is laying it on the others and he's mad as hell. But it's the woman saying she wants to kill me.* With nothing in his favor, Phil felt the slightest twinge of relief when he heard the *Jefe* bellow, *"Esperate. Está en camino."*

Somebody was coming. But who?

191

*

Suffering sinus polyps from his years of allergies and from being gagged so tightly he couldn't swallow, the helpless deputy struggled to breathe. He tried to cry out but to no avail. His life was slipping away. They wouldn't have to shoot him. He was strangling to death. He heard voices but couldn't understand them. They were going to let him die. *Bastards, he thought, dirty rotten bastards.*

He heard someone driving up the hill, coming to a halt a few feet away from him, and then a door slammed. Then, without fanfare or comments, someone loosened the tape from his hands and feet while someone else pulled off the gag and blindfold. He sputtered and blinked his eyes but couldn't see. They were holding a flashlight in his face, but he could hear a familiar voice—Alberto. "Stupid shit," he was barking. "What were you doing?" Someone grabbed Phil's shoulders and pulled him into a sitting position. He blinked as Alberto came into focus. Albrerto had saved his life.

Taking command, Alberto yelled at him, calling him a stupid fuck and a *pinchazo*—a prick. He saw Alberto glance at a teenage girl wearing a cowboy hat and jeans and holding a machete across her chest. Just the sight of her gave him a jolt. She was indescribably beautiful, but the personification of Satan. Even in the near darkness, he felt her eyes ripping his soul from his body.

*

Phil stuttered, sipped again on the water bottle Hamilton had given to him, then continued, "Alma wanted to chop off my head and send it to the Sheriff." The young, demoralized deputy coughed and clasped his hands in an effort to control the shaking. He took a deep breath, then resumed his narrative.

Alberto stood erect, pulled Phil to his feet, and commanded him to start talking or he would let Alma do what she did best—chop off his fucking head.

One of the men standing next to the Yukon handed a water bottle to him, laughed, and told him to drink up while he still had a head on his shoulders. Then all of them laughed at him.

Phil nodded his thanks when he took the water, realizing the *generous* man was the *cabrón* who had skunk's breath. He leaned against his Yukon, drank one, and then another while he explained his predicament through a series of sputters and stammers. He was too nervous to put together two consecutive sentences. Nevertheless, he spat it out and hoped for the best. He meant well.

Alberto nodded a disgusted acceptance of the deputy's pitiful explanation, then directed the others to go to the strip. It was almost time. The loads were almost here. Alberto kicked Phil's boots to him and handed him his gun. *"Pendejo,"* he said, "there'll never be another screwup like this, or I'll kill you myself." Though his mind was fogged, he caught Alberto's statement—*loads,* not a load. There was more than one.

The three men, all in their twenties, and the teenage girl grudgingly turned downhill and walked toward the runway. Alma looked over her shoulder at the humiliated deputy and swiped her blade carefully across her throat. The pretty young girl gave him a soft, intimidating whisper. "Next time, *cuico.*"

*

Phil pulled himself upright in the chair, made eye contact with the agents, and continued with his experience in the heart of Aintry County. "Alberto stepped nose-to-nose with me. He seethed with hate. He told me to take my unit and go to the runway and that my days of having choices were over. I'd do whatever he said and there was no way out. I knew I didn't have any alternative. I was going to help them smuggle whatever it was they were moving."

The deputy leaned forward again and looked down at his feet. His voice was barely audible. "I was a cooked goose."

Servitude is a hunter.

CHAPTER TWENTY-NINE

Deputy Arnold continued his narrative of that dreadful evening in the desert with Alberto and his gang of thugs. His heart had pounded when Alberto screamed at him to follow them to the runway. He knew his life was going from bad to worse. This had turned into a situation beyond anything he could imagine. When he got into the driver's seat, his hands were shaking and perspiring so much he had to dry them on his trousers and force himself to calm down. A feeling he had never experienced was overwhelming him. He was on the verge of hysteria.

Understanding his dire predicament, he concentrated on controlling his breathing and heart rate or he would bring about his own downfall. It was something his grandmother had taught him when he was a little boy—count backward from ten to one; take a deep breath and let it out slowly. Do this two times; then tell yourself you can do anything you want to do.

He did it, and Grandmother Arnold was right. He had control. Knowing what he had to do, he sucked up his tears, bit his lip, and drove to the northern terminus of the runway. Nevertheless, he knew he had taken a giant step and there was no turning back.

*

Phil thought he had been in a perfect vantage point from his hilltop overlook. However, a mesquite grove and a dense growth of ragweed proved otherwise. To his surprise, an old pickup pulled out of the bushes near the end of the airstrip. The worn and battered vehicle passed within a few feet of him and zipped south on the runway. Even more to his surprise, Alma was the driver. The bad breath bandit was in the front with her, and the others were in the bed of the truck.

It made a series of stops approximately every fifty yards where the men in the bed jumped out and placed smudge pots, or what Alberto called, *choofas,* on either side of the runway. They lit the pots, then raced to the south end of the airstrip where Alma swung around facing north with the headlights on.

When the strip was outlined with lights, Alberto ordered Phil to get out and stand aside as the *real Jefe* got into the sheriff's vehicle. He slammed it in gear, turned it south toward Alma's truck and turned on the parking lights.

The deputy stepped alongside Alberto's pickup, the one he drove when he was ticketed for speeding on Highway 90, and leaned against it. By this time, he had regained a smidgen of self-control, dried his eyes, and wiped his brow. He rebuked himself as he slipped his hands into his pockets to conceal his trembling. Even so, he couldn't help but be impressed with the timing and coordination of their plan—military precision at its best. He turned at the sound of a vehicle coming down the road from the highway. Its headlights shot darts between the soft pads of the prickly pear cacti, the mesquite trees, and the mass of ragweed, all of which thrived in this isolated locale with a pocket of groundwater.

The pickup bounced and rattled as it maneuvered between ruts and rocks. A cloud of dust billowed in its wake when it came down the road and stopped near Alberto's vehicle. Phil looked in amazement. It was a Ford Super Duty with sideboards on the bed. He was stunned, but his eyes and ears didn't lie. It was full of goats, bleating and crying from their ride in the countryside.

Goats, he thought, *they can't be shipping goats to Mexico.*

Alberto interrupted his thoughts when he bellowed, "Get over here, *pendejo.*" Phil and Alberto went to the rear of the truck when it turned around with its tailgate toward the runway.

The driver, a hulking, elderly *Campesina,* crawled out from behind the wheel. Wearing a housedress, Dr. Marten boots, and a battered straw hat, she looked first at the deputy and his marked vehicle, then to Alberto. She spoke in English, asking Alberto what was happening with a cop car there and what would his "papa" think of this?

He snarled at her, "Do your job old witch, and shut your fucking mouth."

Phil was silently amused. She wasn't afraid to speak her mind.

"Cabron," she cracked as she turned to the tailgate and started twisting the latch.

Alberto pointed at Phil and ordered him to help the old woman. He continued his rant, telling Phil it was time to get his hands dirty because now he was just like them, a narco—a *Traficante.*

197

Phil took a deep breath and stepped alongside the old woman. She looked at him, nodded her head, and laughed through her toothless mouth. She called him a *"Pendejo,"* and told him to show his hands to her. He complied, and she took his hands palm up in hers. Lifting them close to see, she laughed again, spit on them, and rubbed them together. She nodded approval and spoke. Her voice was soft, almost secretive.

He remembered her words precisely. *"Lo jodiste, ese.* You screwed up. Watch your ass or you'll never leave this desert alive."

She gave him a wry grin, then grabbed the latch on the left side of the lower tailgate and directed Phil to undo the one on the right side. Suddenly he understood what she was doing. The goats were camouflage. The 'product' was stowed in a compartment beneath the goats. The lower tailgate dropped with a heavy metallic clunk clank as Alberto, who had been standing back, turned on a flashlight.

The prize, Phil thought when he looked at the boxes of ammunition, rifles, and handguns. *It's gotta be at least fifty guns. Enough for a small army . . . enough to take out any Federales who get in the way.*

The droning sound of an aircraft engine caught his attention. Turning to the south, he saw the landing lights of a single-engine plane illuminate the runway. It touched down, bounced up, came down, bounced again, then made firm contact with the ground and taxied to the front of his Yukon before it stopped. He looked at his watch. It was 11:02.

Alma's pickup followed the plane up the runway. As she stopped alongside the plane, the two men jumped from the truck bed. Simultaneously, the airplane hatch opened. A man who Phil guessed to be in his late twenties hopped out when someone inside heaved a bail to him. From his distance, Phil could not ascertain whether it was one *large* bail or several smaller bundles taped together. Forming an assembly line, the man from the plane and the two from the pickup built a stack of bails on the ground next to Alma's truck. When they completed the unload, Alberto turned to Phil and pointed to the armaments. "Get to work," he barked.

Phil, the old woman, and the two men formed another assembly line moving the armaments out of the truck and into the plane. With the last crate of ammunition loaded, the man from the plane climbed back in and closed the hatch behind him. Seconds later, the engine started, the plane turned, taxied to the south, turned around again, and took off to the north.

Phil looked at his watch. It was 11:11. They landed, unloaded, loaded, and took off in nine minutes. At that moment he understood that whether he liked it or not, he was now part of their organization and there was no way out.

Alberto gave him a smart-ass grin and pointed to the bundles. Phil recalled his exact wording. "Put the product in your flashy ride. You're our new driver."

Phil hesitated briefly, stunned by the sudden changes in his life. He observed for a moment, too shocked to do anything while Alma, the old woman and the three men went to work. They had practiced it so many times they didn't stop to take a breath. With their assembly line in motion, Phil stood at the rear of his vehicle and loaded the drugs into the Aintry County Sheriff Department SUV. It was twenty

199

bails, each consisting of eight bundles that he assumed were one kilo each.

One subject Phil was good at was mathematics. He loaded more than 350 pounds of hard drugs—not marijuana—into an official government vehicle. He knew he was in deep trouble. The old woman's words echoed in his mind—he didn't want to die in the desert.

Fear is a hunter.

CHAPTER THIRTY

Deputy Arnold's official government vehicle was loaded with contraband when he started back up the road to the highway. He was already familiar with the address and business name Alberto gave him for his delivery. It was the same little family shop where he bought cooler pads for his grandparents' house—Desert Breeze Coolers on Buena Vista Street in Alpine. It wasn't much of a place: a dumpy little adobe building on a dead-end street. The Yanez family had owned it for decades. Old Tiburcio, who Phil knew as Tibo, and his wife, Felipa, were hard-working peóns. There wasn't a crooked bone in their bodies . . . unless arthritic joints counted.

Phil could not conjure up that scrawny little man running a stash house. They lived in a shanty a few blocks from their business. If they were involved in the drug business, it didn't show in their lifestyle. *Somehow,* he thought, *they boxed him into a corner, and he has to do what he's told.*

The deputy chewed his lips as he thought of his predicament. *Me too. What a friggin' idiot I've been.*

*

Pulling onto the highway and leaving Alberto, Alma, and their smelly friends behind, he found a moment of self-deprecating humor. *What if I wrecked and everything burned up? Me too. What a story that would make.*

He took a deep breath and brought himself back to the moment. Everything he did was contrary to his conscience, but he'd gone beyond the point of no return. He was greedy. Money dominated his life. Money, and all the things it could buy. But now, everything was topsy-turvy. He had money and he was more miserable than ever.

He commiserated on where his life was versus where it should be. It was an ugly picture. He was transporting more than $500,000.00 worth of narcotics in the Sheriff's van—just one load: one small, insignificant business in a little college town. His mind was scrambled. How far had he fallen? Alberto was right. There was no way out. Whether he liked it or not, he was a *Traficante*.

*

It was after midnight when the sheriff's vehicle turned onto Buena Vista Street. The rut-filled, narrow dirt road was dark but for the solitary light hanging over the door at Desert Breeze Coolers. Its dim yellow bulb swung to and fro in the night air, tossing whispers of light across the barren landscape. The gate of the six-foot, chain-link fence was wide open. Otherwise, the business appeared closed.

Phil drove through the entrance to what he knew was Tibo's freight door in the rear. As in the front, a nearly lifeless yellow light swung ghostlike over the double-wide doors. They opened as Phil backed his SUV around to unload the contraband. Looking in his

202

side-view mirror, he saw Tibo propping the entryway open. Wearing an undershirt and pajama bottoms, the skinny, barefoot little man looked as though he would blow away if he stepped outside. He waved his hand and was saying something, signaling the deputy to stop when he was parallel with the opening.

Phil strained to hear the old man's raspy voice. *Have another cigarette, you old fart,* he thought.

Climbing out of the patrol vehicle, he caught a bit of Tibo's angry swearing while the old man opened the tailgate. Phil gave him a pat on the back and offered a sincere, "*Hola,* my friend. I'm sorry about dragging you into this."

Tibo stopped and looked into the deputy's eyes. He nodded his head and blurted a question, "They got you, too, uh? The bastards told me to expect a surprise, and you're it." He went on to say they put the pressure on him a couple of years earlier. It was the *chucos* from El Paso. Tibo's grandson, José Luis, was going to be the first member of the family to go to college but fell into the good life selling drugs. One thing led to another. In the end, he was using more than he was selling. When it came time to pay up, he couldn't. Tibo had no choice.

The *chucos* went to his house while Tibo was working. Felipa was an easy target. They slapped her face so hard she was bruised for over a month, knocked out a front tooth, and in the end, desecrated her with a broom handle. "Then they came to my shop," Tibo told Phil. "I could take what they did to me, but I couldn't let them hurt Felipa or José Luis anymore, so now I work for them."

"And you?" Tibo had asked.

203

Phil's response was similar to Tiburcio's grandson's. He got in too deep too fast. He was greedy for the good life and took a shortcut. He didn't think fast enough in his decision-making.

Deputy Lester Phillip Arnold had a new understanding of life. There were no shortcuts. His goal was no more than staying alive. Tiburcio wasn't so fortunate. His two-pack-a-day of cigarettes killed him a few months later.

After his first delivery, Phil went home to his little apartment close to the university. He was no longer interested in seeing the college girls sunning themselves around the swimming pool. There were bigger issues in his life now. Following the most miserable day in his life, he crawled between the sheets but was unable to sleep.

Guilt is a hunter.

CHAPTER THIRTY-ONE

With the interviews behind them, Ricky, Hamilton and Deputy Arnold walked out together. Each in his own way was satisfied with the outcome—the tax matter was secondary to the other matters but opened the door for more serious offenses; the Krutoy and Espinoza death investigations led deep into the New Juarez Cartel. For the deputy, the road was open to turn the corner with his life, but it would not be without peril. Especially in one area—twice at Alberto's direction, Phil used his personal vehicle to meet a plane at the landing strip. Once he transported two teenage girls to a motel in Odessa, and on another trip, he transported a young woman and her baby to a truck stop in Pecos where they were transferred to a waiting 18-wheeler.

He understood the road ahead may be a bumpy ride.

Last, but not least for Phil, the federal liens on his property were removed. Rounding the corner of the Federal Building, the agents caught a smile sweeping across his face. Seeing his pickup was the shot of adrenaline he needed. He turned and spoke as he shook hands with the federal agents. "I'm sorry for the mess I've caused, but I'll do everything possible to make things right. I can't undo the past, but I'll take the straight and narrow from here on. You can count on it."

"Thanks," Hamilton said. "Now, the ball is in your court. Your statements will be used as evidence, but you'll have to testify when the case goes to trial."

"That means I'll be an unindicted co-conspirator?"

"In all likelihood," Hamilton said.

Phil looked down and nodded his understanding. "What about in the meantime? Between now and then? How do I keep Alberto from becoming suspicious?"

"Continue as you have been," Ricky said. "Nothing changes. Don't let on that anything happened here today. If anyone inquires, tell them you went over your tax returns and everything was okay. As far as they're concerned, you're free and clear."

Phil opened the door of his shiny maroon pickup which was loaded with all the extras a vehicle could have—bought and paid for with drug money. Sliding behind the wheel, he turned to face the agents. His expression was somber. He was in over his head with challenges from every side. He knew he had to work his way out . . . if that was possible. "I'm worried about Alberto. What if that bastard tells me to do something crazy? You know, maybe do something to somebody?"

"I've discussed it with the U.S. Attorney," Hamilton said. "She approved a reasonably broad parameter, but there are limits. You can keep doing what you have been doing. However, be sure to notify us on the phone number I gave you: day or night. When you've completed an assignment, make the call. Use the burner phone we provided—never your own. One of us or another agent will answer twenty-four seven."

He took a deep breath and grimaced. "Something all of us know—that son of a bitch may throw a curveball to you. Just remember—don't get yourself killed. Secondly, the prosecutor cannot give you a *Get Out of Jail Free* card if you cause serious bodily injury or death to someone . . . anyone. Do you understand?"

Phil nodded almost imperceptibly, then closed his door. It was a long drive home.

*

Ricky was halfway home when his cell phone buzzed. It was Felix Lugo, the Border Patrol Agent who accompanied him the day of the shooting at Muncie's archaeological location. "My friend," Lugo said, "I've got something you need to see. I'm at your wife's dig site."

"I'll head your way. Give me a hint. What do you have?"

Felix laughed. "Basurto, you'll have to see it to believe it. There's no sense in trying to explain it. You're going to pop your eyes out when you get here."

"10-4. I'll be there in forty-five minutes," Ricky replied.

*

By the time he reached the turnoff from Highway 9, the night sky was an inky blackness punctuated by millions of stars. It was a soothing, beautiful evening in the vast openness of the Chihuahua Desert—but appearances can be deceiving.

He chuckled as he checked his watch—thirty-seven minutes. He slowed when he started down the bumpy dirt road toward the dig site, vividly recalling the day someone took a potshot at his wife and her colleagues. Within minutes, he observed the glow of lights on the southern horizon. Something was amiss. He knew it wasn't a Border Patrol or Task Force operation. That could only mean the Mexicans. For them to be in the open countryside without any effort to conceal their activity screamed volumes. Something huge was happening. Half a mile further he came upon Felix's Border Patrol unit parked in the road. Pulling in behind it, Ricky turned off his lights and loosened his seat belt.

Felix hopped out, his brow furrowed, and lips pursed. "Bodies," he said as he and Ricky met alongside the vehicle. "I came down here an hour ago. I was going over a rise on the highway and saw the lights in the distance. At first, I thought it was your wife and her staff. I was surprised. I thought you would have warned us about them if they were restarting their dig. When I got closer, I shut down my lights and came in where I could get a better view of what was happening. I called into the Communications Center when I saw it was on the other side of the border. They didn't have any knowledge of it, so it was up to me to determine who was doing what.

"I watched for a few minutes and counted at least twenty *Federales* and heavy equipment operators. They've got generators, light stanchions, and a couple of backhoes working like hell." He looked down, kicked a stone, and chuckled, "I turned on my headlights and light bar and called them over my PA system. They answered immediately and invited me down to the fence."

He paused and grimaced, then continued. "They're digging up a major gravesite. I was talking with Captain Mungia who's in charge of the operation. He said an informant provided them with evidence of this being a cartel burial site—supposedly thirty or more corpses. Some are buried; some are in barrels of acid in that shed we saw.

"Mungia said they started digging around two o'clock this afternoon and will stay here until they've recovered what they think is all the bodies." Giving a sick little guffaw, he continued. "Now we understand why the cartel didn't want your wife's people down here. It would interfere with their body disposal system."

Ricky and Felix walked to the fence, taking in a spectacle they had never before witnessed. Captain Mungia was sitting on the hood of his jeep with an unlit cigar in his mouth. Following introductions and an invitation from the captain, Ricky climbed over the fence. Wearing his Border Patrol uniform, Lugo decided to remain within his own jurisdiction.

Walking toward the shed, Ricky and the captain passed a backhoe scooping away the soil from a gravesite. "It's going to be a body . . . or a few bodies," Mungia said. "We've dug up fourteen so far, plus there are six barrels in the shed. We opened one. It looked like at least one person had been stuffed into it. We closed it immediately because of the smell, plus we didn't know what type of liquid they stuffed the person in."

The captain took a cigar from his shirt pocket and handed it to Ricky. "A little trick I learned years ago. Always have a few cheap cigars with you. When you get to these foul-smelling places, stick a cigar in your mouth and don't breathe through your nose."

Ricky accepted it and, without hesitation, took the captain's advice. The stench was overwhelming. "Do you have any identification on these people?" he asked.

Mungia shook his head. "Most likely they're soldiers from the Sinaloa and Jalisco New Generation Cartels—the CJNG. The war damn near wiped out the Juarez Cartel, but they've re-grouped. Now they call themselves the New Juarez Cartel, and they have been killing the competitors like it's the end of the world." He shook his head and spat. "We don't see a happy ending to this story.

"We pushed our ground-penetrating radar device over this whole area to identify plots that indicated an anomaly. An officer followed behind the operator and marked the spot with a traffic cone. When we believed we had covered the entire area," he said with a wave of his arms over the otherwise desolate expanse, "We brought in the heavy equipment and these laborers to do the hands-on work" He took a deep drag on his unlit cigar, leaned forward, and spit into a now empty grave.

Leading his guest to the shed, they took a cursory peek inside but left due to the fetid odor. Moving back outside, Ricky followed him around several dig sites where workers were professionally and respectfully loading bodies and body parts into FEMA standard leak-proof body bags. The body handlers wore hazmat suits and respirator/air filter apparatus as they went about their gruesome task. They worked in teams of two, lifting the decomposed bodies or pieces of human flesh and bones from their resting place, slipping them into a bag, and zipping it shut.

Ricky noticed two men walking slowly among the recovered bodies and the yet-to-be-open burial sites. Wearing hazmat suits and breathing apparatus, they walked together and were talking, but also appeared to be intense about their duties.

210

Mungia guided his guest to the men where they were standing alongside an open grave. It was about three feet deep. They were speaking to the workers as they organized several decapitated bodies and bits of human remains to put in body bags. The captain introduced them as chaplains to the *Federales'* Grave Recovery Team. One was a Baptist minister; the other a Catholic priest. Each of them was reading from The Book of Psalms, "Yea, though I walk through the valley of the shadow of death, I will fear no evil: for thou art with me; thy rod and thy staff they comfort me," repeating the prayer for the deceased, their families, and for the workers who were retrieving the bodies from their unholy gravesites.

It was a sight Ricky would never forget.

*

Again on U.S. soil and trudging back to their vehicles, Ricky asked, "Last time we were here, Dispatch sent you and the Oscar unit to Cloverdale on a search. Whatever happened?"

"It was ugly," Lugo replied. "The man who was found was about thirty years old. They were from *Janos*, about fifty miles south of the border. He and his wife and two children, a two-year-old and a four-year-old hitched a ride to *Rancho El Valle* a few miles west of Antelope Wells. He thought he could get them across the desert to Albuquerque where his brother had a job for him. To make a long story short, the desert won. We did a two-day air and ground search but never found his wife or the kids. We took the dad to the hospital in Deming. He was there for a couple of days, then voluntarily returned to Mexico. End of story. His family died a hard death out there somewhere—just three more bodies for someone to find some day.

*

It was ten o'clock when Ricky pulled into his driveway. It had been a long day. Muncie greeted him at the kitchen door with her upraised finger over her lips. *"Cállate,"* she whispered. "Lupe was wound up and I just got her to sleep."

Ricky tip-toed into the kitchen, sat down, and quietly pulled off his boots.

"Hungry?" she asked.

Leaning back in his chair, he yawned and uttered a soft, "I'm starved."

"Scrambled eggs and toast sound good?"

"A meal fit for a king," he joked.

Standing at the stove with his eggs in the skillet, she looked over her shoulder at her husband, her knight in shining armor with his head drooped onto his chest. "Tell me about your day."

He shrugged. "Just another day at the office."

Fatigue is a hunter.

CHAPTER THIRTY-TWO

Meeting in the breakroom and enjoying a cup of coffee, Ricky briefed Anna and Miguel about yesterday's adventures, ranging from the IRS office to his late-night foray at the gravesites. Finishing their refreshments, Ricky rose from the table and went to the sink. "Freudian," he commented when he dumped the last drops of coffee down the drain.

Rinsing his cup and hanging it on the hook beneath the cabinets, he tossed a wry smile to them, "Curiosity killed the cat, but I've got to go see what's happening."

"Count us in," Miguel replied with a nod to Anna. "Let's all go. This should be educational at least."

*

With Miguel driving, they turned off the highway onto the dirt road leading to the archaeological site. Ricky leaned forward and stared out the windshield as they approached the end of the trail. He was stunned at the changes that had occurred overnight. "Gone," he whispered, "lock, stock, and barrel."

Miguel stopped at what had been the center point of the university dig site. Caught unprepared by the abandoned site, he turned to Ricky. "Did they finish digging up all the graves?"

"Beats me," Ricky said as they exited the SUV. "I assumed they would be here all night and most of today." Looking out over the barren land beyond the border fence, he could see that the creosote bushes, prickly pear cactus, and the smaller mesquite trees were graded into piles of rubble along the edge of the approximate one-acre gravesite. The shed stood as it was—a lone sentinel in a cemetery of the lost. A scattering of mature mesquite trees remained. Otherwise, the land was graded clean.

With his hands on his hips, Miguel shook his head in disbelief. Looking at the cleared land, he mumbled, "Something's wrong. I don't like this. It's too far outside the realm of normal, even in the lopsided world of the cartels."

Ricky's skin crawled as the three agents walked slowly toward the international fence. In his mind, they were approaching a sacred place where no one should tread. Reaching the international boundary, he grasped the top wire of the four-foot fence with both hands and stood stoically, recalling how only a few hours ago it was a hub of activity—the living retrieving the dead. Looking down at the fresh dirt, he could see the tracks of the earthmoving equipment, but no footprints or debris were left behind. Everything and everybody was gone. Nevertheless, a question persisted in his mind, *Did they recover the bodies, or did something happen?*

A cold chill coursed through every fiber of his being. It was as though a spiritless shroud covered the land. The Chihuahuan Desert

214

was desecrated, void of the souls of humanity—dead or alive. "A few tire tracks," he uttered, looking at the lines in the sand. "Last night there were a couple of trucks, Mungia's jeep, a backhoe, and a grader, but now it's an empty land."

"What about the grader?" Anna asked.

"Mungia said they used it to push through a road from the highway about a mile south of the site. Otherwise, they couldn't get their backhoe in here."

With Miguel and Ricky absorbed in studying the cleaned-out gravesite, Anna scanned the southern horizon. "Somebody's coming," she said as she pointed toward the southwest. A cloud of dust rose in the distance, trailing along an unseen path over the top of the low, rolling hills. Ricky and Miguel followed her line of sight and spotted the dust cloud swirling in the distance, but at least a mile away. "Friend or foe?" she asked.

Ricky took a deep breath and exhaled slowly, focusing on the rapidly approaching cloud of dust. He offered a grim comment, "No friend of ours."

Miguel loosened the mic from his belt and broadcasted his radio designator, "This is 406. Is the helicopter unit available?"

The squelching burp of the Oscar unit responded immediately. "Oscar-7 to 406, what's your location?"

"South of Highway 9. Three miles west of our office."

"10-4," Oscar responded. "We're a few minutes away."

Miguel and the helicopter operator stayed in communication while Ricky and Anna watched the dust cloud grow closer to what remained of the cartel disposal ground.

Simultaneous to hearing the chopping sound of the helicopter's rotor blades in the distance, a white pickup truck loomed over the crest of a knoll and came to a halt. It was about 300 yards beyond the international border. It was not a *Federales'* vehicle. Two men stood in the truck bed, each holding an AK-47 type weapon across their chest with one hand while the other hand grasped a roll bar over the top of the cab.

With her binoculars on a lanyard around her neck, Anna sighted in on the visitors. "Shit," she mumbled as she pulled them off her neck and passed them to Miguel.

"Bastards," he said as he lifted his left hand over his head and extended the middle finger. "That son of a bitch is flipping us the bone."

Ricky watched the happenings with his naked eye. Moments later, he saw the second man in the bed of the truck lift his rifle over his head and shoot a burst of automatic fire into the air. At that same moment, the helicopter came in low overhead from the north but remained in U.S. territory.

The cartel's pickup accelerated away in a cloud of dust over the hilltop and out of sight. The helicopter observer came on the radio, laughing, but also serious. "The idiots went too fast and one of the people in the back fell out. They stopped, and he's climbing back in." There was a brief pause before Oscar transmitted again. "They're hightailing it out of here."

"Oscar," Mungia said, "Is there any construction equipment or vehicles over the top of the rise that we can't see from here."

"10-4. There's a burned-out jeep in a wash about 400 yards south of the fence."

"Any signs of life anywhere besides the pickup truck?"

"Negative. No life at all, but there appears to be a body near the jeep. One person wearing a military-type uniform." Oscar hovered at the border, then slipped back to the north. "Without crossing the line, we can't confirm anything for certain, but through our glasses, it looks like someone with their head blown off. He's about ten yards from the jeep. We have a good view at 500 feet. Other than the corpse and a burned-out Jeep, there's nothing else. Your actors in the pickup have cleared the area. We last saw them when they reached the highway, turned right and went out of sight."

"10-4," Miguel replied. "Thanks for your help. We're going 10-8 now."

"10-4," Oscar responded, then turned sharply and departed to the north.

Death is a hunter.

CHAPTER THIRTY-THREE

For the remainder of the day, Anna and Ricky communicated with the El Paso Fusion Center, New Mexico State Police, and the city police and sheriff departments of southern New Mexico. Their efforts were fruitless. No one had any information about the cartel's Chihuahua disposal area. Furthermore, there were no news reports from Mexican or U.S. media outlets. There wasn't a hint of a rumor anywhere.

Ricky leaned back in his office chair, stretched, and looked at Anna still buried in her computer screen. "Give it up," he blurted. "It's as if it never happened. We were never there. Neither were the *Federales* or the preachers. It was just our imagination."

Completely frustrated, Anna turned and faced him. "*We* know Captain Mungia is dead, but nobody cares. As far as they're concerned, he stuck his nose into somebody's business and paid the price." She raised her hands in surrender and bellowed her fury, "You and I understand the reality of the situation. Dozens of people were buried there. What happened to them and Mungia's troops? Did they turn on him or run off? There're a lot of mysteries about that burial ground and we don't have the answers."

Anger scorched her face. "How can anyone say, *Que sera, sera?* People were murdered and the Mexican government closed their eyes to it." She blew a hearty exhale and shook her head. "But we care, and we'll do something about it." Giving a pitiful chuckle, she offered a closing touch of deprecating humor. "It may not be much, but we'll give it our best shot . . . and *that's* Freudian."

Ricky pushed back from his desk and looked pensively at her. "Let's refocus and not allow ourselves to get too deep in the graveyard." He paused for effect, then continued. "That's not Freudian. It's a cold, hard fact. Sure, it was a disaster, but we can't let it deter us from where we were and our original goals—Oleg Krutoy's murder, Maria Espinoza's death, the Russian handgun, the Salinas family, and the cartel.

"If we can pull it off, we will have done extraordinarily well. Take a moment and look at how all this came together—a man we never heard of was murdered in Saguaro National Park; a young woman was found dead 400 miles away at Antelope Wells; a handgun was found beneath her body, and all of it jelled into a major international case."

He smiled and brushed the hair from his brow. "I'd say we've done everything we could have hoped for. We've exposed a Russian Mafia/New Juarez Cartel connection, white slavery, drug running, murder, gun running, and official corruption. Finally, we'll do a RICO case and confiscate as much Salinas property and holdings as we can link to their operations." He gave a devilish chuckle, "RICO. Whoever came up with the original legislation was a genius—the Racketeer Influenced and Corrupt Organizations Act. Not only do we put the bad guys in prison, but we confiscate their wealth and that hits them where it really hurts."

"Thanks for keeping us sighted in," Anna said. "What happened to Mungia and those other people was tragic, but we need to keep our eyes on the moving target." She lifted an eyebrow and continued, "RICO? Absolutely. So, where do you see us going from this point forward?"

Sitting down again and gazing at the ceiling, she spoke thoughtfully, answering her own question. "The DNA samples on Nicolas Salinas are in the lab, so we're on hold for confirmation of his connection with the Russian handgun. Plus, we're on hold to see if he wants to utilize our proposed laundering scheme and start sending cartel money to us. Third, we have our statements from Deputy Arnold. And lastly, the same gun was used in both of their deaths." She paused and smiled confidently at Ricky. "I think that's about it. Do you have any ideas?"

"Your informant, Chico. When did you last hear from him?"

"Last week. He's convinced Salinas wants us to launder the money, but we don't know his schedule. Chico and Nicolas Salinas know they have to contact me ahead of time when they want to make a deposit. Nevertheless, I've coordinated with my DEA colleagues and the FBI. The undercover office is on the fourth floor of La Placita Santa Monica on Pico Boulevard in Los Angeles. Everything and everybody is in place. When someone from the cartel shows up, we'll be ready. The office space has a reception area, a large private office, two smaller offices, and a workroom. The bureau has an interior design staff who stages the setting, so it's a professional appearing office.

"The currency counter is in the workroom, and that's where our heavily armed security agents will be . . . all of them expert shooters and trained in martial arts." She rose from her chair and gazed out the window at the stark Chihuahuan Desert. Her voice was soft and introspective. "'Expect the unexpected.' My coordinator taught us that little credo at the academy." She turned and looked into Ricky's eyes. "As a precautionary note, we have a command-and-control center in the office next door. We'll also have extra personnel there if needed. This deep into our case, we can't relax our guard. These are badasses supposedly bringing money to us, but we can't trust them for a moment. Additionally, we have no idea who else may know their plan and pull some sort of a double cross. One way or another, we'll be locked and loaded."

"Tell me about the counter," Ricky said. "How much can it process on a single run?"

She moistened her lips and gave a sarcastic smile. "More money than you and I will make in a lifetime. It'll count over 50,000 bills an hour and it scans for counterfeit money at the same time. We assume Salinas or his mule will bring in the money by the pound. Whatever their game plan, we'll be ready. If they're stupid enough to try anything, one of our guys already told me what he'll say . . . 'Go ahead. Make my day.'"

Ricky smiled and nodded his approval.

Revenge is a hunter.

CHAPTER THIRTY-FOUR

Sunday afternoon at the Basurto home was a casual, family-oriented occasion. Today was no different—temperate weather with a few puffy clouds dotting the azure sky; backyard grass cut, trimmed, and watered; raised flower beds displayed the last vestiges of color; and after a night in the smoker, a brisket was ready for an early afternoon feast.

Ricky, Muncie, and two-year-old Guadalupe sat at a table beneath an awning upwind from the column of smoke rising from the stack. His sister, Lupe, had come from Denver for the weekend. Wearing a halter, shorts, and a Rockies' baseball cap, she sat with her feet in Guadalupe's wading pool.

To complete the family gathering, their mother Sophie had come from Hachita. She sat on a lawn chair alongside the smoker, wearing an oversized sombrero to shade her from the sunlight. Having assumed responsibility for the brisket, she had risen twice during the night to care for the fire and meat. It was a task she loved, and the loss of sleep was well worth the outcome of what would be a delicious family meal.

Sophie's voice had a gentle, melodic tone when she called out, "*Escúchame*, children. It's not often we have time together and there's something I must say." Rising from her chair, she picked up Guadalupe and held her tightly as she returned to her seat. "Today has been my reward from Almighty God for having such a blessed family. Of course, we don't know how long it will be before we are together again, so I want to take this moment to tell each of you—"

She paused and held Guadalupe at arm's length, looked at her, then to Muncie, on to Ricky, and finally to Lupe who was lifting her feet from the water and drying them on a towel. "Your Papa was taken from us many years ago, but together, each of us has risen to face life—sometimes with great risk, but always with the grace of God and our honorable intent. Now, though," she paused and looked into the youngster's eyes, kissed her forehead, and squeezed her tightly. "Tonight, I will go home. Tomorrow, Lupe will go back to Denver, and Muncie, Ricky, and precious little Guadalupe will resume their daily routines." She offered a soft chuckle and smiled. "But having a two-year-old, and her daddy doing what he does for a living, I'm not sure what routine is. Nevertheless, I want you to know that wherever you are, whatever you are doing, I pray for you every day. We live in uncertain times. You must always remember the love your father gave to you and the love I give to you every moment of my life." She took a deep breath, sat up straight, and tossed her sombrero on the grass. "Today, I want to announce that I am making a lifestyle change." She paused and nervously wet her lips. "I'm moving."

Lupe jumped to her feet, "What?" she clamored. "*Mamacita*, where are you going?"

Sophie leaned back, holding Guadalupe tightly to her bosom. "I'm so alone out there at our house—the home where each of you grew up." Glancing back and forth to Lupe and Ricky, she continued. "*Los narcos* and the illegal immigrants control the land around Hachita and throughout the Chihuahuan Desert. The few remaining people are doing what I am doing—getting out. It's not a place to live anymore."

Guadalupe began to squirm, so Sophie placed her on the grass where she immediately rose on unsteady feet and ran to her mother.

"*Preciosista*, if life was only so easy," Sophie said as she beheld the grandchild with her eyes and her heart. "Nevertheless," she continued, "I've sold our home to the Molina family from Animas. Mr. Molina was looking for a place to live and raise his German Shepherds, and our property fit him like skin on bone," she chuckled, throwing a glance at the smoker.

"But Mamma," Ricky interjected, "what about you? Where are you going?"

"Not far away," she said. "I bought a modest townhouse here in Columbus." With a broad smile creasing her lips, she continued, "I'll always be nearby when you need me. It's *La Casa Bien*, not more than a mile from where we sit this very moment."

Lupe rose from her seat and moved to the grass at her mother's feet. "Mother," she intoned, "Our house. Our home."

"Yes," Sophie replied as tears rolled down her cheeks. "Ricky knows how hard this land has become. It is not safe for a woman to live out there on the plains with nothing but a grouchy old dog and a single-shot .410 shotgun." Dabbing her eyes with her apron, her voice quaked when she spoke. "Ricky and his colleagues are fighting an unending war with the most violent people on Earth. I simply can't stay there any longer. There are no other ladies my age alone in Hachita. All of them have moved out. Only our tiny general store and gas pump are left, and about the only customers they have are the Border Patrol and Customs officers. Everyone else is gone."

Ricky looked at his mother, then glanced down at his vibrating cell phone. Snapping it off his belt, he rose from the picnic table and walked away from his family. "*Hola*, Miguel, what do you have for me?"

Sophie looked mournfully at her son. "The desert is calling him."

Passion is a hunter.

CHAPTER THIRTY-FIVE

"I hope I'm not interrupting your Sunday," Miguel said.

"That's all right," Ricky replied. "We're having a little reunion, but what do you have for me? I know it's important or you wouldn't call on a Sunday."

Miguel's voice hinted his regrets. Nevertheless, he delivered the message. "The DEA Communications Center called me. They heard from your informant and thought it sounded critical, so they called me—and me to you. Sorry."

Ricky had moved to the shade of the back porch where he leaned against the wall, propping himself with a foot tucked behind him against the adobe bricks. He spoke professionally, but his heart was elsewhere. "Give it to me. I wouldn't know what to do with a complete weekend off anyway."

"Your informant was leaving the Blazing Saddles Truck Stop in Amarillo where he dropped off a couple of teenage girls. He's heading home now but wants to talk to you."

"Call it done," Ricky said as he clicked off and hit the *contacts* directory on his cell phone. Seconds later, he was speaking with Deputy Arnold on the burner phone.

"Damn it," Arnold said. "Alfredo called me at seven o'clock last night and he was specific with his orders. I was to drive my pickup and get to the landing strip at one o'clock this morning, so I did what he told me. I never question him. I learned that long ago. When he says jump, I jump.

"Go ahead," Ricky replied.

"I was scared out of my boots when I saw what was happening. The plane landed as I drove up to the parking area. I was expecting a load of dope, but *no*, the guy from the plane gets out with two little girls."

Ricky listened patiently as Deputy Arnold paused. His breathing was deep and irregular.

Moments later, Arnold continued, "When I saw them, I didn't know what I was supposed to do." He hesitated and breathed deeply. "Mr. Basurto, I knew I was allowed by you and Mr. Hamilton to move some dope, but not little girls. They couldn't have been older than fifteen. I don't want to get in any more trouble than what I'm in now." He paused and coughed.

Ricky heard him struggle to control his emotions, then swallow hard.

Deputy Arnold continued in halting words and phrases, "Alberto . . . he didn't waste any time. He grabbed those kids and pushed them . . . pushed them over to my truck, then screamed at me . . . to get my ass . . . my ass in gear and get out of there. 'Go to the Blazing Saddles Truck Stop on I-40 in Amarillo,' he said. He told me there would be a box truck with the name Enchantment Groceries on it. His orders were very precise. 'Park next to it. Get out by yourself, go inside the café, and don't look back,' and that's exactly what I did. I had a cup of coffee. When I went out to my pickup, the grocery truck and girls were gone. That's it, and I'm afraid I'm in deep trouble."

"Where are you now?" Ricky asked.

"On I-27 south of Amarillo. I want to go home, but I don't know what's going to happen to me. I couldn't call you when the girls were in the truck, so I did exactly as he ordered me to do. I took two little girls and delivered them to be somebodies' whores. They're children," he sobbed. "I want to die, Mr. Basurto. I've done evil and I just want it over with."

"Calm down," Ricky interjected. "Take a deep breath and let it out. You're going to be fine, and we'll get that S.O.B." Ricky paused and listened while the deputy faltered with his deep sobbing and breathing. After a few moments of silence, Ricky spoke again. "Did Alberto give you any other instructions?"

"Not a thing. Today and tomorrow are my days off, so I'm thinking of laying low—maybe go camping or something like that. Just get my butt out of town and not let them find me. I'm scheduled to work my patrol job Tuesday day shift, so I'll just get out of Dodge for a couple of days."

"Okay," Ricky replied. "Keep your burner phone charged. Call us if you need anything, and I'll call you if something comes up."

The deputy choked his comments between mournful sobs. "I'll be cool and just stay out of sight. Until them . . ." The phone clicked off.

*

Ricky caught his mother's eye as he walked back to his family gathering.

"Can you stay long enough to eat with us?" she asked.

A smile creased his lips. "Mamma, if you stayed up all night smoking this brisket, I'd have to be *loco* to say I didn't have time to eat."

Thirty minutes later, they were seated at the picnic table beneath the umbrella with their plates of brisket, beans, potato salad, and fresh hot tortillas in front of them. The meal was perfect. By four o'clock, they had finished eating, the dishes were done, and the trash had been emptied. It was an almost perfect day until Ricky's cell phone buzzed again.

Looking at the caller ID, he saw Anna's initials on his screen. Thirty seconds later, he had his answer. Nicolas wanted to make a deposit.

Greed is a hunter.

CHAPTER THIRTY-SIX

Anna and Ricky caught a Monday morning flight from El Paso to Los Angeles. To further their undercover guise, they went separate ways, each to a car rental agency and from there to the undercover office of Golden State Finance. When he entered, Ricky was surprised to find FBI Special Agent Larry Summers sitting behind the reception counter. "Larry," Ricky exclaimed, "It's been months. How did you happen to be assigned back on this case?"

The two shook hands as Larry offered a quick account of the recent months. "I was in Phoenix for a few weeks, then back to Tucson where I picked up a couple of high-priority cases. Once we cleared our backlog, I was reassigned to my old cases. Of course, Krutoy was my priority, so here I am. When the request for this office space came in, our information system notified me about the multiple links between Krutoy and your Juarez Cartel case, so *zip*, here I am. Just like I hadn't been AWOL."

*

Gathering for a mid-day lunch of Subway sandwiches and soft drinks, the Golden State Finance staff sat around the workroom conference table. The room was a modern conference setting—an eight-foot, mahogany veneer table, three upholstered/countered back chairs on each side with another at each end, a dropdown video screen on the far end wall, and windows facing out to the ocean in the distance. The centerpiece was unique—a 14" x 14" x 20" black- and silver-colored portable currency counter.

Summers gave the introductions, FBI Agent Patrick Mahoney, a professionally dressed middle-aged man, will be at the reception desk; Special Agent Emily Patterson, a petite twenty-six-year-old African American is assigned to be at a desk in an open side office; DEA Agent Randolph Meier, a gangster-looking German American and DEA Agent Sean O'Boyle, a battered looking former rugby player, will be in the workroom.

Summers's and Anna's primary responsibility will be handling the money and the currency counter. Ricky will meet the courier at the door and initiate the reception and counting of the money. All of them will carry concealed handguns, and Meier and O'Boyle will each carry a .223 semi-automatic rifle clearly visible to dissuade any inopportune thoughts."

Patterson pointed out two concealed microphones and cameras in opposing corners to record audio and video documentation of the transaction. "Additionally, three DEA agents will be in the adjoining office if an emergency occurs. They also will have monitors that allow them to have live-action audio and visual from the entire surveillance system.

Besides the discreet audio and video systems in the workroom, the FBI placed surveillance cameras in the fourth-floor hallway and stationed a team in a parked van on the second floor of the parking garage across the street. That camera provided a 180-degree view up and down the street and the front entrance of the building."

After discussing the surveillance system, the entire team conducted a walk-through of the cameras and recording equipment. When they were confident the equipment was functioning correctly, they called it a day—especially for Anna and Ricky.

*

As did the other businesses in the building when it was five o'clock, the agents filtered out and went their respective ways. Ricky and Anna left at different times, each going to their rented vehicle where they traveled in different directions to separate hotels.

Ricky battled the afternoon traffic to the Pacific Inn two miles away. Reaching the quiet of his room, he pulled off his boots, slipped his concealed 9mm pistol from his belt, and laid it on the bathroom counter. Taking a deep breath and mentally reviewing the afternoon activities, he leaned over the basin to wash his face. His solitude was short lived. His cell phone buzzed. It was a message from Marta Bravo at the Santa Fe crime lab. They had a match. Her note was terse, "Positive DNA on Nicolas Salinas and an unfired bullet plus the magazine in the handgun."

After sending a quick response, Ricky opted for some fresh air and a walk to the Santa Monica Pier for a California meal—no tacos or burritos. Maybe Bubba Gump.

Two hours later, he lay back across the bed and closed his eyes. It had been a long day.

*

Rising at the buzz of the alarm clock, he climbed out of bed and flicked on the morning news—politics, murders, and traffic jams on the infamous Los Angeles freeways. He smirked, shook his head, and turned it off. He would have enough excitement today without getting absorbed in the world's problems.

Minutes later, with a soothing hot shower cascading over his head, his mind raced ahead to today's undertaking. The rehearsal was over. This would be a pivotal event in the financial activity of the New Juarez Cartel.

Following a complimentary sweet roll and juice in the coffee shop, Ricky was in the Golden State Finance office at 7:30. With the planning embedded in their minds, the staff was ready for the courier or couriers to make their grand entry. Even though Chico had said they (whoever *they* were) would arrive at 9:00, the agents were prepared well ahead of time.

The wait was short lived. At 8:42, the parking garage surveillance crew notified the office of a white Ford SUV that stopped in the freight loading zone at the front of the building. Two men, each dressed in casual Mexican attire of *guayabera* shirts and Levi's, exited the vehicle. They removed two office-supply-type boxes and a dolly from the rear baggage space, stacked the containers on the dolly, and entered the building. A third person was driving. As quickly as the cart was loaded, the SUV pulled out of sight. The cameras did not get a viable image of the driver.

Mahoney cracked the tension with a quick barb. "Let the games begin."

Agent Patterson, sitting at her desk with Ricky standing alongside, observed the activity on her computer. Ricky recognized the men immediately—Nicolas and Chico. Speaking in a muted tone, he announced to the others that he and Anna knew both men—the man in the blue shirt was the informant, the other man was their primary target.

Nicolas and Chico were out of sight from the time they entered the front doors until they exited the elevator on the fourth floor. Stepping into the hallway, they paused to look at the wall directory, then pushed their dolly toward Golden State Finance in Suite 407. When they reached the office door, Patterson switched her screen to a dummy business display and Ricky moved to the entrance.

There was a quick knock and the door opened. Chico pushed the dolly into the outer office with Nicolas directly behind him. Each was carrying a not-so-well-concealed handgun beneath their loose-fitting shirts.

Ricky spoke first, greeting them in English. "Good morning, gentleman." Ignoring Chico, he bowed his head slightly to Nicolas Salinas and gave a hint of a polite smile. "We're glad to see you, sir."

Salinas returned a forced smile. His voice was curt. "Let's get on with business."

Nodding toward the closed workroom door, Ricky gestured to it and spoke equally tersely, "This way."

Mahoney spoke from behind the reception desk, "If you gentlemen need anything, just let me know and I can take care of it." Giving them a broad smile, he continued. "May I get you some coffee?"

Chico looked at him coldly, then responded. "Two coffees, black."

*

Pushing the dolly into the workroom, Chico and Nicolas found Anna and Larry Summers standing by the conference table. Nicolas's eyes sparkled when he looked at the money counter. He had arrived! Only big-money people needed a machine to count their cash. He turned and glanced at the armed agents standing in the corner. He raised an eyebrow, smirked, and commented, "Big boys, aren't they?"

Ricky broke his normal, servile role, "We don't play games when we do business. We're *deadly* serious."

Anna interjected a softer, businesslike approach, directing her remarks to Nicolas. "Good morning, Mr. Salinas."

Pointing to a spot adjacent to the table, she gestured for Chico to push the dolly near the counter. Anna waited while he placed the load by the conference table; then she gave Nicolas an equally hard scowl. "What's your count?"

He shrugged, "How the hell should I know. That's your job."

She nodded with a Cheshire cat grin. "We'll conduct a count and that's what it is—no debate. "

Salinas returned her gesture and barked, "Just do it."

The workroom door opened briefly as Mahoney delivered the coffee, gave it to Chico, then turned and left.

Summers went down on one knee, slipped the blade of his pocketknife under the taped edges of the boxes, and opened them. He paused momentarily. They were filled with used, filthy, and

235

scuffed bills. He looked up and spoke to Salinas who stood over him. "Twenties, fifties, or are there any others?"

"You've got it," Salinas snapped. "There shouldn't be any larger denominations nor any currency other than U.S. bills."

Summers stood straight and looked down at the money. "Before we start, I need to know if there is anything other than rubber bands or money wrappers banding them together?"

Salinas gave a hearty laugh. "U.S.-approved currency wrappers. Nothing but the best."

Anna looked at her watch when she spoke. "It's almost nine o'clock. This will take most of the morning. Nobody leaves the room once we start the count—no piss call, no phone calls. Your cell phones must be turned off, put on the table, and the SIM cards removed." She nodded at their sidearms, saying, "You can keep those." Offering an amiable smile, she continued. "Any questions?" She paused momentarily, then resumed her directions. "Hearing none then let's get down to business." Extending her hand, the two men removed their cell phones from their pockets and gave them to her.

Meier stepped forward, took the phones, removed the SIM cards, and put them on the table. He stepped back as Summers went to a closet and rolled out a set of scales. Without hesitation, Summers directed Chico to remove the bills from the first box and stack them on the scales. Simultaneously, Anna took latex gloves from a box on the table, handed a pair to Summers; then he and she each donned them. The purpose was twofold—sanitation, and the money would be forensically searched at the crime lab for trace evidence of whoever had handled the currency.

Minutes later, Anna, Summers, Chico, and Salinas moved closer to read the weight—eighty-one pounds. Moving the money aside, Chico loaded the second box of bills onto the scales and noted the weight—seventy-nine pounds.

At Anna's direction, Chico and Summers removed the wrappers from the currency and placed the unbound money lengthwise on the table.

Anna stepped to an ice chest in the corner, removed a water bottle for herself, then offered one to the others. All of them accepted. She made eye contact with Salinas and Chico, then commented, "Before we begin, are there any questions?"

Nicolas pulled up a chair and leaned back, put a toothpick in his mouth, and snarled, "Let's see you get busy."

It was noon when the final pack of money went into the counter. Thirty seconds later, the count was finished. "$1,450,800," Summers said as he tossed an empty water bottle into the trash can. Looking directly at Salinas, he asked, "Do you accept the count?"

"I do," Nicolas replied. "I certainly do."

Arrogance is a hunter.

CHAPTER THIRTY-SEVEN

With the counting complete, the currency repacked in the boxes, and their cell phones returned, Nicolas and Chico departed. *El Patron* would return in exactly forty-five days to collect his eighty percent in cash, stocks, commodities, and/or real property amounting to $1,160,640.00 in laundered assets. Golden State Finance would profit $290,160.00.

With no further need for the dolly, the *traficantes* left it as a humorous jest.

The FBI personnel in the parking garage watched the pair exit the building with Nicolas holding the cell phone to his ear. Moments later, the white SUV pulled to the curb. The agents were ready this time. Special Agent Agnes Moorhead, a fiftyish bag woman, trudged down the sidewalk with a discreet surveillance camera on her floppy hatband. Her little stroll recorded the front license plate of the vehicle and a burst of still pictures of a comely thirtysomething Hispanic female behind the wheel. By the time the SUV reached the far corner from the building, the agents had the registration information—a 2021 Ford Expedition registered to Calexico Automotive, Calexico, California.

Armed with an emergency telephonic search warrant from a Federal Magistrate, the FBI Forensic Technology Division hacked the rental agency computer service and forwarded their findings to Special Agent Summers. The car was rented two days earlier to Gilbert Henke. Additional information from the rental contract showed that Henke gave a Tucson home address and an Arizona driver's license.

Technology staff conducted a computerized search and determined that the Tucson address was non-existent, and the drivers' license number was of a ninety-two-year-old man. Searching public records, they determined he had died three years earlier. His name was Gilbert Henke.

The surveillance team went to the Golden State office and shared their information and photographs with the undercover agents. Ricky and Anna immediately recognized Henke's name. The same name appeared on the passport Maria Espinoza saw in the El Paso hotel where Nicolas forced himself on her. They didn't recognize the picture of the woman driving the SUV; nor did any of them have any insight about the car rental agency.

Ricky smiled inwardly, remembering an ancient Greek tale from a college Philosophy class—*The wheels of justice grind oh so slowly, but oh so fine.*

The noose was tightening around Nicolas Salinas's neck. The charges he would face were overwhelming—Murder; Use of a Firearm Involved in Drug Offenses; Sexual Exploitation of Children; and Drug Trafficking. He would spend the rest of his life behind bars.

*

Ricky and Anna had a morning flight out of Burbank and landed in El Paso in the early afternoon. Two hours later, they were in the Task Force conference room with Miguel O'Rourke and Acacia Rios to review the details of the investigation. It was a slow, plodding process detailing the minutiae beginning with Krutoy's death and culminating with the financial transaction with Nicolas Salinas.

As Ricky was wont to do, he reminded himself and the others that the focus of the investigation was the murder of Oleg Krutoy. Serious, but light-hearted, he emphasized that despite the numerous federal and state offenses and the number of people involved, their primary goal was to hold accountable those who planned or carried out the murder of Mr. Krutoy—mafia henchman or not. The importation of narcotics, public corruption, exploitation of children, and gun-running crimes were subordinate to the primary matter— murder.

Following an afternoon of drinking coffee and nibbling on a bag of Acacia's pork rinds, they finalized a step-by-step analysis of the physical evidence, the specific crimes, witnesses, and the corresponding statutes and case law.

The golden rays of the setting sun swept across the azure sky, tossing its natural beauty into the stark federal office building where Miguel was shutting down his computer. Giving his *off* button the *coup de grâce,* he rose from his chair and stepped to the window. Breathing deeply, he inhaled the serenity of the landscape, then turned to his colleagues. His demeanor returned to the task at hand as he grinned and commented. "That son of a bitch is done. Lock, stock, and barrel."

It was time for a Grand Jury and a host of federal charges.

Justice is a hunter.

CHAPTER THIRTY-EIGHT

The currency, totaling 36,280 individual bills, was boxed, tagged as evidence, transported by federal courier service, and submitted to the FBI Crime Lab in Washington D. C. The sheer amount of money would not allow each bill to be analyzed, but seventy-five bills serving as a random sample were set aside for forensic examination. Over the next two weeks, trace evidence from those twenty- and fifty-dollar bills provided evidence of a wide variety of illegal substances ranging from marijuana, heroin, cocaine, methamphetamine, and phencyclidine. Additionally, fingerprints and/or DNA profiles were linked to eighty-eight individuals, fourteen of whom were identified through the Integrated Automated Fingerprint Identification System (AFIS), and the Combined DNA Identification System (CODIS). The remaining seventy-four persons were not found in the bureau's identification systems.

Thirteen of the fourteen people had felony records in the United States, but no current outstanding warrants for their arrest. Neither Nicolas Salinas nor Gilbert Henke had a record, but Nicolas's prints were identified several times on the money. Additionally, prints of the informant, identified by his true name, were found on multiple bills.

DNA on two twenty-dollar bills was determined to belong to Manuel Estrada, a former Arizona certified law enforcement officer. He had been terminated from his position for twice failing a mandatory employee drug test. His information was set aside for potential future investigation separate from the Krutoy case.

*

Three weeks after the financial transaction in California, Ricky, Anna, Summers, and Deputy Pepe Anaya met with Assistant U.S. Attorney Malcolm Bridwell in his Tucson office. Beginning at nine o'clock and breaking at noon for take-out sandwiches, they spent the entire day reviewing the evidence.

Their critique of the evidence and witnesses who would corroborate the connection to a crime started with the spent bullet taken from Krutoy's body. From that point, they proceeded to the Russian handgun found with Maria Espinoza's corpse. Following a linear timeline, they reviewed the information from Boquillas del Carmen, Alpine; the deputy's relationship with Maria Espinoza; her employment at the Rio Lobo Outdoor Adventures; her encounter with Nicolas Salinas and his son Alberto; then to the sworn statements from Deputy Arnold about the drug importation, exploitation of minors, weapons and sex offenses; and finally to the money laundering scheme. They completed their assessment with a review of Nicolas and Alberto Salinas's DNA and fingerprints, and the FBI lab test results from the money.

*

The setting sun shone a golden hue over the city as it slipped behind the barren Tucson Mountains. Bridwell paused and gazed out the window, allowing his mind to blend with the peaceful interlude of nature. Taking a deep breath, he leaned back, interlocked his fingers behind his head and stretched. He made eye contact with each investigator and spoke softly but with a touch of humor. "I'd say you've got 'em by the balls. Like father, like son." He pitched forward with his chair legs slamming on the floor. "We have a Grand Jury next week. I'll need all of you, plus Deputy Arnold."

Titling his head like a puppy listening to a distant siren, he gave a wily grin and voiced his solitary concern. "From what you say, that young deputy is going to have a hard life. But," he said with a shrug as he turned to face the officers, "those are the cards he dealt us, so that's the hand we'll play."

Thirty minutes later, the prosecutor and the agents gathered around a table in the *Las Hermanas Famosa Bar and Café* midway between the federal building and the city police department. It was the ideal after-work watering hole for cops, lawyers, and the ever-present journalist hoping for a scoop.

*

Benny Ronquillo, a reporter for the Nogales twin-cities *Ambos Periodico,* and his fellow investigative reporter, Estella Mojica, sat quietly in a corner booth. The overhead party lights and the subdued daylight passing through the stained-glass windows twinkled off the couple's ice cubes and tumblers of rum and coke.

"Are you getting any pictures in this crummy light?" he asked.

Estella shifted around in the booth with her compact in hand, ostensibly freshening her lips and nose. "They pay me for my work. I never failed before and I'm not going to fail this afternoon." She glanced at Benny. "I recognize the lawyer and Mr. Anaya, but who are the other three?"

Benny smothered his laugh. "Foreigners?"

She gave him a sexy smile and blow kiss, then continued with her discreet photography. Moments later and satisfied with her work, she returned her compact to her purse, tossed a quick, cheerful nod to her partner, and slipped out of the booth.

"Qué pasa?" he asked.

She leaned over and whispered in his ear, "We're working, Benny. This isn't a date, and that *Chica* just went to the potty, so I am too." Passing through the door marked *Damas,* Estella saw the foreigner entering a stall, so she did likewise. Taking the appropriate time and the sounds of a busy lavatory, she exited the stall moments after hearing her target leave hers.

As was fitting, the two ladies stood only feet apart while washing their hands and refreshing themselves. Estella quickly dabbled the water, then with compact in hand, she coiffed her hair while turning slightly to face the other woman. Speaking casually, she offered a standard, "Beautiful day, isn't it?" still holding her compact.

Anna tilted her head slightly to the lady. "Oh yes, *perfecto,*" she said, unknowingly looking directly into the camera lens.

The two ladies completed their *deberes de baño,* and returned to their tables, Anna ready to go to the hotel. Estella was ready to send her photographs to the editorial counsel of news agencies and cartel soldiers in Nogales, Sonora.

Deception is a hunter.

CHAPTER THIRTY-NINE

B ridwell was an early riser. The glory of the sunrise soothed his inner being as he stood on his patio and admired the distant Tanque Verde Peak. His mind basked in the beauty of the day. The mountains and the giant saguaro cacti were a gift of creation, not a place for the sordidness of human deeds.

However, the realization of today's toil became paramount to his thoughts. In a few hours, he would deliver a somber picture to the Grand Jury. The magnificent elegance of nature had been sacrificed to settle a debt between Krutoy, the Russian Mafia, and the New Juarez Cartel.

It was not nature's plan.

*

A week had passed since his meeting with the officers who would testify regarding the complex murder and sundry other charges stemming from the Krutoy investigation. Standing in his office and gazing out the window, his view differed from that of an hour ago. He looked out over *El Barrio Viejo*, Tucson's historic city center. From its early days as the hub of civilization in the Arizona Territory, it had seen more than its share of scoundrels, preachers, and politicians. Times had changed, but the cross section of the citizenry had not. The proof lay in the documents on his desk—murderers, thieves, liars, gun runners, sex offenders, and some upright citizens doing their best against the tide of greed and corruption. And this was just one case.

He scanned his list of witnesses and the order in which they would be called before the sixteen men and women of the Grand Jury. The prosecutor would lead with Pima County Sheriff Detective Pepe Anaya and New Mexico State Trooper Enrique Basurto. They would be followed by FBI Special Agent Larry Summers and IRS Agent Paul Hamilton, then DEA Agent Anna Fernandez, and Aintry County Texas Sheriff Deputy Lester Arnold.

On one hand, it was an ideal picture of the success brought about by inter-agency cooperation. On the other, it exposed the extent to which those with a distorted moral compass would go to satisfy their voracious appetite for money and power.

As a safety measure, Arnold would hold Basurto as a follow-up witness. Should the jury have doubts about Arnold's veracity, the trooper could be available to substantiate Arnold's testimony.

A cliché ran through Bridwell's mind, *You can indict a ham sandwich with a Grand Jury.* Nevertheless, the Texas deputy was the weak link. To salvage himself, Arnold had agreed to become an unindicted co-conspirator. A choice he didn't like but he had few alternatives.

*

The morning of the Grand Jury, each of the witnesses met to summarize their testimony with Bridwell and his assistant, Brina Epstein, a University of Arizona law student interning with the U. S. Attorney's Office. After their interviews, they adjourned to the witness waiting room—the dreaded abyss where officers and agents had whiled away untold hours in Limbo before giving a few minutes of testimony to the Grand Jury.

Today was no different. It was an interior room—no windows, nothing but a six-foot conference table, eight straight-backed mahogany veneer chairs, and a stack of old magazines on a corner table.

If there was an allegory of hell, this was it.

*

No sooner had they made themselves comfortable in the witness room than Brina stuck her head in the door. She smiled at Pepe with a soft, "Ready?"

He tossed his copy of the morning paper on the table, nodded "goodbye" to his colleagues, and followed the young woman out the door.

Thirty minutes later, Brina was back. With a broad smile, she tilted her head and looked at Ricky. "They're ready for you, Mr. Basurto."

Following her clicking heels down the otherwise deathly quiet hall, they entered the windowless jury room. Ricky did as cops are prone to do—he took quick stock of the room. Fittingly, it was a majestic setting of wood-paneled, floor-to-ceiling walls; the jury box of seven men and nine women was a reasonable balance of Chicanos, Blacks, Anglos, and one Asian; a projector and screen were situated so as to be viewed by the witness and the jury; and there were mahogany tables for the two attorneys, each with two upholstered contoured chairs; and a witness stand and chair.

The flag of the United States was in one corner, and the wall opposite the jury held a photographic display of the president and each of his predecessors.

Ricky was humbled. This Grand Jury chamber was the manifestation of the American judicial system, and he was an important cog in the wheel of justice. This was where the future of Nicolas and Alberto Salinas would be determined.

He took the witness stand after being sworn in by the court clerk. As prompted by Bridwell, he gave a brief overview of his life from Hachita to the Marines to the Law Enforcement Academy and his specialized DEA training. He closed his oratory with a description of his assignment to the Joint Federal and State Task Force on Human and Drug Interdiction, housed between Columbus and Hachita, New Mexico.

The next forty-five minutes were spellbinding for members of the jury. Ricky was an expert witness, making eye contact with the jurors and displaying his personal and professional self. He was knowledgeable and articulate, but not overly confident or cocky, as he described meeting Border Patrol Agents Armando Ochoa and Axel Wolff in the *Cañón de la Muerte*; the condition and photos of the body later identified as Maria Espinoza; the bloodstained handgun

250

found beneath her body, and the staff from the Medical Examiner's Office who were dressed in hazmat suits, preparing the remains for transit to the morgue.

Ricky's tone and facial expressions took on a somber air as he continued with the woes of his findings in *Boquillas del Carmen*—the painful story from Father McGuire, and the equally heartbreaking tale by *El Abuelo*.

As deeply as he had been touched by his conversations with those two elderly gentlemen, he felt and saw the jurors' expressions when they, too, absorbed the depth of passion those old men suffered because of their futility at helping Maria.

In her death, Maria reached out and touched the jurors, especially juror number 14, a stoic but elegant, middle-aged Hispanic woman. She wore a simple black dress with a silver grommet in her hair. Tears filled her eyes when she looked upon the grotesque photograph of what once was a beautiful, young *Chicana* who may have looked like she herself did at that age.

Number 14 continually dabbed her eyes from the moment she saw the first photograph of the maggot-infested body of that once lovely and charming young woman dead and forgotten in the bottom of the *Cañón de la Muerte*. There was no doubt juror 14 would vote to indict the Salinases. There weren't enough charges in the book to restore the horror they had committed.

Ricky continued testifying, now focused on the Rio Lobo Outdoor Adventures, obtaining Alberto's DNA and fingerprint-laden business card, and the search of Maria's apartment in Alpine.

Following Bridwell's direction, he moved his testimony to Culiacán, Mexico, and their meeting with Nicolas Salinas and how they obtained his DNA and fingerprints at the *La Plaza del Rey*.

He closed his testimony with a description of the California money-laundering event and the lab results obtained from the examination of a sample of the currency.

At four o'clock in the afternoon, it was over. Deputy Arnold had passed his first test.

A week later, Ricky and Anna received a copy of the sealed indictments issued by the Grand Jury. It was a catalog of crimes, the most serious of which was the murder charge against Nicolas Salinas and his son Alberto. There also was a civil filing against all assets owned by the two men ordering the officers to seize all assets reasonably believed to be obtained as a result of a continuing criminal enterprise.

Sitting alongside Anna in Miguel's office, they reviewed the indictments and began their plan to carry out the apprehensions and seizure.

"Eleven days," Anna said. "That's when Nicolas should show up to collect his share of the laundered assets, so I say that's when we should snap him up."

Ricky nodded. "I agree. We can set up surveillance on Alberto a couple of days ahead of time so we know his exact location. Then we can coordinate the arrests and confiscate Rio Lobo and any bank accounts or other assets we know of—all in one swoop."

Miguel nodded approval, then asked, "Exactly what's the plan for Salinas to show up to collect his assets?"

Anna responded, "I'm to contact our informant three days ahead of time and give him the go-ahead, and he will relay it to Nicolas. We expect him to show up for his collection, and we'll scoop him up. Then," she said with a glance at Ricky, "another team will snatch Alberto wherever he happens to be."

Miguel smiled and nodded approval. "Keep me posted."

*

Tuesday of the following week, Anna contacted her informant on his cell phone and relayed the information to him.

"*Esta buena,*" he replied. "I'll get in touch with him." He paused for a moment, then spoke. "My money?"

"You'll be paid in full when Nicolas is busted."

Chico gave a casual guffaw. "You're good, lady."

"Have him there on time. We'll arrest you along with him, then we will arrange for your bail and you and your money can ride into the sunset."

He chuckled again and clicked off.

Dishonor is a hunter.

CHAPTER FORTY

It was Thursday afternoon. Ricky, Anna, and Miguel gathered in Miguel's office to finalize next week's plan for the arrest of Nicolas and Alberto Salinas.

Ricky could not stop the thought from running through his mind. He didn't believe in karma or Ouija boards, but the memory persisted. Throughout his career, Thursdays were always a bad luck day for him. He chuckled to himself. *I'm turning over a new leaf today. We're going to string those bastards up.*

When the evidence had begun to coalesce, Miguel reacted to Ricky's comment with a name for their investigation: "*Operación Encadenarlos*, to string 'em up."

The plan was straightforward. With D-Day scheduled the following Tuesday, agents planned around-the-clock surveillance on Alberto to begin Saturday. Friday evening before the full-scale operation, discreet cameras would be set up to provide a clear view of the front and rear doors, plus the access and egress routes to Rio Lobo Outdoor Adventures. The second set of cameras would cover Alberto's single-story home on Tumamoc Hill, two miles northwest of Alpine.

An upscale home of burnt adobe with a swimming pool and jacuzzi, it was surrounded by a stucco patio wall like the *hacienda* where he grew up in the Chihuahuan Desert. Natural landscaping gave it a touch of oneness with nature, a gorgeous and peaceful home overlooking Alpine and the Cuyamaca Mountain Plateau below. Like his life, it was a visual deception of his true colors—a murderer, white slave trader, and drug trafficker.

The agents' drone flyover provided not only a picture of luxury in the desert but also showed numerous surveillance cameras covering every potential approach to his home. No one could slip in undetected. It was not simply a luxurious home; it was a fortress.

*

Federal Agents from Midland and Laredo DEA and ICE were assigned to conduct the Alpine surveillance and subsequent apprehension and asset seizure.

Miguel O'Rourke was responsible for the overall coordination of both arms of the case in Texas and California.

Anna and Ricky were scheduled to fly from El Paso to Los Angeles on Monday morning. FBI Special Agent Larry Summers would arrive Sunday evening. He and the other agents would set up their discreet audio and video system, test them and each other, and prepare for things to go smoothly, or possibly not. Either way, the entire system would be operational in Texas and California. The noose was tightening on Nicolas and Alberto.

Operación Encadenarlos was a trap door ready to snap shut.

*

Ricky's cell phone buzzed when they disembarked in Los Angeles. It was Miguel. "What's up," he said when he punched the *talk* button.

Miguel fired back, "We've got a problem. They can't find Alberto anywhere—home, work, getting drunk or getting laid. He's gone."

"Did you look in church?" Ricky wisecracked.

Miguel smirked. "Don't be a smartass. Where the fuck will we find him?"

Pulling his carry-on bag behind him, Ricky guided Anna into a relatively quiet corner of the airport. "When did they last see him?"

"That's the problem. They didn't. The video surveillance system was set up Friday evening. The store was closed, and there was no in-or-out traffic from his house, but that didn't cause our people any alarm. He's single and we know he's sexually active, so no alarm bells went off when they didn't see him Friday night. The Outdoor Adventure store is normally open on Saturday, but no one showed up. A couple of customers stopped by but left without getting inside the place. By that time, the surveillance crew was nervous. They sent their drone over the house but there wasn't any activity, and his pickup truck was nowhere to be found."

"*Malo, muy malo,*" Ricky mumbled.

"There's more," Miguel replied. "By Sunday, our people were desperate. They checked every system available—car wreck, sick or dead in a hospital, got arrested somewhere for something else, anything. They ran the system dry but couldn't come up with anything. They checked every second on every camera. Zilch. He disappeared."

Ricky heard him taking a deep breath before he continued. "There's more. Aintry County put out a BOLO—be on the lookout. Our *good* Deputy Arnold is missing."

"What do you mean, missing?" Ricky shot back.

"As in *disappeared*. Sunday he was scheduled to work from 7 a.m. to 3 p.m., but he never made it. One of their sergeants went to his apartment. His pickup was gone, and no one answered the door. He checked with the landlady. She got visibly upset and started to cry. She liked having Phil, as she called him, around the property. She thought he was not just a good tenant, but a nice guy—very personable and polite. She went with the sergeant to the apartment and unlocked the door. He went inside, but nothing looked out of place. Phil's clothes and miscellaneous stuff were there. The bed was unmade; groceries in the fridge; no signs of a struggle; and no neighbors saw or heard anything unusual. Puff the Magic Dragon, and he was gone."

"This isn't good," Ricky said as he let out a deep exhale. "Not good at all."

Anna was standing alongside and read his body language. He was up the creek without a paddle.

*

An hour later, they sat around the conference table in the La Placita building with the entire team. There was no glad-handing or high-fives. It was a somber atmosphere as Ricky updated them on Alberto and Deputy Arnold.

"What about your informant?" Summers asked.

257

Anna's lips pursed. Her brow furrowed as she spoke more to herself than to the others. "I can't risk calling him. If he's alive and okay, he knows how to contact me. If he's alive, but not okay, I would only further jeopardize him by calling his cell phone." She wet her lips and tossed a sidelong glance at Summers. "It's wait and see."

He acquiesced agreement with a nod and a long, slow blink of his eyes.

The remainder of the day was a tense holding pattern. It was after six o'clock when Summers gave the final order of the day, "Let's fold our tent and see what tomorrow brings." He turned in his chair and looked at Anna. "Let us know if you hear anything. Otherwise, we'll meet here at seven o'clock tomorrow morning and be ready for whatever happens."

Ricky and Anna's eyes met. They were unhappy. Their case was unraveling.

Impatience is a hunter.

CHAPTER FORTY-ONE

Ricky had a restless night. He knew from experience that traffickers were infamous for either not being on time or disappearing completely if they smelled a rat. That was a hazard of the business, but this was different. There was nothing normal about it. Nicolas had given them $1,450,800 to launder, and a cartel leader wouldn't take the loss of that much money sitting down. One way or another, he would want it back or someone's life would be forfeited.

His thoughts jumped to Oleg Krutoy. The cartel collected on his Russian Mafia debt. Now, what about Anna's informant and Deputy Arnold? What had they offered up to assuage Nicolas's anger and frustration?

There would be no sleep for Ricky tonight.

*

With a box of Spud Nuts and a dozen coffees-to-go from the barista on the first floor, the agents met in the conference room. There was no drama. Everyone was a realist. Some things go according to plan. Some don't.

Summers started the meeting with a question to Anna. "What're your thoughts about the informant?"

She shook her head. "There's no update. I can guess, but that doesn't do us any good. Either he's alive and wishing he was dead, or he's already dead."

Summers glanced back and forth between Anna and Ricky. "It's your call about how we play this out today. What do you think?"

"We've gone this far," Anna said. "There's no value in turning back now. I say we play this out for a few hours and see where it takes us." She looked at Ricky, "We can throw guesses around, but that isn't going to do us any good. My call is we stick with our game plan and see what happens—see it through until midafternoon. Then, if it hasn't come together, we call it off."

Ricky grimaced and nodded.

Summers went around the table, making eye contact with each agent. All gave simple nods of approval. No one was pleased, but the facts were the facts. Either play it out or call it off.

"Okay," Summers said. "Let's put everything and everybody in position. We assume it's *a go* until Nicolas shows up, and in the meantime we check all our sources for any updates, and then if he doesn't show, we officially back off for today."

FBI Special Agent James Horowitz, a burly Tactical Operations Specialist, leaned forward with his elbows on the table. He spoke with a commanding voice befitting his cauliflower ears and flat nose, "This son of a bitch is too dangerous to take any chance on letting him come into the building should he decide to show up." He locked eyes with Summers. "With your permission, I'm calling in another Tactical Team. I've surveilled the building and I'm not too comfortable with our plans as they are. I suggest we keep in place everybody we already have assigned in this office and next door, plus the surveillance team across the street." Shaking his head and looking at each of his colleagues, he described his adjustments to the security plan. "There's too much of a likelihood that your bandit knows he got screwed. Maybe he has taken it out on the deputy and the snitch, but he's out over a million bucks and is pissed." Nodding his head in approval of his own thoughts, he continued. "I think that bastard might be crazy enough to come here or send a cartel team to do his dirty work for him."

"Good thoughts," Summers replied.

Horowitz grimaced and looked again at his coworkers. "I'll have the other team cover the rear entrance from the alley and some of them will be undercover in one guise or another close to the front door. If that asshole shows up, or if someone we think might be his muscle, we take them down before they get to the doorway—front or rear."

Summers nodded his approval. "Okay, everyone. You know the plan. Let's get in place, be patient, and see if someone shows up." He gestured to Anna and Ricky. "Get on the line. Run down what you can as fast as you can and keep us posted."

*

Recalling how small the border crossing station between Big Bend and Boquillas del Carmen was, Ricky hoped that whoever was on duty might be able to help him pin down Alberto Salinas. He called the discreet number the Border Patrol had in each station—a number reserved for confidential matters. It was answered on the first ring by a woman. Ricky's heart pounded. Could it possibly be the same agent he spoke to when he crossed there?

"Border Patrol, Agent Sensing speaking?"

Luck was with him. Sandra Sensing was the same duty agent he spoke to the day he went to Boquillas del Carmen. "Agent Sensing, my name is Trooper Enrique Basurto with the New Mexico State Police. I'm a member of the Joint Federal Task Force on Human and Drug Trafficking. A few weeks ago, I came through your crossing and interviewed some witnesses in Boquillas del Carmen—a Father McGuire, and an older gentleman, *El Abuelo."*

"Yes, I know both of the men, but I have to validate who you are."

"Of course," he said. "At the moment, we are in Los Angeles, but you can contact my supervisor, Miguel O'Rourke."

"Certainly," she replied. "I know Agent O'Rourke. I'll speak with him and if he approves, then I'll call you back at this number you're calling from."

"Perfect," he said. "we'll be waiting."

Twenty minutes later, Sensing was back. "Mr. Basurto, I've spoken with Agent O'Rourke. He gave me a quick version of what you're working on, so how can I help you?"

"We are trying to find Alberto Salinas. He's a prime suspect in our case and has dropped out of sight—very unexpectedly. He has used your crossing station on business many times over the years. Would you happen to know him?"

"For sure. I used to see him quite often. He was a tour guide, so I'd see him at least a couple of times a month, but recently he seldom comes this way. That is, until Friday. He crossed over just before we closed at six o'clock. He knew our schedule and that we were about to close. I reminded him that if he crossed, he wouldn't be able to get back until the next day. He seemed to be in a happy mood and said, 'No problem. I'll be gone a couple of days.'" She paused briefly. The tone of her voice changed dramatically when she spoke again. "His pickup truck is in our parking lot and he hasn't come back yet. I sense there's a problem. Do I need to be on guard?"

"Indeed," Ricky replied. "He's wanted for murder."

*

The Placita office was quiet the remainder of the morning. The surveillance teams around the building gave periodic reports of people coming and going, but there was nothing of significance to show the cartel had any activity in the area.

The Alpine crew did not have success in tracking down Alberto; the FBI surveillance teams found nothing to arouse their suspicions; and as a last resort, Miguel threw in his opinion: "He flew the coop."

It was shortly after one in the afternoon when the front surveillance team offered one of their many comments on people going in and out of La Placita. "You've got a Pacific Punch Pizza delivery girl coming in with a couple of pizza boxes."

"Roger," Special Agent Patterson replied.

Each of the bored Placita agents was going about looking like they had something to do when the door opened abruptly. Caught unaware, the room exploded in a burst of activity as the agents pulled their weapons screaming, "Federal Agent!" and in a variety of expressions, ordered the female to slowly put the pizza boxes on the floor.

The young lady stiffened and her face froze in fear. She wore a Pacific Pizza orange and red shirt and her bright red pants suddenly darkened as she peed. She tried to speak, but in her terror, she could only continue to soil herself. Tears poured from her eyes and she dropped the pizza boxes as Horowitz and Meier pounced on her, took her to the floor, and in one swift motion, handcuffed her hands behind her back.

The sausage and cheese pizzas spilled out onto the floor.

*

It took only moments for the surprise to be clarified. A call-in order for two pizzas, paid with a credit card belonging to Lester Phillip Arnold, was delivered to room 401 of the La Placita Building.

The terrified eighteen-year-old delivery driver, Sandy Marchant, was on her second day as a pizza delivery driver. She decided the job was not one for career development.

*

It was early evening by the time they closed the office, removed the surveillance equipment, and made the necessary notifications for the potential fallout from Ms. Marchant's unpleasant day.

Ricky and Anna had a late flight to El Paso. He was home and in the arms of his lover at two o'clock in the morning. Tomorrow would be another adventure.

Disappointment is a hunter.

CHAPTER FORTY-TWO

Ricky and Muncie planned a late but casual meal of *huevos rancheros* and tortillas for breakfast. Ricky had left a message for Miguel saying that he would be in after lunch; Muncie had done the same with Dr. Gerber.

The morning was theirs to do as they pleased. Still in their pajamas, they moved to the rear patio where Lupe played on her swing while her mamma and daddy each sipped a long, slow cup of Piñón coffee. It was a wonderful and refreshing start to the day. Ricky mused: *This is how life is supposed to be lived.* He paused and took a deep breath. *But I don't live in a fairyland.*

It was a picture-perfect start to what he knew was going to be a less than satisfactory end to his workweek. He couldn't escape the feeling that the Salinas father/son duo would escape justice for their deeds. Adding to his misery was the possibility that Aintry Deputy Lester Phillip Arnold and Chico, the confidential informant, had met a tortuous death.

He struggled mentally, conflicted. *A hell of a way to think when I'm sitting here with my queen and the little princess.*

*

Ricky was on edge, grinding his teeth and biting his lip. His clothes felt like they didn't fit. Maybe he was getting fat. Maybe he was getting older but denying it.

Maybe nothing, he decided.

It was another Thursday, and he was digging into a final remnant of hope of finding Alfredo Salinas. He hitched a ride on a U.S. Custom plane that was delivering new communications systems to the Big Bend area stations. They would fly directly into Marfa, arriving at 10 a.m. and departing at 5 p.m. He gladly accepted the offer and was behind the wheel of a Border Patrol SUV at 10:30 a.m., bound for the smallest U.S./Mexico border crossings on the Rio Grande River.

It was noon when he pulled into the unpaved parking lot at the crossing station, a 30' x 30' block building bearing a sign, "USA/Republic of Mexico Border Crossing." He immediately recognized Alberto's pickup gathering dust in the parking lot. Shaking his head in disgust, he realized he may never see Alberto again.

It stung.

Inside the building, he met again with his new, old friend, Sandra Sensing. *"Que tal?"* she joked when he entered. "Now I get to meet the real Enrique Basurto." She chuckled, then continued. "The day you crossed and showed me that bullshit ID, I knew something was up but didn't have any idea what it was."

"You're good," he said with a broad smile creasing his lips. "We've gone really deep to make a case on these Salinas men. Now that we have the warrants, we need to find them, but they got wind and rode into the sunset."

"Speaking of," she said, "I assume you'll be back before we close at six o'clock?"

Checking his sidearm and holster into Sensing's file cabinet, he turned toward the lone door that led to the Republic of Mexico. "If I'm not back, send in the cavalry."

Bowing in mockery of his official trip, she opened the door opposite the one through which he entered. They made eye contact as he passed through the portal. She spoke with deadly earnestness. "Be careful. This is the safest crossing on the entire border, but I'm familiar with those cartel bastards." Shaking her head, she offered a parting comment, "In all seriousness, once you cross the river, we can't help you." She paused and wet her lips. *"Vaya con Dios, Amigo."*

Twenty minutes later and twenty dollars lighter, thanks to the boat trip and burro ride, Ricky rode into the desolate hilltop village of Boquillas del Carmen. Although he trusted the priest and Abuelo, he intentionally had not called ahead. At this level of criminal activity and being out of his jurisdiction, safety was paramount. It would be better to show up unexpectedly than to chance the cartel having advance notice of his plans.

Sliding down from the back of *Maya*, a red roan mare, Ricky was greeted by the sound of *mariachi* music coming from what they referred to as *La Plaza*, even though it was only a city block with small businesses and a few kiosks on either side. To them, it was the square, and the hand-painted signs adorning the booths proclaimed it to be the celebration of *San Isidore,* the patron of their church.

Wearing a straw Stetson hat, blue chambray shirt, an old pair of boots and Levi's, Ricky fit the ambience of the square—farmers,

267

cowboys, truck drivers, *tias y tios, abuelas y abuelos,* and *los ninos en todo partes.* It was party time in Boquillas del Carmen.

Following the loud chatter of the children, he found Father McGuire and Juana, his housekeeper, overwhelmed by the flurry of little hands and arms. It was the free *empanadas,* compliments of Juana and her mother who had worked through the night to prepare the pumpkin-filled fried turnovers for the kids.

Safely at the rear of the hungry *ninos y ninas,* he gestured to the old priest who slipped out of the booth and nodded toward the relative peace and quiet of the church. Walking side by side up the dirt road, the priest commented, "Sir, this is a joyful day in our little town, but your expression tells me a different story."

Ricky nodded as they climbed the steps and entered the blessed quiet of the sanctuary. Taking a seat in the last row of pews, the priest spoke again. "I know you do not bear good news for us, but what is it that I can help you with?"

Ricky spoke as he turned to face the priest. "Father, I need to talk with you and Abuelo. We can talk together. I just need a little information, then I will bid you a wonderful evening." He smiled from ear to ear. "It's too good a day to stay inside and talk about the devil's handiwork."

"I agree. C'mon. Let's go find Abuelo." He chuckled. "I know exactly where to find him. He'll be napping beneath his ramada." Minutes later, the three sat in the shade of the ramada, sipping tin cups of cold water from Abuelo's well.

"Alberto Salinas," Ricky said. "He's wanted for murder, and he crossed over here last Friday."

"*Seguro*," Abuelo replied. "I got to know him over the years before he took little Maria into his devil's lair. We saw him Friday."

"*Tambien*," Father McGuire said. "I thought for a moment there was going to be trouble, but everything was fine."

"Why? What happened?" Ricky asked.

"I had just come out the front door of the church and saw a white Toyota pickup and a black Chevy Yukon pull up by the bar—Benny's Place." He paused momentarily and bit his lips. "They looked like they were going to war. Two *hombres* in the truck bed had rifles and they went inside the bar. I listened, but nothing happened. I was afraid they were going to kill somebody, but they didn't. Two more men got out of the Yukon and also went in Benny's."

"For a priest, you're a crazy old fart," Abuelo wisecracked.

Both of them laughed.

"Well, I'm not afraid, but this isn't their town, and they had no business scaring people—driving like idiots and carrying those big guns. So, I walked over there and went in like I owned the place, but it turned out very nice. They were sitting at the bar and looked at me when I approached them. They were very polite. '*Padre, Venga aca,*' they said. One got up and offered his stool to me, so I sat and had a glass of water. They each had a beer. Didn't say much. They offered to buy me dinner, but I declined. After a few minutes, I told them *adios*, and came home."

Abuelo laughed again. "Father, I still think you were crazy to do that."

"Like an old fox," the priest replied.

"That's when I came around front and found you sweeping the sidewalk?" Abuelo asked.

"*Sí*. And we sat together on the step and watched the rest of it. Then they left."

"I'm sorry, Father," Ricky said. "The rest of it?"

"Yes. Not long after we sat down, we saw Alberto coming down the street. It was about that time when the men came out of the bar. It was like old times for them—shaking hands, hugging each other, and then they left. Alberto was in the Yukon, and the Toyota and the gun bearers followed them out of town."

*

It was nine o'clock when Ricky pulled into his driveway. He saw Muncie through the kitchen window, doing dishes—as beautiful as ever. He tapped his horn. She looked out and waved to him. They were both glad he was home.

Love is a hunter.

El Fin

EPILOGUE

Samuel Baca

The legal proprietor of the property housing Rio Lobo Outdoor Adventures, Samuel was never linked to any ongoing investigation. He has thrived as the operator of the business. Due to the language of the RICO statute, the government was barred from seizing the company.

Nicolas Salinas

Federal warrants for his arrest were issued but never served. He remains in the State of *Coahuila*, Mexico, and serves in the New Juarez Cartel.

Alberto Salinas

Two months after leaving Boquillas del Carmen, Alberto was killed in a gun battle with the Sinaloa Cartel in the coastal city of Sayulita on the Riviera Nayarit.

Chico

His tortured body was hung on a Juarez railroad overpass. A scrawled message was pinned to his shirt, Rata. His tongue had been cut out and was pinned to the sign.

Deputy Lester Phillip Arnold

His pickup truck was found abandoned in the Dallas/Ft. Worth Airport parking lot. He was never located.

New Mexico State Trooper Enrique Basurto

Promoted to the rank of Sergeant, Tony remains with the Task Force. Due to the influx of immigrants, the Task Force is temporarily reassigned to care for the housing, education, and medical treatment of unaccompanied minors.

Their desert compound on Highway 9 has been repurposed to serve as a holding/treatment center for children.

The Aspen Groves

The aspen is a deciduous tree. It grows in a stand and can live more than one hundred years. The real story is their root system. The aspens are a connected family through their roots. They can be chopped down or burned to the ground, but the secret is in the roots. They spread and grow sprouts, and sprouts become trees, and life continues.

The aspens and the cartels are a lesson in real life. They have roots and sprouts and cannot be killed.

And that, my friend, is why the cartel is like an aspen grove.

Made in the USA
Middletown, DE
10 March 2022